Chekhov
The Comic Stories

Chekhov
The Comic Stories

*Translated from the Russian
and with an Introduction by*

Harvey Pitcher

Ivan R. Dee
Chicago 1999

Library of Congress Cataloging-in-Publication Data:
Chekhov, Anton Pavlovich, 1860–1904.
    [Short stories. English. Selections]
    The comic stories / Chekhov ; translated from the Russian and
with an introduction by Harvey Pitcher.
       p. cm.
    ISBN 1-56663-241-2 (cloth : alk. paper). — ISBN 1-56663-242-0
(paper : alk. paper)
    1. Chekhov, Anton Pavlovich, 1860–1904—Translations into
English. I. Pitcher, Harvey J. II. Title.
PG3456.A15P58 1999
891.73'3—dc21   98-49198

Contents

Chekhov
The Comic Stories

Introduction

There it was, on the theatre page of that highly respectable news-paper, the *Independent*, an advertisement for 'Britain's Biggest Bottled Beer' and above it, in eye-catching capitals, the words: HEAVIER THAN CHEKHOV.

Chekhov would have loved this. In Russia, he predicted, his work would not be read for more than a few years after his death, and he was sure it could never be understood in the West. How amazing, then, to be so well known in Britain almost a century later! An avid newspaper reader and not one to skip the adverts (they might give him an idea for a comic story), he would cheer-fully have agreed to promote 'The One and Only Newcastle Brown Ale'. As for 'heavier than Chekhov', that would have amused him most of all: were my plays really so boring, he would have asked, throwing up his hands in mock despair.

They weren't, but that makes no difference. Labels stick and images lead a life of their own. Chekhov has been especially vulnerable to labelling. Beware of the ubiquitous adjective 'Chekhovian': the more confidently people use it, the profounder their ignorance. The present volume, the first substantial collec-tion in English to be devoted solely to his comic stories, is intended to provide a counterbalance to the worn-out image of Chekhov as a heavy writer.

As a man, he was anything but heavy. His friend and fellow-writer, Ivan Bunin, described him figuratively as 'very light on his feet'. Easily bored, he was mistrustful of anyone solemn or preten-tious, preferring the company of people who were lively and amusing, unpredictable and good fun; he loved comic banter and was forever inventing comic nicknames for himself and other people, assigning them comic roles and weaving comic fantasies around them; and he had his own laconic conversational style, with an offbeat, understated sense of humour. Few people were

1

able to resist his infectious laughter. All this, however, was not simply a matter of temperament or disposition. Chekhov adopted the humorous stance deliberately, as a means of distancing himself from other people and avoiding unwanted intimacy. Often, he seems to conduct the relationships of real life as if they were comic fiction.

As a writer, too, Chekhov does not reveal himself. His great gift is to reveal others. It is no accident that 'The Chameleon' (1884) is one of his best-known early stories, for he himself has a chameleon-like, mimetic gift. His lowly origins and social mobility meant that throughout his life he was constantly participating in different worlds, meeting different kinds of people. He seems to have developed an almost uncanny ability to absorb how other people behaved, how they viewed the world, how they talked, all of which he later reproduced imaginatively in his fiction. These acts of impersonation mean that readers of Chekhov, as William Gerhardie put it, may congratulate themselves when they die 'on having lived a hundred lives – but paid for one!'

From 1879 to 1884 he led a double life. 'I began contributing to the journals during my first year at university,' he wrote later, 'and as a student had hundreds of stories published under the pseudonym "A. Chekhonte", which, as you see, is very similar to my own name. And not one of my fellow students knew that I was "A. Chekhonte", none of them was interested.' That he successfully combined these contrasting lives – as a medical student (so unassuming that his contemporaries remembered only that he attended lectures regularly and sat somewhere near the window) and as a literary Bohemian – was a tribute to his remarkable energy, chameleon quality and a strength of character lacking in his elder brothers. When the father's grocery business in Taganrog, a port in the south of Russia, failed in 1876, the family decamped hurriedly to Moscow, all except Anton, who stayed on for three years, tutoring younger pupils to help pay for his own schooling and acquiring an independence of mind and action.

In Moscow the family were very dependent on his income from writing, and as a result he had a go at everything, 'except a novel, poetry and denunciations to the police'. He soon learned to be succinct (better to cut a story yourself than leave it to an editor) and never forgot the lesson: the mature Chekhov is the least flowery or self-indulgent of writers. He seemed not so much to invent stories as to find them everywhere in the life around him. All those flighty young girls and downtrodden civil servants step straight on to his pages from the streets of 1880s Moscow.

To the serious business of comic writing, for which there was a regular demand from the popular press, he applied himself assiduously, happy to turn his hand to anything in the humour line: captions to cartoons, comic advertisements and announcements, menus, questionnaires, mathematical problems ('My mother-in-law is 75 and my wife 42. What time is it?') and calendars of past and future events ('Sarah Bernhardt [who toured Russia in 1881] is about to marry an assistant secretary at the Chinese Embassy'). Most frequently, though, he contributed short stories, seldom more than a few pages long.

Certain conventions had to be followed. Merchants, priests and usually civil servants had to be given funny names. Chekhov fell in with this, but brought his own originality to bear. Only certain comic genres were acceptable. Here, too, he had to toe the line, but with distinctive variations of his own. His first published story was in the well-established genre of parody. 'The Swedish Match' (1883), one of his best-known and longest early stories, he also refers to as a parody (of the crime stories so popular at the time), but it is more than that: the lively writing turns it into a comedy thriller, and in exploiting the interplay of character between the inspector and his bright young assistant ('That's enough of your fancy theories. Get on with your lunch.') Chekhov was anticipating every television crime series you can think of in the late twentieth century. In 'From the Diary of a Book-keeper's Assistant' (1883) he takes another well-worn genre, the comic diary or memoir, and does something quite distinctive with it: this sketch with its 'zero ending', still unusual then, hovers precariously between humour and pathos. In the many stories that involve simple mistakes, errors of judgement, mistaken identity, jumping to false conclusions, misinterpreting other people's behaviour and so on, Chekhov is making use of seemingly universal sources of humour, which at its most basic level is all to do with expectations. In 'Overdoing It' (1885) he goes a step further by showing how both protagonists build up a false picture of the other; mutual incomprehension, here happily resolved, will be a later, non-humorous Chekhov theme. Very often these error-based stories are resolved by means of a comic twist. Here Chekhov could be highly ingenious and produced some of his most wonderful comic effects. Especially unforgettable are the endings of stories like 'Revenge' (1886) and 'No Comment' (1888),

3

where the reader is not only taken completely by surprise, but has to admit that the outcome is entirely plausible. 'The Burbot' (1885) ends with a comic twist of a literal kind.

Far less inspired are those stories – over fifty of them – in which Chekhov takes a facetious look at (nearly always thwarted) romance. They are represented here by two comic memoir stories, where much of the fun derives from the use of a narrator's mask. 'Notes from the Memoirs of a Man of Ideals' (1885) is a simple story with a cast of two and a comic twist, whereas 'Notes from the Journal of a Quick-tempered Man' (1887) is full of invention, has an unusually large cast and reverses many a romantic cliché, whether that of romantic atmosphere – 'The revolting moon was creeping up from behind the shrubbery. The air was still, with an unpleasant smell of fresh hay . . .' – or the delights of the first kiss: 'So there was nothing else for it – I got up and put my lips to her elongated face, experiencing the same sensation I had as a child when I was made to kiss my dead grandmother's face at her funeral.'

Almost as numerous, not so overtly comic, but more satirical and in their own way subversive, are those stories in which the central character is a 'little man', usually a minor civil servant, a literary descendant of Gogol's Akaky Akakiyevich in 'The Overcoat' (1842). His view of the world is imposed upon him by society's rules and regulations, by his place within a strict hierarchy in which social rank is all-important. All is well until some chance happening disrupts the fabric of his life. The humour of 'The Civil Service Exam' (1884) and 'The Exclamation Mark' (1885) is very gentle, but Chekhov also produces disturbingly original variations on the theme. In 'The Malefactor' (1885), a story much admired by Tolstoy, no contact is ever made between the simple world of the uneducated peasant and the magistrate's world of civilized legal procedures. In the famous 'Fat and Thin' (1883) the natural world of friendship yields at once to the unnatural world of social hierarchy. The rank-conscious central character in 'The Chameleon' (1884) can no longer 'see' the world properly: his inability to sort out who owns the dog makes it impossible for him to decide whether he should be looking up or down. As for 'Sergeant Prishibeyev' (1885), he is the dangerous little man who identifies with the bosses and turns dictator, only to find that his view of the world has nothing in common with theirs, either.

Chekhov's distinctive mimetic gift shows up in stories where the humour derives from the highly individual way in which the central character construes the world. In 'Kashtanka' (1887) the young dog 'divided the human race into two very unequal classes, masters and customers . . . the former had the right to beat her, whereas she herself had the right to seize the latter by the calves.' For the very young child, the sole purpose of the clock 'is to swing its pendulum and strike' ('Grisha', 1886). The would-be runaways in 'Boys' (1887) simplify the world: once they reach America, 'California's no distance'. These two boys are dreamers, constructing an ideal world of the imagination, youthful representatives of a type found elsewhere in Chekhov; the defiant ten-year-old at the end of the story has all the makings of a future revolutionary.

One other element in the comic stories peculiar to Chekhov is that of the absurd. This ranges from the incongruous and the ridiculous to the bizarre, the grotesque and even black humour. Here everyday expectations of the world are turned completely upside down. In 'The Daughter of Albion' (1883) grotesque physical description of the English governess, with her nose that looks like a hook and her rotten smell, is combined with a bizarrely improbable situation. This absurd element takes over at the climaxes of 'The Death of a Civil Servant' (1883), 'A Drama' (1887) and 'Encased' (1898). Like several of the more sophisticated comic stories, 'A Drama' operates on different levels. It combines a parody of a cliché-ridden play, the potentially serious theme of the abyss that separates the two characters, and a bizarre climax that is immediately overtaken by a comic twist.

By March 1888 Chekhov had published an incredible 528 stories, about half of them comic. Critics in his lifetime were quick to distinguish what they regarded as the lightweight outpourings of Antosha Chekhonte from the serious work of Anton Chekhov, who published only 60 stories between 1888 and his death in 1904, and gave up comic writing altogether, apart from the one-act farce-vaudevilles of 1888–91. This contrast was inevitable, especially given the very variable quality of the early stories, but it had the unfortunate effect of making it seem as if Chekhonte and Chekhov were two different people, rather than different manifestations of one person. Most Russian critics in the Soviet era concentrated on the handful of comic stories that could be made to yield a strong socio-political message, and likewise failed to look for any deeper continuity. But in 1979 V.B. Kataev wrote that 'it was in the humorous stories of 1884–7 that Chekhov found himself as an artist. Their aim is no longer to make the reader laugh at all costs, but to formulate in comic terms Chekhov's central underlying theme.' That theme, he argues, is philosophical: Chekhov is preoccupied with how each person makes sense of the world differently, and with what happens when these different world-pictures are juxtaposed or come into conflict.

The comic twists of Chekhonte may disappear, but what stands out very clearly in the later Chekhov is a highly developed sense of irony. Story after story turns on some kind of ironic reversal (often that was how the plot suggested itself to him), as if his mind were always patterning the world in that kind of way. The heroine of 'The Grasshopper' (1898) spends all her time collecting 'remarkable' people, only to discover, too late, that the one truly remarkable person in her life was her very 'ordinary' doctor-husband; Dr Ragin in 'Ward No.6' (1892) finds himself incarcerated in the very ward that he has presided over with such calm indifference for so many years; while Belikov in 'Encased' finally discovers the ideal case that he has been searching for all his life – in his coffin. At the start of 'Lady with a Little Dog' (1899) the womanizing Gurov is unattractive, but by the end he has become a sympathetic, even a pathetic, figure.

If Chekhonte is preoccupied with social rank and the unnatural attitudes and relationships it engenders, in Chekhov this theme has a much wider application. He rejects authoritarian attitudes of every kind. He deflates the pretensions of all those who are self-centred, self-satisfied or self-important, and is quick to see through their self-deceits and double standards. He is suspicious of all those who seek to interfere with other people's lives, even when, as in the case of Lida, the elder sister in 'The House with a Mezzanine' (1896), they seem to be well intentioned. In 'Encased', a late story full of comic details that might have been invented by Chekhonte, Chekhov makes a psychological link between Belikov's own insecurity and the role that he feels compelled to play in the outside world as a guardian of public morals. How many more Belikovs there are still to come, the narrator comments, giving the story the widest possible application.

The imaginative empathy that can lead to comic effects when applied by Chekhonte to children and animals is used seriously by Chekhov to depict other 'minority viewpoints', like that of the *déclassée* village schoolmistress in 'A Journey by Cart' (1897) or the closed community of the 'Horse Thieves' (1890), and most effectively in 'Peasants' (1897). To *see* accurately was of great importance to Chekhov, and in this story a whole marginalized class of Russian society is brought miraculously to life from within. No wonder it provoked such a furore.

As for the comic-absurd element in Chekhonte's writing, that surfaces again magnificently in Chekhov's major plays, especially *Three Sisters* (1901) and *The Cherry Orchard* (1904). Among the events and prophecies in the weekly comic *Calendar* that Chekhonte compiled in March–April 1882 we read: 'In Tambov [a well-known provincial railway junction, a place of extreme ordinariness] a volcano is going to erupt'; 'In Berdichev [an important commercial centre in the Ukraine] the refraction of light will take place'; 'On the island of Borneo [here the place is exotic, the event ordinary] there's an outbreak of diphtheria'. Anyone familiar with *Three Sisters* will be reminded at once of the old army doctor Chebutykin. When he first wanders on to the stage, he is copying down in his notebook a formula from the newspaper to prevent hair falling out. In Act II, still carrying his newspaper, he announces that 'Balzac was married in Berdichev', and follows this up soon after with the information that 'in Tsitsikar they've got a smallpox epidemic'.

Without his early experience of comic-absurd writing, it is unlikely that Chekhov would have made a character read out irrelevant scraps of information from a newspaper, although it needed a touch of genius to perceive how this would at once fix him in the audience's mind. The very incongruity of his remarks makes them stand out so sharply that we remember where Balzac was married long after more serious lines have been forgotten. Indeed, the unconventional (and highly influential) approach to stage dialogue that Chekhov perfected could probably *only* have occurred to someone with a taste for the comic-absurd. Faced by conventional dialogue, so neat and rational and orderly, Chekhov said: that's not what conversation is like, it's haphazard and unpredictable, people are having a serious discussion, then someone else reads out something totally irrelevant from a newspaper.

If Chekhonte appears only at odd moments in *Three Sisters*, in *The Cherry Orchard* he is seldom absent for long. The improbable name Simeonov-Pishchik is a combination of the ordinary Simeonov and the absurd Pishchik, 'Squeaker'. Squeaker describes himself as 'an old horse': his constitution and appetite are horse-like, and his father used to joke that the ancient stock of the Simeonov-Squeakers was descended from the horse that Caligula made into a senator. On his first appearance Yepikhodov drops the bunch of flowers he is carrying and is unable to stop his new boots from squeaking; when not dropping something, he is knocking something over or squashing something flat. Chekhonte creates the memorable image of the governess Charlotta, reminiscent of the strikingly visual portrait of the Daughter of Albion. He stage-manages her conjuring tricks and her ventriloquism. He is the instigator of lost galoshes and of sticks that come down over the wrong person's head.

Just as *The Cherry Orchard* resists all attempts to give it a simple comic or serious label, so not every story in this volume will be seen as purely comic. Often, however, critics look too hard for the undercurrent of sadness or the serious implication. It is difficult to accept Gorky's view that in 'The Daughter of Albion' Chekhov wanted to show up the abominable behaviour of the Russian landowner 'towards a lonely, alienated human being', while to comment on 'Vint' (1884) that the little men's obsession with their ridiculous card game only shows up the futility of their lives seems to miss the point: what makes the story delightful is that for once distinctions of rank break down, and the head of department becomes even more enthusiastic about the game than his subordinates ('Sit down, gentlemen, let's have one more rubber!') With 'The Darling' (1899), the last story in this collection, the comic or serious question is especially delicate. Chekhov in a letter describes it as 'a humorous story'. The heroine perfectly illustrates the thesis that we are nothing more than how we view the world. Because she has no view of her own, she can only make sense of the world through other people; without them she collapses. Tolstoy found Olenka's selfless love very moving, but the story is told in a comically deadpan style that makes such an emotional response seem inappropriate; it is equally possible to see in 'the darling' a sinister figure, who feeds on other people and buries two husbands. I prefer to accept Chekhov's own description and to see the story as a light-hearted exploration of what happens when the idea of the chameleon figure is taken to an absurd extreme.

Who is to say what will make a person laugh, or what will make people laugh in one society and not another?

Chekhov's humour has always seemed to me very accessible to people in the English-speaking world. It is not slick or contrived, does not depend on verbal or logical gymnastics, does not shout or show off. It is very much person-oriented. That his characters are Russian is irrelevant: they are immediately recognizable people in easily understood situations.

Introduction

Why, then, are his comic stories not better known? Partly it is a matter of translation. It is much harder to translate the short comic stories than the serious long ones. The former are often full of dialogue, which is difficult to translate at the best of times and especially so if the speakers are not very literate; in the latter there is less dialogue and the speakers are more educated. Translating the long stories with their smooth narrative flow gives you the feeling of driving along in top gear, with only occasional interruptions to negotiate a roundabout or check the map. Not so the short ones: with them it is a matter of constant stops and starts, of jumping out to look under the bonnet, of being endlessly patient and resourceful. Few translators can be bothered. Such translations as exist are often painfully inadequate. Small wonder that Chekhov's numerous commentators in the West who manage to function without a knowledge of Russian conclude that the comic stories deserve no more than a passing glance.

Then there are publishers. In the 1970s, trying to interest a publisher in Chekhov's comic stories, I took along a pile of translations to leave with her. On top was 'An Incident at Law' (1883), at that time unknown in the West. Since it was so short, I suggested she might like to read it on the spot. The massed editions of Virginia Woolf lining her shelves looked down with interest. Two or three minutes passed in silence. Then she suddenly went very red in the face, her eyes filled with tears, and she began choking. A secretary was sent out for a glass of water. Had this been an example of Chekhov's black humour, she would have had a heart attack and died, but since it was real life, she soon recovered her composure. Surely, I thought, after a response like that she will not be able to turn the stories down? But she did. With a literary flourish now rare among publishers, she wrote of her fears of being 'hauled over the coals in offering them to the world'. In the background the voice of Belikov in 'Encased' can be heard whining: 'Yes, it's a good idea, of course, but what will the critics say?' The Chekhov of the comic stories was not sufficiently 'literary', he was not the high culture figure whose short stories had influenced Virginia Woolf and Katherine Mansfield, and whose plays had changed the course of world drama. As if the author of 'Ward No.6' or *The Cherry Orchard* might in some way be diminished by being revealed as the author of 'The Complaints Book' or 'A Horsy Name'! No use protesting, though. Haven't I heard, Chekhov's been labelled, Chekhov's a *heavy* writer.

This introduction is becoming heavy, too. It might have been

9

more effective to write: here are forty of Chekhov's comic stories, I've chosen the ones I like best, they cover a wide range, read them for their own sake and see how you enjoy them. They start from the simple and unsophisticated, and proceed to the more sophisticated and complex; the resulting order is roughly but not strictly chronological.

Nineteen of the stories appeared originally in *Chekhov: The Early Stories 1883–88*, a joint translation by Patrick Miles and myself, first published by John Murray in 1982, reprinted in 1984 by Sphere Books under their Abacus imprint, and in 1994 by Oxford University Press in their World's Classics series. These stories are indicated by an asterisk in the Notes. I am very grateful to Patrick Miles and to Oxford University Press for granting me permission to include them in the present volume.

It is a pleasure to acknowledge my debt to Professor V.B. Kataev of Moscow University for responding with such patience and expertise to my tedious lists of queries; to Richard Davies of the Leeds Russian Archive, together with Tamara Kulikova and Kirill Degtiarenko, for answering queries and especially for making corrections and suggesting improvements to my original versions; and to Patrick Miles for helping a non-angler in his attempts to catch the elusive 'Burbot', which was by far the most difficult story to translate.

Harvey Pitcher

He Quarrelled with his Wife
An Incident

'To hell with you! A chap comes home from the office as hungry as a horse and look at the rubbish he's offered! And if he dares say anything, we have floods of tears! I wish to God I'd never married!'

So saying, he banged his spoon down on his plate, jumped up and went out, slamming the door furiously behind him. She began sobbing, clasped her serviette to her face and also left the room. End of meal.

On reaching his study, he threw himself down on the sofa and buried his face in the cushion.

'What on earth possessed me to get married?' he thought. 'If this is "family life", you can keep it! I'm no sooner married than I want to shoot myself!'

A quarter of an hour later soft footsteps were heard outside the door . . .

'Oh yes, the usual pattern . . . She insults me, behaves outrageously, and now she's out there wanting to make it up . . . Well, blow that, I'd rather hang myself!'

The door opened with a faint squeak and did not close again. Someone had come into the room and approached the sofa with quiet timid footsteps.

'That's right! Beg my forgiveness, implore me, start sobbing . . . A fat lot of good that'll do you! You won't get a word out of me and that's final . . . Can't you see I'm asleep and don't want to talk?'

He buried his head deeper in the cushion and snored quietly. But men are as weak as women. It's easy to thaw them out and make them sweet again. Aware of a warm body behind him, he stubbornly shifted his position closer to the back of the sofa and twitched his leg.

11

'Oh yes, now we creep in and snuggle up to me and start fawning. Soon we'll start kissing my shoulder and kneeling in front of me. I can't stand these endearments! Still, I'll have to forgive her. It's bad for her to worry in her condition. I'll let her stew for an hour as a punishment and then forgive her.'

A profound sigh flew quietly right past his ear. Then a second and a third . . . He felt the touch of a small hand on his shoulder.

'To hell with it, I'll forgive her this last time. I've tormented her long enough, poor thing! Especially as it was my fault! Making a fuss over nothing!'

'Let's call it a day, then, my little pet!' he said, stretching his arm out behind him and clasping a warm body.

'Ugh!'

Beside him lay his large dog Diana.

1884

Notes from the Memoirs of a Man of Ideals

On the 10th of May I took twenty-eight days' leave, scrounged a hundred roubles on credit from our cashier and made up my mind that come what may I'd live 'the good life', live it right up to the hilt, so that for the next ten years I'd be able to live on memories alone.

You do know, don't you, what is meant by 'the good life' in the best sense of the term? It doesn't mean going to the operetta at a summer theatre, dining out and returning home tipsy in the early hours. It doesn't mean going to an exhibition, then on to the races and throwing your money about round the tote. No, if you want to live the good life, board a train and go to a place where the scent of lilac and bird cherry permeates the air, where lilies of the valley and butterfly orchids compete to caress your eye with their delicate whiteness and gleaming diamond-coloured dewdrops. That's where you'll understand what life is all about – in the wide open

12

spaces, beneath the blue vault of heaven, amidst the green woods and babbling brooks, in the society of birds and green beetles! Throw in two or three encounters with a wide-brimmed hat, darting eyes and a little white apron . . . All these thoughts, I'm bound to say, were in my mind as I moved out to the country, holiday permit in my pocket and basking in the generosity of our cashier.

On the advice of a friend, I rented a datcha from Sofya Pavlovna Knigina. It consisted of a spare room in her own datcha, equipped with a table, furniture and other conveniences. Renting it couldn't have been simpler. On reaching Pererva and going to look for Knigina's datcha, I remember mounting a terrace – and stopping in confusion. It was a nice, cosy, charming little terrace, but even nicer and cosier (if you'll pardon the expression) was the buxom young lady sitting at a table on the terrace drinking tea. She peered up at me and said:

'How can I help you?'

'Do forgive me,' I began. 'I think – I think I must be in the wrong place. I'm looking for Knigina's datcha . . .'

'I *am* Knigina . . . How can I help you?'

I was taken aback . . . I was used to thinking of the landladies of apartments or datchas as rheumaticky old individuals smelling of stale coffee grounds, but here – 'angels and ministers of grace defend us,' as Hamlet says – here sat this wonderful, splendid, astonishing, captivating individual. I stammered out an explanation of what I wanted.

'How delightful! Do sit down! Your friend wrote to me. Would you like some tea? Cream or lemon?'

There is a certain kind of female (most frequently blonde) with whom you feel quite at home, like old friends, in no more than a couple of minutes. Sofya Pavlovna was just such a one. After the first glass of tea I already knew that she was unmarried and living on the interest from capital, and that she was expecting a visit from her aunt; and I knew the reasons that had prompted her to let one of her rooms. To begin with, 120 roubles was a lot for one person to pay, and then being alone was a bit scary: a thief might break in during the night, or some crazy peasant stumble in during the day! And it was perfectly proper for a single lady or gentleman to occupy the corner room.

'Still, I prefer men!' sighed the landlady, licking jam off a spoon. 'They're less bother and I feel safer . . .'

In a word, within an hour or so Sofya Pavlovna and I had become friends.

'Oh!' I suddenly thought as I said goodbye. 'We've talked about everything except the most important thing of all. How much should I pay you? I shall only be with you for twenty-eight days . . . I'd like a meal, of course . . . and tea, and so on.'

'Do we have to talk about that? Pay me what you can . . . I'm not letting the room for money, but just . . . for the company . . . Is 25 roubles all right?'

Naturally, I agreed, and so my datcha life began. The interesting thing about datcha life is that each day and each night is like the one before – yet this very monotony is so delightful, and what days and nights they are! Reader, I'm in raptures, allow me to embrace you! In the morning I'd wake up without a single thought of work and drink tea with cream. At 11 I'd go in to wish my landlady good morning and join her in drinking coffee with rich warmed-up cream on top. Between coffee and dinner we'd chat. At two dinner, and what a dinner! Imagine you're feeling as hungry as a horse, you sit down at table, knock back a large glass of blackcurrant vodka and follow it with hot salted beef and horse-radish. Then imagine cold kvass soup or green shchi with sour cream etc., etc. After dinner a quiet lie-down, reading a novel, and having to jump up every other minute, as my land-lady keeps appearing by my door, saying 'don't move, don't move!' Then a bathe. In the evening until well into the night a walk with Sofya Pavlovna. Imagine yourself at eventide, when everything is asleep except the nightingale and a heron crying from time to time, when the sound of a distant train barely reaches you on the faintly stirring breeze – imagine walking in the woods or along the railway embankment with a buxom little blonde, who hugs herself coquettishly in the cool evening air and every so often turns her pale moonlit face towards you . . . Terrific!

Within a week that event occurred which the reader has long been anticipating and which no decent story can do without . . . I was unable to resist . . . Sofya Pavlovna listened to my declarations indifferently, almost coldly, as if she had long been anticipating them, and merely pouted sweetly, as if to say:

'I don't know why you're making such a fuss about it!'

Those twenty-eight days flashed past in a second. When my leave expired, feeling miserable and dissatisfied, I had to say goodbye to the datcha and to Sonya. As I packed my suitcase, my landlady was sitting on the sofa wiping her eyes. Almost in tears myself, I comforted her and promised to come and see her at the datcha on my days off and to visit her during the winter in Moscow.

'Oh!' I suddenly thought, 'when are we going to settle up, dear heart? How much do I owe you?'

'Later, later . . .' said the object of my affections, sobbing.

'Why later? Never mix business and pleasure, as the saying goes, and besides I'd hate to feel I was living at your expense. Don't make things difficult, Sonya . . . How much?'

'It's . . . a trifling sum,' said my landlady, sobbing and opening a table drawer. 'You could always pay me later.'

Sonya rummaged in the drawer, pulled out a piece of paper and handed it to me.

'Is this the bill?' I asked. 'Splendid, absolutely splendid . . . (I put on my glasses) we'll settle up and that'll be fine . . . (I glanced through the bill.) Grand total . . . Hang on, what's this? Grand total . . . But this can't be right, Sonya! It says "212 roubles 44 kopecks". That's not my bill.'

'It's yours, Doodie! You check!'

'But – why is it so much? Board and lodging 25 roubles, agreed . . . Use of servant 3 roubles, well, yes, I agree to that . . .'

'I don't understand, Doodie,' my landlady said slowly, looking at me in astonishment with her tear-filled eyes. 'Surely you believe me? Count it up if you don't! You drank blackcurrant vodka . . . I could hardly give you vodka for dinner at that price! You had cream with your tea and coffee . . . then there were strawberries, cucumbers, cherries . . . As for coffee, you hadn't said you wanted any, but drank it every day! Still, they're such trifling items that I can knock off 12 roubles if you wish. Let's just say 200.'

'But – there's an item here for 75 roubles without any details . . . What's that for?'

'What's that for? Well, I ask you!'

I looked at her pretty little face. It had such an open, sincere and astonished expression that my tongue couldn't utter a single word. I gave Sonya a hundred roubles and a promissory note for another hundred, humped my suitcase on to my shoulders and set off for the station.

Can anyone out there lend me a hundred roubles?

1885

15

A Dreadful Night

Ivan Petrovich Spektroff's face grew pale and his voice quavered as he turned down the lamp and began his story:

'It was Christmas Eve 1883. The earth lay shrouded in impenetrable darkness. I was returning home from the house of a friend (who has since died), where we had all been sitting up late attending a seance. For some reason the streets through which I was passing were unlit, and I had almost to grope my way along. I was living in Moscow, near the Church of St Mary-in-the-Tombstones, in a house belonging to the civil servant Kadavroff – in other words, in one of the remotest parts of the Arbat district. My thoughts as I walked along were gloomy and depressing . . .

"The end of your life is at hand . . . Repent . . ."

Such had been the words addressed to me at the seance by Spinoza, whose spirit we had succeeded in calling up. I asked for confirmation, and the saucer not only repeated the words, but added: "This very night." I am not a believer in spiritualism, but the thought of death, or even the merest allusion to it, is enough to plunge me into despondency. Death is inevitable, my friends, it is commonplace, but nevertheless the thought of death is repugnant to human nature . . . Now, as cold, unfathomable darkness hemmed me in and raindrops whirled madly before my eyes, as the wind groaned plaintively above my head and I could neither see a single living soul nor hear a single human sound around me, my heart filled with a vague, inexplicable dread. I, a man free from superstition, hurried through the streets afraid to look around or glance to either side. I felt sure that if I did look round, I would see an apparition of death close behind me.'

Spektroff gulped for breath, drank some water and continued:

'This feeling of dread, which despite its vagueness you will all recognize, did not leave me even when I climbed to the third floor of Kadavroff's house, unlocked the door and entered my room. It was dark in my humble abode. The wind was moaning in the stove and tapping on the damper, almost as though it were

16

begging to be let into the warm.

If Spinoza was telling the truth, I reflected with a smile, then I am to die this night to the accompaniment of these moans. What a gruesome thought!

I lit a match . . . A violent gust of wind raced across the roof. The quiet moaning turned to a ferocious roar. Somewhere down below a half-loose shutter started banging, and the damper began whining plaintively for help . . .

Pity the poor devils, I thought, without a roof over their heads on a night like this.

The moment was to prove inopportune, however, for reflections of that kind. When the sulphur of my match flared up with a blue flame and I looked round the room, an unexpected, a terrifying spectacle met my eyes . . . Oh, why didn't that gust of wind blow out my match? Then perhaps I should have seen nothing and my hair would not have stood on end. I gave a wild cry, took a step backwards towards the door, and filled with terror, amazement and despair, closed my eyes . . .

In the centre of the room stood a coffin.

The blue flame did not last long, but I had time to make out the coffin's main features . . . I saw its richly shimmering pink brocade, I saw the gold-embroidered cross on its lid. There are certain things, my friends, which imprint themselves on one's memory, even when one has glimpsed them but for a single moment. So it was with that coffin. I saw it but for a second, yet I recall it in the most minute detail. It was a coffin made for a person of medium height, and judging by the pink colour, for a young girl. The expensive silk brocade, the feet, the bronze handles – all these suggested that the deceased came from a wealthy family.

I rushed headlong from my room, not stopping to think or consider but experiencing only unutterable fear, and flew downstairs. The staircase and corridors were in darkness, I kept tripping over my coat-tails, and how I avoided tumbling head-over-heels down the stairs and breaking my neck, I shall never know. Finding myself in the street, I leant up against a wet lamp-post and tried to recover my composure. My heart was thumping horribly and I had a tight feeling across the chest . . .'

One of the listeners turned up the lamp and moved her chair closer to the narrator, who continued:

'I would not have been so taken aback if I had discovered in my room a fire, a thief or a mad dog . . . I would not have been so taken aback if the ceiling had come down, the floor had collapsed or the walls had caved in . . . All that is natural and comprehensible. But how could a coffin have turned up in my room? Where had it come from? How had an expensive coffin, evidently made for a young girl of noble birth, found its way into the miserable room of a minor civil servant? Was the coffin empty or was it – occupied? And who was this *she*, this rich young aristocrat who had quitted life so prematurely and paid me this dread, disturbing visit? It was a tantalizing mystery!

If it's not a case of the supernatural, the thought flashed through my mind, then there's foul play involved.

I became lost in conjecture. My door had been locked while I was out, and only my very close friends knew where I kept the key. But the coffin certainly hadn't been left by friends. Then it was also conceivable that the undertakers had delivered the coffin to me in error. They might have muddled up the names, mistaken the floor number or the door, and taken the coffin to the wrong place. But who ever heard of Moscow undertakers leaving a room without being paid, or at least waiting for a tip?

The spirits foretold my death, I thought. Perhaps they've already set about providing me with a coffin, too?

I am not a believer in spiritualism, my friends, nor was I then, but such a coincidence is enough to plunge even a philosopher into a mood of mysticism.

But all this is absurd, I decided, and I'm being as cowardly as a schoolboy. It was an optical illusion – no more than that! On my way home I was in such a gloomy state of mind that it's hardly surprising my overwrought nerves thought they saw a coffin . . . Of course, an optical illusion! What else could it be?

The rain was lashing my face, and the wind kept tugging angrily at my hat and coat-tails . . . I was wet through and chilled to the bone. I would have to find shelter – but where? To go back home would mean running the risk of seeing the coffin again, and that was a spectacle beyond my powers of endurance. Not seeing a single living soul or hearing a single human sound around me, left alone in the company of a coffin which perhaps contained a dead body, I might easily lose my reason. But to remain on the street in the cold and pouring rain was equally impossible.

I decided to go and spend the night with my friend Lugubrovitch (who, as you know, was later to shoot himself). He lived in a block of furnished rooms belonging to the merchant Skeletoff – the ones on the corner of Deadman's Passage.'

Spektroff wiped away the beads of cold perspiration that had gathered on his pallid brow, and with a deep sigh continued:
'I did not find my friend at home. After knocking on his door and deciding he must be out, I felt for his key on the lintel, unlocked the door and went in. I flung my wet coat on the floor, and feeling my way to the sofa, sat down to recuperate. It was very dark ... The wind droned mournfully in the ventilator. Behind the stove a cricket chirped over and over again its monotonous song. The Kremlin bells had begun to ring for Christmas morning communion. Hastily I struck a match. But its light did not dispel my gloomy mood; on the contrary. A dreadful, unutterable terror seized me again ... I cried out, staggered backwards, and rushed blindly from the apartment ...

In my friend's room I had seen the same as in my own – a coffin!

My friend's coffin was almost twice as large as mine, and its subfusc upholstery gave it a peculiarly gloomy appearance. How had it got there? That it was an optical illusion now seemed quite certain – there couldn't be a coffin in every room! I was obviously suffering from a nervous disorder, from hallucinations. Wherever I now went, I would see before me the dreadful dwelling-place of death. In other words I was going mad, I was suffering from a kind of "coffinomania", and the cause of my derangement was not hard to find: I had only to recall the spiritualist seance and the words of Spinoza ...

I'm going mad! I thought to myself with terror, clutching my head. Oh my God! What am I to do?

My head was splitting and my knees shaking ... The rain was pouring down in buckets, the wind was piercing right through me, and I had neither coat nor hat. To go back to the apartment for them was impossible, beyond my powers of endurance ... Fear gripped me firmly in her cold embrace. My hair was standing on end and cold perspiration streamed down my face, even though I believed that the coffin was only a hallucination.'

'What was I to do?' Spektroff continued. 'I was going mad and in danger of catching a violent cold. Fortunately I remembered that not far from Deadman's Passage lived my good friend Kryptin, a recently qualified doctor, who had also been at the seance with me that night. I hurried round to his place. This was before he married his merchant heiress, and he was still living on the fourth floor of a house belonging to state counsellor Nekropolsky.

At Kryptin's my nerves were fated to undergo yet another ordeal. As I was climbing to the fourth floor, I heard above me a terrible din of running footsteps and slamming doors.

"Help!" I heard a soul-piercing cry. "Help! Porter!"

And a moment later a dark figure in a coat and battered top-hat came hurtling down the stairs towards me . . .

"Kryptin!" I exclaimed, recognizing my friend. "Is that you, Kryptin? Whatever's wrong?"

Kryptin pulled up short and clutched my hand convulsively. He was pale, breathing heavily and trembling. His eyes were rolling wildly and his chest was heaving . . .

"Is that you, Spektroff?" he asked in a sepulchral voice. "Is that really you? You're as white as a ghost . . . Are you quite sure you're not a hallucination? . . . My God . . . you scare me stiff . . ."

"But what about you? You look ghastly!"

"Phew, let me get my breath back, old chap . . . It's wonderful to see you, if it really is you and not an optical illusion. That damned seance . . . Would you believe it, my nerves were so overwrought that when I got back to my room just now I thought I saw – a coffin!"

I could not believe my ears and asked for confirmation.

"A coffin, a real coffin!" said the doctor, sitting down exhausted on one of the stairs. "I'm no coward, but the devil himself would get a fright if he came home after a seance and bumped into a coffin in the dark!"

Stumbling and stammering, I told the doctor about the coffins I had seen . . .

For a moment we gazed at each other, our eyes popping and our mouths gaping in astonishment. Then, to make sure we were not seeing hallucinations, we began pinching each other.

"We both feel pain," said the doctor, "which means that we're not asleep and seeing each other in a dream. And that means the coffins – mine and your two – are not optical illusions but really do exist. So what's our next move, old man?"

After standing for a solid hour on the cold staircase and losing ourselves in conjecture and surmise, we were chilled to the bone and made up our minds to cast aside cowardly fear and wake up the floor porter, in order to return with him to the doctor's room. This we did. On entering the apartment, we lit a candle and there indeed we saw a coffin, covered in white silk brocade, with a gold fringe and tassels. The porter crossed himself reverently.

"Now we can find out," said the doctor, pale faced and

trembling all over, "whether this coffin is empty, or – or – inhabited!"

After an understandably long period of indecision, the doctor bent over, and gritting his teeth in dread and anticipation, wrenched off the lid of the coffin. We looked inside and . . .

The coffin was empty.

There was no dead body, but we did find a letter which read as follows:

"My dear Kryptin! As you know, my father-in-law's business has been going from bad to worse. He's up to his neck in debt. Tomorrow or the day after they're coming to make an inventory of all his stock, which will deal the death blow to his family and mine, and to our honour, which is dearer to me than anything. At our family conference yesterday we decided to hide everything precious and valuable. As my father-in-law's stock consists entirely of coffins (he is, as you know, a master coffin-maker, the best in town), we decided to hide away all the best coffins. I appeal to you as a friend to help me save our fortune and our honour! In the hope that you will assist us in preserving our stock, I am sending you one coffin, old chap, with the request that you keep it until it is required. Without the help of our friends and acquaintances we shall certainly perish. I hope this is not too much to ask, especially as the coffin will not be with you for more than a week. I have sent a coffin each to all those I consider our true friends and am relying on their nobility and generosity.

Affectionately yours, Ivan Nekstovkin."

For three months afterwards I was under a specialist in nervous disorders, whilst our friend, the coffin-maker's son-in-law, not only saved his honour and his stock, but set up a funeral parlour and deals in memorials and tombstones. His business is none too healthy, and now, when I come home each evening, I am always afraid I'm going to see a white marble memorial or a catafalque by my bedside.'

1884

21

From the Diary of an Assistant Book-keeper

11 May 1863. Glotkin, our sixty-year-old book-keeper, took brandy and milk on account of his cough, and had an attack of delirium tremens in consequence. The doctors are maintaining with their usual self-confidence that he'll be dead by tomorrow. So I'll be book-keeper at last! It was promised me ages ago.

Collegiate Secretary Grabsky is going to be charged with assaulting a petitioner who called him a bureaucrat. It seems definite.

Took a decoction for catarrh of the stomach.

3 August 1865. Glotkin the book-keeper has a bad chest again. He's coughing and on brandy and milk. If he dies, I'll replace him. Only a faint hope, though, as apparently delirium tremens isn't always fatal!

Grabsky snatched a promissory note from an Armenian and tore it up. The case may well come to court.

An old woman (Guryevna) was saying yesterday I've not got catarrh of the stomach, but concealed haemorrhoids. Very likely!

30 June 1867. According to the papers there's cholera in Arabia. If it reaches Russia, there'll be lots of vacancies. If old man Glotkin dies, I'll get the book-keeper's job. How people do hang on! I reckon it's quite reprehensible for anyone to live as long as that.

What can I take for my catarrh of the stomach? Should I try worm-seed?

2 January 1870. A dog was howling all night in Glotkin's yard. My cook Pelageya says it's a sure sign, and we sat up until two talking about how I'll buy myself a racoon coat and a dressing-gown once I'm book-keeper. And I may well get married. Not to a young girl, of course, in view of my age, but to a widow.

Grabsky was turned out of the club yesterday for telling a dirty story out loud and laughing at Sniffkin, a member of the trade deputation, for his patriotism. I hear the latter's taking him to court.

Must take my catarrh of the stomach to see Doctor Botkin. They say he's very good.

4 June 1878. According to the papers, there's plague in Vetlyanka. People going down like ninepins, they say. Glotkin's taking pepper-brandy on account of it. Well, pepper-brandy's hardly going to be much help to a man of his age. If the plague comes, I'm sure to be book-keeper.

4 June 1883. Glotkin's dying. I went to see him and with tears in my eyes begged his forgiveness for being in such a hurry to see him die. He forgave me magnanimously with tears in his eyes and recommended acorn coffee for catarrh of the stomach.

Grabsky nearly landed up in court again. He pawned a hired piano with a Jew. In spite of it all he's already a collegiate assessor and has his St Stanislas. Amazing what goes on in this world!

For catarrh of the stomach: take 2 *zolotniks* of ginger, 1½ of galingale, 1 of nitric acid, and 5 of seven brothers blood, mix together, infuse in a *shtof* of vodka, and drink by the glass on an empty stomach.

7 June ditto. Glotkin was buried yesterday. Alas, this ancient's death did nothing for me! At night I dream of him all draped in white, beckoning me with his finger. And wretched, wretched sinner that I am, the job of book-keeper didn't go to me, but Chalikov. Not to me, but to a young man whose aunt is married to a general and pulled strings on his behalf. All my hopes are dashed!

10 June 1886. Chalikov's wife has run off. He's miserable, poor fellow. In his grief he may lay hands on himself. If he does, I'm book-keeper. It's being talked about already. So there's still hope, I can go on living, and the racoon coat may well not be far off. As for getting married, I'm not averse. If a good opportunity arises, why not take it, only I need to consult someone; marriage is a serious step.

Grabsky took Privy Councillor Lirmans's galoshes instead of his own. What a to-do!

Païsy the porter recommended mercuric chloride for catarrh of the stomach. Must try it.

1883

An Incident at Law

The case occurred at a recent session of the N. district court.

In the dock was Sidor Felonovsky, resident of N., a fellow of about thirty, with restless gypsy features and shifty little eyes. He was accused of burglary, fraud and obtaining a false passport, and coupled with the latter was a further charge of impersonation. The case was being brought by the deputy prosecutor. The name of his tribe is Legion. He's totally devoid of any special features or qualities that might make him popular or bring him huge fees: he's just average. He has a nasal voice, doesn't sound his k's properly, and is forever blowing his nose.

Whereas defending was a fantastically celebrated and popular advocate, known throughout the land, whose wonderful speeches are always being quoted, whose name is uttered in tones of awe . . .

The role that he plays at the end of cheap novels, where the hero is completely vindicated and the public bursts into applause, is not inconsiderable. In such novels he is given a surname derived from thunder, lightning and other equally awe-inspiring forces of nature.

When the deputy prosecutor had succeeded in proving that Felonovsky was guilty and deserved no mercy, when he had finished defining and persuading and said: 'The case for the prosecution rests' – then defence counsel rose to his feet. Everyone pricked up their ears. Dead silence reigned. Counsel began his speech . . . and in the public gallery their nerves ran riot! Sticking out his swarthy neck and cocking his head to one side, with eyes a-flashing and hand upraised, he poured his mellifluous magic into their expectant ears. His words plucked at their nerves as though he were playing the balalaika . . . Scarcely had he uttered a couple of sentences than there was a loud sigh and a woman had to be carried out ashen-faced. Only three minutes elapsed before the judge was obliged to reach over for his bell and ring three times for order. The red-nosed clerk of the court swivelled round on his chair and began to glare menacingly at the animated faces of the public.

Eyes dilated, cheeks drained of colour, everyone craned forward in an agony of suspense to hear what he would say next . . . And need I describe what was happening to the ladies' hearts?!

'Gentlemen of the jury, you and I are human beings! Let us therefore judge as human beings!' said defence counsel *inter alia*. 'Before appearing in front of you today, this human being had to endure the agony of six months on remand. For six months his wife has been deprived of the husband she cherishes so fondly, for six months his children's eyes have been wet with tears at the thought that their dear father was no longer beside them. Oh, if only you could see those children! They are starving because there is no one to feed them. They are crying because they are so deeply unhappy . . . Yes, look at them, look at them! See how they stretch their tiny arms towards you, imploring you to give them back their father! They are not here in person, but can you not picture them? (*Pause.*) Six months on remand . . . Six . . . They put him in with thieves and murderers . . . a man like this! (*Pause.*) One need only imagine the moral torment of that imprisonment, far from his wife and children, to . . . But need I say more?!'

Sobs were heard in the gallery . . . A girl with a large brooch on her bosom had burst into tears. Then the little old lady next to her began snivelling.

Defence counsel went on and on . . . He tended to ignore the facts, concentrating more on the psychological aspect.

'Shall I tell you what it means to know this man's soul? It means knowing a unique and individual world, a world full of varied impulses. I have made a study of that world, and I tell you frankly that as I did so, I felt I was studying Man for the first time . . . I understood what Man is . . . And every impulse of my client's soul convinces me that in him I have the honour of observing a perfect human being . . .'

The clerk of the court stopped staring so menacingly and fished around in his pocket for a handkerchief. Two more women were carried out. The judge forgot all about the bell and put on his glasses, so that no one would notice the large tear welling up in his right eye. Handkerchiefs appeared on every side. The deputy prosecutor, that rock, that iceberg, that most insensitive of organisms, shifted about in his chair, turned red, and started gazing at the floor . . . Tears were glistening behind his glasses.

'Why on earth did I go ahead with the case?' he thought to himself. 'How am I ever going to live down a fiasco like this!'

'Just look at his eyes!' defence counsel continued (his chin was trembling, his voice was trembling, and his eyes showed how much his soul was suffering). 'Can those meek, tender eyes look upon a crime without flinching? No, I tell you, those are the eyes of a man who weeps! There are sensitive nerves concealed behind those Asiatic cheekbones! And the heart that beats within that coarse, misshapen breast – that heart is as honest as the day is long! Members of the jury, can you dare as human beings to say that this man is guilty?'

At this point the accused himself could bear it no longer. Now it was his turn to start crying. He blinked, burst into tears and began fidgeting restlessly . . .

'All right!' he blurted out, interrupting defence counsel. 'All right! I *am* guilty! It was me done the burglary and the fraud. Miserable wretch that I am! I took the money from the trunk and got my sister-in-law to hide the fur coat. I confess! Guilty on all counts!'

Accused then made a detailed confession and was convicted.

1883

The Daughter of Albion

A handsome barouche with rubber tyres, a fat coachman and velvet-upholstered seats drew up in front of Gryabov's manor house. Out jumped the local Marshal of Nobility, Fyodor Andreich Ottsov. He was met in the anteroom by a sleepy-looking footman.

'Family at home?' asked the Marshal.

'No, sir. Mistress has took the children visiting, sir, and Master's out fishing with mamselle the governess. Went out first thing, sir.'

Ottsov stood and pondered, then set off for the river to look for Gryabov. He came upon him a couple of versts from the house. On looking down from the steep river bank and catching sight of him, Ottsov burst out laughing . . . A big fat man with a very big head, Gryabov was sitting cross-legged on the sand in Turkish fashion. He was fishing. His hat was perched on the back of his head and his tie had slid over to one side. Next to him stood a tall thin Englishwoman with bulging eyes like a lobster's and a large bird-nose that looked more like a hook than a nose. She was wearing a white muslin dress, through which her yellow, scraggy shoulders showed quite clearly. On her gold belt hung a little gold watch. She too was fishing. They were both as silent as the grave and as still as the river in which their floats were suspended.

'Strong was his wish, but sad his lot!' said Ottsov, laughing. 'Good day, Ivan Kuzmich!'

'Oh . . . it's you, is it?' asked Gryabov, without taking his eyes off the water. 'You've arrived then?'

'As you see . . . Still sold on this nonsense, are you? Not tired of it yet?'

'Been here since morning, damn it . . . They don't seem to be biting today. I haven't caught a thing, nor's this scarecrow here either. Sit sit sit, and not so much as a nibble! It's been torture, I can tell you.'

'Well, chuck it then. Let's go and have a glass of vodka!'

'No, hang on . . . We may still catch something. They bite better towards dusk . . . You know, I've been sitting here since first thing this morning – I'm bored stiff! God knows what put this fishing bug into me. I know it's a stupid waste of time but still I go on with it! I sit here chained to this bank like a convict and stare at the water as if I was daft. I ought to be out haymaking and here I am fishing. Yesterday the bishop was taking the service at Khaponyevo, but I didn't go, I sat here all day with this . . . this trout . . . this old hag . . .'

'Are you crazy?' Ottsov asked in embarrassment, glancing sideways at the Englishwoman. 'Swearing in front of a lady . . . calling her names . . .'

'To hell with her! She doesn't understand a word of Russian anyway. You can pay her compliments or call her names for all she cares. And look at that nose! Her nose alone is enough to freeze your blood. We fish here for days on end and she doesn't say a word. Just stands there like a stuffed dummy, staring at the water with those goggle eyes.'

The Englishwoman yawned, changed the worm on her line and cast out again.

'You know, it's a very funny thing,' Gryabov continued. 'This fool of a woman has lived over here for ten years and you'd think she'd be able to say *something* in Russian. Any tinpot aristocrat of ours can go over there and start jabbering away in their lingo in no time, but not them – oh no! Just look at her nose! Take a really good look at that nose!'

'Oh come now, this is embarrassing . . . Stop going on at the woman . . .'

'She's not a woman, she's a spinster. I expect she spends all day dreaming of a fiancé, the witch. And there's a kind of rotten smell about her . . . I tell you, old man, I hate her guts! I can't look at her without getting worked up! When she turns those huge eyes on me, I get this jarring sensation all over, as if I'd knocked my funny-bone. She's another one who likes fishing. And look at the way she goes about it: as if it were some holy rite! Turning up her nose at everything, damn her . . . Here am I, she says to herself, a member of the human race, so that makes me superior to the rest of creation. And do you know what her name is? Wilka Charlesovna Tvice! Ugh, I can't even say it properly!'

Hearing her name, the Englishwoman slowly brought her nose round in Gryabov's direction and measured him with a look of contempt. Then, raising her glance from Gryabov to Ottsov, she poured contempt over him too. And all of this was done in silence, solemnly and slowly.

'You see?' said Gryabov, roaring with laughter. 'That's what she thinks of us! Old hag! I only keep the codfish because of the children. But for them, I wouldn't let her within a hundred versts of the estate . . . Just like a hawk's beak, that nose . . . And what about her waist? The witch reminds me of a tent-peg – you know, take hold of her and bang her into the ground. Hang on, I think I've got a bite . . .'

Gryabov jumped up and lifted his rod. The line went taut . . . He gave a tug but could not pull the hook out.

'It's snagged!' he said, frowning. 'Caught behind a stone, I expect . . . Blast!'

Gryabov looked worried. Sighing, scuttling from side to side and muttering oaths, he tugged and tugged at the line – but to no effect. Gryabov paled.

'Blow it! I'll have to get into the water.'

'Oh, give it up!'

'Can't do that . . . They bite so well towards dusk . . . What a ruddy mess! I'll simply have to get into the water. Nothing else for it! And I'd do anything not to have to undress! It means I'll have to get rid of the Englishwoman . . . I can't undress in front of her. She is a lady, after all!'

Gryabov threw off his hat and tie.

'Miss ... er ... Miss Tvice!' he said, turning to the Englishwoman. *'Je vous prie* ... Now how can I put it? How can I put it so you'll understand? Listen ... over there! Go over there! Got it?'

Miss Tvice poured a look of contempt over Gryabov and emitted a nasal sound.

'Oh, you don't understand? Clear off, I'm telling you! I've got to undress, you old hag! Go on! Over there!'

Tugging at the governess's sleeve, Gryabov pointed to the bushes and crouched down – meaning, of course, go behind the bushes and keep out of sight ... Twitching her eyebrows energetically, the Englishwoman delivered herself of a long sentence in English. The landowners burst out laughing.

'That's the first time I've heard her voice. It's a voice all right! What am I going to do with her? She just doesn't understand.'

'Forget it! Let's go and have some vodka.'

'Can't do that, this is when they should start biting ... At dusk ... Well, what do you propose I do? It's no good! I'll have to undress in front of her ...'

Gryabov removed his jacket and waistcoat, and sat down on the sand to take off his boots.

'Look, Ivan Kuzmich,' said the Marshal, spluttering with laughter. 'Now you're actually insulting her, my friend, you're making a mockery of her.'

'No one asked her not to understand, did they? Let this be a lesson to these foreigners!'

Gryabov took off his boots and trousers, removed his underwear, and stood there in a state of nature. Ottsov doubled up, his face scarlet from a mixture of laughter and embarrassment. The Englishwoman twitched her eyebrows and blinked ... Then a haughty, contemptuous smile passed over her yellow face.

'Must cool down first,' said Gryabov, slapping his thighs. 'Do tell me, Fyodor Andreich, why is it I get this rash on my chest every summer?'

'Oh hurry up and get in the water, you great brute, or cover yourself with something!'

'She might at least show some embarrassment, the hussy!' said Gryabov, getting into the water and crossing himself. 'Brrr ... this water's cold ... Look at those eyebrows of hers twitching! She's not going away ... She's above the crowd! Ha, ha, ha! She doesn't even regard us as human beings!'

When he was up to his knees in the water, he drew himself up to his full enormous height, winked and said:

'Bit different from England, eh?!'

Miss Tvice coolly changed her worm, gave a yawn and cast her line. Ottsov turned aside. Gryabov detached the hook, immersed himself and came puffing out of the water. Two minutes later he was sitting on the sand again, fishing.

1883

Foiled!

Mr Elias Dregs and his wife Cleopatra were standing by the door, straining to catch every word. In a small room on the other side a declaration of love was apparently taking place, those involved being their daughter, Natashenka, and Gropin, a local schoolmaster.

'He's nibbling!' whispered Dregs, trembling with impatience and rubbing his hands. 'Now look, Mother, as soon as they start talking about their feelings, whip down the icon from the wall and in we go to bless them. Once we've put the icon over them, that's absolutely final and sacred. He can't wriggle out then, even if he goes to court.'

Meanwhile, behind the door, the following conversation was taking place:

'Leave your *caractère* out of it,' Gropin was saying, striking a match on his check trousers. 'I say I never wrote you any letters.'

'Oh no, of *course* you didn't! As if I wouldn't recognize your handwriting,' the girl answered, giving a shrill affected laugh and glancing at herself every so often in the mirror. 'I knew it straight away! And aren't you the funny one! A teacher of calligraphy and you write just like a chimpanzee! How can you teach handwriting when you can't write yourself?'

'Hm! . . . That's not the point. The main thing in calligraphy isn't handwriting, it's keeping the class in order. Bang 'em on the head with a ruler, make 'em kneel in the corner. What's handwriting, anyway? Doesn't mean a thing! Nekrasov was a famous writer, but it's quite shameful, the way he wrote. They show you his handwriting in the collected edition.'

'Yes, but you're not Nekrasov . . . (sighs). I'd be quite happy to marry a writer. He'd spend all his time writing poems to me!'

'I could write you verses, too, if you liked.'

'You? What could *you* write about?'

'About love . . . about feelings . . . about your eyes. You'd go crazy when you read them. They'd make you weep. And if I wrote you poetic verses, would you let me kiss your little hand?'

'That's nothing, you can kiss it now if you want!'

Gropin jumped to his feet and with eyes popping, threw himself upon her plump little hand which smelt of egg soap.

'Get the icon down,' said Dregs, pale with excitement, giving his wife a swift dig in the ribs and buttoning up his coat. 'Right. *Now!*'

And without a moment's delay, Dregs flung open the door.

'My children . . .' he murmured, throwing up his arms and blinking back the tears. 'May the Lord bless you, my children! Live . . . be fruitful . . . multiply . . .'

'And my . . . my blessings upon you, too,' said Mamma, weeping with happiness. 'Be happy, my dear ones! Oh, you're depriving me of my one and only treasure,' she went on, turning to Gropin. 'You must love my daughter and be kind to her . . .'

Gropin gaped in fear and astonishment. The parents' attack had been so daring and unexpected that he could not utter a single word.

'Done for! They've got me at last!' he thought, feeling faint with terror. 'Curtains for you, mate! You've had it!'

And he bowed his head obediently, as if to say: 'Right, you've won!'

'I . . . I give you my blessing,' Papa continued, also bursting into tears. 'Natashenka, daughter, stand beside him . . . The icon, please, Mother . . .'

But at this point the fond parent suddenly stopped crying and his face became distorted with rage.

'Blockhead!' he said angrily to his wife. 'You fool, you! Call that an icon?'

'Oh, saints alive!'

What had happened? The teacher of calligraphy cautiously raised his eyes and saw that he was saved: instead of an icon Mamma in her hurry had taken down a portrait of Lazhechnikov the historical novelist. Old Dregs and his wife Cleopatra stood there sheepishly holding the portrait, not knowing what to do or say next. The teacher of calligraphy took advantage of their confusion and ran.

1886

A Woman Without Prejudices

A Novel

Maxim Kuzmich Salyutov is tall, broad-shouldered and well built. His physique, you can confidently say, is athletic, his strength phenomenal. He can bend coins, pull up young trees by the roots and lift weights with his teeth, and he swears that no man would dare wrestle with him. He is brave and courageous. No one has ever seen him scared of anything. Other people, though, are scared enough of him and turn pale if he is angry. Men and women squeal and blush when he shakes their hands: ouch! His fine baritone is so powerful it deafens you. A rock of a man! I've never met anyone like him.

But when Maxim Kuzmich, this prodigy of nature, this ox-like force, was declaring his love for Yelena Gavrilovna, he resembled nothing so much as a squashed rat! He turned pale, blushed, trembled and was in no fit state to lift up a chair when he had to squeeze the words 'I love you!' from his large mouth. All his strength disappeared, and his large body turned into one big hollow shell.

He declared his love on the skating-rink. She was skimming about the ice as light as a feather, while he chased after her, trembling, feeling faint and speaking inaudibly. His face was a picture of misery. His quick, nimble feet gave way and became tangled up whenever he had to trace some intricate pattern on the ice. You think he was scared she'd turn him down? You're wrong. Yelena Gavrilovna, a pretty little brunette, loved him, was longing to be offered his hand and heart, and could scarcely restrain her impatience. He was already thirty, he might not be very high up or well

32

off, but he was so handsome, witty and agile! A wonderful dancer, a superb shot, and unrivalled as a rider. Once when they were out together, he had jumped over a ditch that would have tested the best English steeplechaser. How could you fail to love a man like that?

And he knew his love was returned. He was sure of it. But there was one thought that made him suffer. It pressed on his brain, making him rage and cry, not letting him eat or drink or sleep. It was poisoning his life. Here he was swearing his love, yet all the time it was swarming round in his brain and pounding at his temples.

'Marry me!' he was saying to Yelena Gavrilovna. 'I'm so madly in love with you!'

And at the same time he was thinking:

'Have I any right to marry her? No, I haven't! If she knew about my origins, if anyone told her about my past, she'd slap me in the face! My miserable, infamous past! A rich, educated, upper-class girl like that would wash her hands of me if she knew what I am!'

When Yelena Gavrilovna threw herself round his neck and swore that she loved him, he did not feel happy. The thought poisoned everything. 'I'm a scoundrel,' he said to himself, returning home from the rink and biting his lips. 'Had I been an honest man, I'd have told her the lot, the lot! Before saying I loved her, I should have entrusted my secret to her! But I didn't, so what am I? A wretch, a scoundrel!'

Yelena Gavrilovna's parents agreed to her marriage to Maxim Kuzmich. They liked the athlete: he was respectful and his prospects in the civil service were excellent. Yelena Gavrilovna was in the seventh heaven. She was happy. Not so the poor athlete! Right up to the marriage he was tormented by the same thought as when he proposed. He was tormented also by a friend of his who knew everything there was to know about his past. He had to give this friend almost all his salary. 'Treat me to dinner at the Hermitage!' the friend would say. 'Or I'll tell everyone. And lend me twenty-five roubles!'

Poor Maxim Kuzmich lost weight, looked pinched and hollow-cheeked, and the veins stood out on his fists. The thought made him ill. But for his beloved, he'd have shot himself.

'I'm a worthless rascal!' he said to himself. 'I must explain to her before the wedding! Let her throw me over!'

But he said nothing, he didn't have the courage. The thought of having to part from his beloved afterwards terrified him more than anything!

Came the wedding evening. The young couple were married and congratulated, everyone was overjoyed. Poor Maxim Kuzmich accepted the congratulations, drank, danced and laughed, but felt terribly unhappy. 'I must make myself tell her, beast that I am! We may be married, but it's not too late! We can still part.'

And he did tell her. When the longed-for moment arrived and the young couple were accompanied to their bedroom, his conscience and sense of honour finally prevailed. Pale and trembling, in a daze and scarcely able to breathe, Maxim Kuzmich went timidly up to her, took her by the hand and said:

'Before we – before we belong to each other – there's something – something I must tell you . . .'

'What's the matter, Max?! You're so pale! You've been pale and silent for days now. Are you ill?'

'I – I must tell you everything, Lyolya. Let's sit down . . . It'll be a blow to you and poison your happiness, but what else can I do? It's my duty . . . I must tell you about my past . . .'

Lyolya opened her eyes wide and grinned.

'Well, go on then . . . Only do get a move on. And stop trembling like a leaf.'

'I was b-born in Tam-tam-bov . . . My parents were lower class and terribly poor. I must tell you what I am. You'll be shocked. Wait till you hear. I was a beggar. As a boy I used to sell apples . . . apples and pears . . .'

'You?'

'You're shocked? But, my dear, there's far worse to come. Oh, I'm so wretched, you'll curse me when you find out!'

'Find out what?'

'When I was twenty . . . twenty . . . I was . . . I'm sorry, please don't send me away! I was – a circus clown!'

'You?! A clown?'

Salyutov covered his pale face in his hands, waiting for the expected slap. He was close to fainting.

'You were – a clown?'

Lyola rolled off the couch, jumped up and began running round the room, clutching her stomach. What was the matter? Laughter filled every corner of the bedroom. It sounded hysterical . . .

'You were a clown, Maxie? You? Oh darling, do a trick for me! Show me what you did! Darling!'

She ran up to Salyutov and embraced him.

'Do show me something! Go on, darling!'

'You're making fun of me, I know you are. You despise me?'

'*Do* something! Can you walk the tightrope? Oh come *on*!'

She showered her husband's face with kisses and snuggled up close to him. She showed no sign of being angry. Bewildered but happy, he acceded to his wife's request. Going up to the bed, he counted three and stood on his head, with his brow resting on the edge of the bed.

'Bravo, Max! Encore! Ha-ha! More, darling, more!'

Max swayed slightly, jumped down in one go onto the floor and started walking on his hands . . .

Next morning Lyolya's parents got the shock of their lives.

'Who's that banging upstairs?' they asked each other. 'The newly weds are still asleep. It must be the servants up to mischief. What a din the devils are making!'

Papa went upstairs but did not find any servants. Much to his astonishment the noise was coming from the newly weds' room. He stood for a moment by the door, shrugged his shoulders and opened it very slightly. Glancing into the bedroom, he shrank back and almost died of astonishment. Maxim Kuzmich was standing in the middle of the bedroom performing the most reckless *salto mortale* in the air. Lyolya was standing beside him applauding. They both looked blissfully happy.

1883

The Complaints Book

It lies, this book, in a special little desk inside the railway station. To get at it you have to 'Apply to the Station Policeman for Key' – but it's all nonsense about the key, since the desk is always unlocked. Open the book and you will read:

'Dear Sir! Just testing the pen?!'

Below this is a funny face with a long nose and horns. Underneath it says:

'I'm a picture, you're a blot, you're a pig, I'm not. I am your ugly mug.'

'Approaching this station and admiring the seenery, my hat blue off. I. Harmonkin.'

'I know not who it was that writ, but him that reads it is a twit.'

'Fobbemoff, Head of Small Claims Office, was here.'

'I wish to register a complaint against Ticket Collector Krumpkin for rudeness with respect to my wife. My wife <u>wasn't</u> kicking up a row but on the contrary was trying to keep it all as quiet as possible. Also against Constable Kuffkin for Grabbing me by the shoulder. My place of residence is the estate of Andrey Ivanovich Snoopin who knows my mode of behaviour. Paragonsky, estate clerk.'

'Nikandroff's a Socialist!'

'Whilst the impression of this disgraceful incident is still fresh – (crossed out). Passing through this station I was shocked to the depths of my being by the following – (crossed out). I witnessed with my own eyes the following disgraceful occurrence, vividly illustrating the state of affairs pertaining on our railways – (everything else crossed out, except for the signature –) Ivan Svot, Upper Sixth Form, Kursk Grammar School.'

'While awaiting the departure of the train I studied the station-master's physiognomy and was not at all pleased by what I saw. Am passing this information along the line. An undespairing nine-to-fiver.'

'I know who wrote that. It was M.D.'

36

'Gentlemen! Teltsovsky's a card-sharp!'

'The station policeman's wife took a trip over the river with Kostka the barman yesterday. Good luck to them! Chin up, constable!'

'Passing through this station and requiring sustenance in the form of something to eat I was unable to obtain any lenten fare. Deacon Cheruboff.'

'Stuff in what they've got, mate!' ...

'Will anyone finding a leather cigar-case kindly hand it in to Andrey Yegorych at the ticket office.'

'Right, if you're sacking me because you say I get drunk, I'm telling everyone you're a load of dirty rogues and swindlers. Kozmodemyansky, telegraph operator.'

'Rejoice in good deeds.'

'Katinka, I love you madly!'

'Please refrain from making irrelevant entries in this complaints book. B.A. Ivanoff (pp. Stationmaster).'

'B.F. Ivanoff, more like.'

1884

The Swedish Match
A Crime Story

On the morning of 6 October 1885, a respectably dressed young man presented himself at the office of the head of No.2 police district in the region of S. and announced that his employer, Mark Ivanovich Klauzov, a retired lieutenant in the Horse Guards, had been murdered. The young man making this announcement was pale and extremely agitated, his hands trembled and his eyes looked terror-stricken.

'To whom have I the honour of speaking?' asked the district officer.

'I'm his estate manager, Psekov. I'm an agronomist and mechanical engineer.'

When the district officer and witnesses returned with Psekov to the scene of the incident, they encountered the following. A huge mob of people was crowding round the fliegel where Klauzov lived in the grounds of the estate. News of the incident had spread through the surrounding countryside like wildfire, and since it was a Sunday, peasants from all the neighbouring villages had converged on the fliegel. A hubbub filled the air, and pale, tear-stained faces could be glimpsed among the crowd.

Klauzov's bedroom door was found to be locked with the key on the inside. 'The villains must have got in through the window,' Psekov remarked as the door was being examined.

They went outside. From the garden the bedroom window had a gloomy, sinister appearance. It was covered by a faded green curtain, one corner of which was slightly turned back, making it possible to peep inside.

'Has anyone looked through the window?' asked the district officer.

'Oh no sir,' replied Ephraim the gardener, a little old man with grey hair and the face of a retired N.C.O. 'How could we think of doing that, your honour, when our knees are all a-knocking with fear!'

'Ah, Mark Ivanych, Mark Ivanych!' sighed the district officer, gazing at the window. 'I told you you'd come to a bad end! I told you, old friend, but you wouldn't heed! No good ever comes from a life of dissipation.'

'If it hadn't been for Ephraim,' said Psekov, 'we wouldn't have suspected. He was the first to realize something was wrong. He came to me this morning and said: "What's the master sleeping so long for? He's not been out of his bedroom a whole week!" His words struck me like a thunderbolt. The thought flashed through my mind . . . he hasn't been seen since last Saturday, and today's Sunday! A whole seven days!'

'Poor old chap,' the district officer sighed again. 'A clever fellow, too, well educated, kind to others. The life and soul of the party, you might say. But a libertine, God forgive him, so nothing would surprise me. Stepan,' he said, turning to one of the witnesses, 'get back to my place right away and send young Andryusha over to the superintendent to report. Say that Mark Ivanych has been murdered. And find me the local constable – what's he taking it so easy for? Send him along here. Then go on yourself as fast as you can to the inspector, Nikolay Yermolaich, and tell him to come over! No, wait, I'll write him a note.'

The district officer posted guards round the fliegel, wrote a note to the inspector and went off to the estate manager's office for a cup of tea. Ten minutes later he was sitting on a stool cautiously nibbling lumps of sugar and sipping scalding hot tea.

'So that's how it goes,' he was saying to Psekov. 'One of the gentry, well off, a darling of the gods, you might say, in Pushkin's famous phrase, and what did he do with it all? Nothing. Drank too much, ran after the women, and now look – he's been murdered!'

The detective inspector drove up two hours later. Nikolay Yermolayevich Chubikov (for that is the inspector's name) is a tall, solidly built old man of about sixty who has been active in his profession for a quarter of a century. He is known throughout the region as an honest, clever, energetic man who loves his job. On his arrival at the scene of the incident, he was accompanied as always by his assistant and secretary, Dyukovsky, a tall young man of about twenty-six.

'So, gentlemen, has it come to this?' said Chubikov, shaking hands briskly with all those in Psekov's room. 'Mark Ivanych murdered? I cannot believe it. I simply *cannot* believe it.'

'Who would have thought it?' sighed the district officer.

'Why, good heavens, it's only a week last Friday that I saw him at Tarabankov Fair! Even drank the odd glass of vodka with him, God forgive me.'

'Yes, who would have thought it?' the district officer sighed again.

After more sighs and expressions of horror and a glass of tea each, they set off for the fliegel.

'Clear the way!' the constable yelled at the crowd.

The inspector's first task on entering the fliegel was to examine the bedroom door. This proved to be of pine, painted yellow, and was undamaged. No special marks were found on it that might serve as evidence of any kind. They proceeded to break it down.

'Gentlemen, I must ask all unauthorized persons to withdraw!' said the inspector, when after much banging and splintering the door gave way to the axe and chisel. 'Correct procedures must be followed. Constable, let no one in!'

Chubikov, his assistant and the district officer opened the door and filed cautiously into the bedroom, where the following sight met their eyes. Next to the only window stood a large wooden bedstead with a huge feather bed. In a tangle on top of the crumpled feather bed lay a crumpled quilt. A pillow in a patterned pillowcase, likewise much rumpled, was lying on the floor. A silver pocket watch and a twenty-kopeck silver coin were lying on a small bedside table; here, too, lay a box of sulphur matches. Apart from the bed, the bedside table and a single chair, the room was devoid of furniture. Glancing under the bed, the district officer found a couple of dozen empty bottles, an old straw hat and a half-bottle of vodka. One dusty boot was lying under the bedside table.

Taking in the room at a glance, the inspector frowned and coloured.

'The scoundrels!' he muttered, clenching his fists.

'But where's Mark Ivanych?' Dyukovsky asked quietly.

'Don't try teaching me my job!' Chubikov answered brusquely. 'Kindly examine the floor!' Turning to the district officer, he lowered his voice and said: 'This isn't the first case of its kind I've had, Yevgraf Kuzmich. I had a similar one in 1870. Remember the murder of Portretov the merchant? Identical features. The scoundrels murdered him and dragged his body out of the window.'

Going up to the window, Chubikov drew the curtain aside and gave the window a cautious push. The window swung open.

'It opens, which means it can't have been locked . . . And look at these marks on the windowsill. See them? Made by someone's knee. Someone must have climbed in. This window will have to be thoroughly examined.'

'Nothing especially worthy of note on the floor,' said Dyukovsky. 'No stains or scratches. The only thing I have found is this single used Swedish match. Look! So far as I remember, Mark Ivanych didn't smoke, and in daily life he always used sulphur matches, never Swedish ones. This match may be a useful clue.'

'Oh, do be quiet!' said the inspector with an impatient gesture. 'Bothering me with your match. I can't stand hotheads. Instead of looking for matches, you'd be better employed examining the bedding.'

Having examined the bedding, Dyukovsky reported:

'There are no signs of blood or any other stains. And there are no fresh tears, either. But there are tooth marks on the pillow. The quilt's been soaked in a liquid having the smell and taste of beer. The general appearance of the bed justifies the conclusion that a struggle took place upon it.'

'I don't need you to tell me there was a struggle! You weren't asked about a struggle. Instead of looking for signs of a struggle, you'd be better employed –'

'And one of his boots is here, but the other one's missing.'

'So?'

'So, he was smothered while taking off his boots. Before he had time to take the second one off, he –'

'Oh, here we go! And what makes you think he was smothered?'

'The tooth marks on the pillow. The pillow itself is badly rumpled and has been thrown from the bed to a distance of six feet.'

'Windbag! We'd better take a look at the garden. You'd have been better employed looking in the garden than poking about here. I don't need your help for that.'

On proceeding to the garden, the first task of the investigating team was to examine the grass. The grass under the window had been trampled down, as had a burdock plant growing under the window up against the wall. Dyukovsky succeeded in finding on the burdock several broken stems and a scrap of wadding, while on its upper heads fine strands of dark blue wool were found.

'What colour was his most recent suit?' Dyukovsky asked Psekov.

'Light brown linen.'

'Splendid. So they were wearing blue.'

Several burdock heads were cut off and carefully wrapped in paper. At this point Superintendent Artsybashev-Svistakovsky and Doctor Tyutyuyev arrived. After greeting everyone, the superintendent immediately asked to be put fully in the picture, whereas the doctor, a tall and exceptionally skinny man with sunken eyes, a long nose and pointed chin, greeted no one and asked no questions, but sat down on a tree stump and said with a sigh:

'Those Serbs are stirring things up again. God knows what they're after. And who's behind it all? Austria, of course, Austria!'

Examination of the window from the outside produced absolutely nothing, whereas that of the grass and bushes growing closest to the window yielded much useful evidence. For instance, Dyukovsky succeeded in tracing on the grass a long trail of dark stains stretching several yards from the window into the garden. The trail ended in a large dark brown patch under one of the lilac bushes. Under the same bush a boot was found that matched the one in the bedroom.

'Dried blood!' said Dyukovsky, examining the stains.

At the word 'blood' the doctor stood up, took a brief half-hearted glance at the stains and mumbled: 'Yes, blood.'

'He can't have been smothered then, can he, if there's blood?' Chubikov said with a spiteful glance at Dyukovsky.

'They smothered him in the bedroom, but once they got him here, they were afraid he'd recover consciousness, so they struck him with a sharp object. The patch under the lilac shows that he lay there a relatively long time while they were searching for ways and means of getting him out of the garden.'

'And the boot?'

'The boot lends even greater weight to my idea that he was killed while taking his boots off before going to bed. He got one off, but the other one, this one, was still half on. While he was being bumped along and dumped, the half-removed boot came off of its own accord . . .'

'Oh, brilliant!' Chubikov sneered. 'How he does run on and on! When are you going to learn to keep your theories to yourself? Instead of theorizing, you'd be better employed collecting some specimens of bloodstained grass for analysis.'

After examining the area and making a sketch-plan, the investigating team adjourned to the estate manager's office to draw up their report and have lunch. Over lunch they got talking.

'His watch, the money and so on are all intact,' Chubikov began the conversation, 'so it's as clear as daylight that the murder wasn't carried out for gain.'

'And it was carried out by an educated person,' put in Dyukovsky.

'What leads you to that conclusion?'

'The Swedish match favours my theory. The use of matches of that kind hasn't spread to the local peasantry yet. They're used only by the landowning class, and not by all of them. I should also add that he was killed not by one person, but at least three. Two held him down, and the third smothered him. Klauzov was a strong man, and the murderers must have known that.'

'And of what use was his strength to him, if, as we assume, he was asleep?'

'The murderers found him taking off his boots. If he was taking off his boots, he was not asleep.'

'That's enough of your fancy theories. Get on with your lunch.'

'If you ask me, your honour,' said Ephraim the gardener,

setting the samovar down on the table, 'it was Nikolashka that done this dirty deed.'

'More than likely,' said Psekov.

'Who's this Nikolashka?'

'The master's valet, your honour,' Ephraim replied. 'Who else done it if not him? He's a proper villain, your honour. Drinks and runs after the women like nobody's business, lord preserve us! He was the one always took the master his vodka, he was the one put him to bed. Who else if not him? And what's more, begging your honour's pardon, I heard the rascal boasting in the pub once that he'd kill the master. It was all on account of a woman. He had this woman Akulka – her man's in the army. The master took a fancy to her and became friends with her, so of course Nikolashka got mad . . . He's lying about drunk in the kitchen now, weeping and pretending he's sorry about the master.'

'Well, you can certainly understand anyone getting mad over Akulka,' said Psekov. 'She may be a peasant and a soldier's wife, but she's . . . Mark Ivanych used to call her Nana and you could see why . . . She's got something attractive about her that really does make you think of Nana . . .'

'Yes . . . I have seen the lady,' said the inspector, blowing his nose in a red handkerchief.

Dyukovsky blushed and looked down. The district officer began drumming his finger on a saucer. The superintendent had a fit of coughing and for some reason started rummaging in his briefcase. Only one person appeared quite unaffected by the mention of Akulka and Nana, and that was the doctor. The inspector sent for Nikolashka. He was a gangling young fellow with a long pockmarked nose and sunken chest, wearing one of his master's cast-off jackets. On entering Psekov's room, he bowed very low to the inspector. His face was sleepy and tear-stained, and he was so drunk he could scarcely stand upright.

'Where is your master?' Chubikov asked him.

'Been murdered, your honour,' Nikolashka said, then blinked and burst into tears.

'We know he's been murdered, but where is he now? Where is his body?'

'They say he got dragged out of the window and buried in the garden.'

'Hm. So the results of the investigation are already common knowledge below stairs. Most irregular. Tell me, my good man, where were you on the night your master was murdered? Last

Saturday evening, that is?'

Nikolashka gazed upwards, craning his neck, and pondered.

'I can't say, your honour. I were drunk and can't remember.'

'An alibi,' Dyukovsky whispered, rubbing his hands gleefully.

'I see. And how do you explain the blood under your master's window?'

Nikolashka tilted his head upwards again and pondered.

'Think, man!' said the inspector.

'Just a tick. That blood's nothing, your honour. It was me killing a chicken. I was killing it same way I always do, when didn't it get it into its head to break free and make a run for it . . . That's where the blood come from.'

Ephraim confirmed that Nikolashka did kill chickens every evening, choosing a different spot each time, but no one had seen a half-killed chicken running round the garden, although you couldn't rule it out completely.

'An alibi,' Dyukovsky grinned, 'and a pretty half-baked one.'

'You were friendly with Akulka?'

'So help me.'

'And your master enticed her away from you?'

'Oh no! It was Mr Psekov there, Ivan Mikhaylych, who took her off me, and then the master took her off him. That's the way it was.'

Psekov looked embarrassed and started rubbing his left eye. Dyukovsky stared at him hard, noted his embarrassment and gave a sudden start. Only now did he appreciate the fact that the estate manager was wearing dark blue trousers. They reminded him of the strands of dark blue wool found on the burdock. Chubikov also gave Psekov a suspicious glance.

'You can go,' he said to Nikolashka. 'Now let me ask you a question or two, Mr Psekov. I presume you were here last Saturday night?'

'Yes, I had supper with Mark Ivanych at ten o'clock.'

'And then?'

Psekov looked embarrassed and got up from the table.

'Then I . . . then I . . . I honestly can't remember,' he mumbled. 'I'd had a lot to drink. I can't remember where and when I fell asleep. What are you all looking at me like that for? Anyone would think I'd killed him.'

'Where did you wake up?'

'Lying on the stove in the servants' kitchen. They'll all confirm that. But how I got there I can't think . . .'

'Just keep calm, please. You knew Akulka, then?'

'And what if I did . . .'

'But she left you for Klauzov?'

'Yes . . . Ephraim, bring us some more mushrooms. Another cup of tea, Yevgraf Kuzmich?'

There followed an awkward, eerie silence lasting about five minutes. Dyukovsky sat silently with his piercing eyes fixed on Psekov's now colourless face. It was the inspector who broke the silence.

'We shall have to call at the house,' he said, 'and have a word with Marya Ivanovna, the deceased's sister, in case she can give us any leads.'

Chubikov and his assistant thanked Psekov for the lunch and walked up to the big house. They found Marya Ivanovna, Klauzov's forty-five-year-old unmarried sister, praying in front of the tall family icon case. When she saw her visitors' briefcases and official caps, her face turned pale.

'May I begin by offering my apologies for this infringement, so to speak, of your private devotions,' Chubikov said with a gallant bow. 'We have a request to make. No doubt you will have heard the news . . . There are grounds for suspecting that your unfortunate brother has been, as it were, murdered. The Lord giveth and the Lord taketh away. Death cometh to us all, to king and beggar alike . . . We wondered if you might be able to help us clear up a few points . . .'

'Please don't ask me, please!' said Marya Ivanovna, turning even paler and covering her face in her hands. 'I have nothing at all to say to you, nothing! Believe me, nothing . . . What could I say? No, no, no, I shall not say a word about my brother! I would rather die than speak!'

Marya Ivanovna burst into tears and retired to the next room. The investigators exchanged glances, shrugged their shoulders and withdrew.

'Damned woman!' Dyukovsky swore as they left the house. 'She obviously knows something and is covering up. And the maid had a funny expression, too. But just you wait, damn you, we'll sort it all out.'

That evening, beneath the pale gaze of the moon, Chubikov and his assistant were making their way home. Sitting in the gig, they went over in their minds the results of the day's work. Both men were tired and silent. Chubikov preferred not to talk in any case while travelling, and Dyukovsky respected the older man's wishes by restraining his natural inclination to prattle. But as their journey neared its end, the assistant could remain silent no longer.

'Nikolashka is implicated in this affair – *non dubitandum est*,' he began. 'You can tell from his face what kind of fellow he is, and his alibi gives him away lock, stock and barrel. Nor is there any doubt that he is not the instigator, but merely a foolish hired instrument. Agreed? And the part played by the modest Psekov is clearly also central – what with the blue trousers, his embarrassment, the way he was cowering on the stove after the murder, his alibi and Akulka.'

'Go on, make a meal of it. I suppose that in your opinion anyone who knew Akulka must be the murderer? Hothead! You should still be sucking a teat instead of investigating crimes! You were running after Akulka yourself, so does that mean you're involved in this affair?'

'Come to that, she worked for a month as a cook at your place – but I refrain from further comment. If I hadn't been playing cards with you that Saturday night, I might have suspected you, too. It's not so much the woman, old man. It's more a question of a nasty, mean, sordid little human emotion. Our modest young man didn't like it, did he, when someone else came out on top. He had his pride, you see. He desired vengeance. And those fleshy lips of his clearly indicate sensuality. Remember how he licked them when he was comparing Akulka to Nana? It's quite obvious the wretch is consumed with passion. Wounded pride, then, and frustrated passion: they're quite enough to make a man commit murder. Two of them are in the bag, but who's number three? Nikolashka and Psekov held him down, but who smothered him? Psekov is too timid and nervous, he's a coward at heart. And the likes of Nikolashka don't smother people with pillows, their weapon is a hatchet or the butt-end of an axe. A third man smothered him – but who?'

Dyukovsky pulled his hat down over his eyes and pondered. He remained silent until the gig drew up at the inspector's house.

'Eureka!' he exclaimed, going in and taking off his coat. 'I've got it, chief! Why ever didn't I think of it before? Do you know who our third man is?'

'Oh, do give me some peace. Supper's on the table. Sit down and eat.'

The inspector and Dyukovsky sat down to eat. Dyukovsky poured himself a glass of vodka, stood up very straight, his eyes flashing, and said:

'I shall tell you, then, the identity of the third person who acted in concert with the wretched Psekov and did the smothering: *it was a woman*! It was none other than the victim's sister, Marya Ivanovna!'

Chubikov choked on his vodka and gaped at Dyukovsky.

'Are you feeling . . .? I mean, your head's not feeling – a bit funny?'

'I am quite well. But let's suppose I am off my head, how do you explain her confusion when we appeared? How do you explain her unwillingness to give evidence? Nothing much in that, you'll say – very well, I agree – but don't forget what their relationship was like. She hated her brother! She an Old Believer, he a godless fornicator – that's at the bottom of all the hatred. They say he'd convinced her he was a servant of Beelzebub, that he dabbled in spiritualism in her presence.'

'Well, what of it?'

'Don't you *see*? As an Old Believer, she killed him out of fanaticism. Not only was she rooting out a rank weed, a fornicator, she was delivering the world from the Antichrist. That'll be my contribution, she thought, my great religious deed! Oh, you don't know what they're like, these devout old maids. You should read your Dostoyevsky – not to mention Leskov and Pechersky. She's the one, I'm positive! She did the smothering. And what a cunning old hag! All that kneeling before the icons as we went in was just to pull the wool over our eyes. I'll kneel down and pray, and that way they'll think I'm calm and wasn't expecting them. It's a method used by all beginners in crime. Nikolay Yermolaich, dear old chap, hand the case over to me! Be a good fellow, let me handle the rest of it. Let me finish it off as I began.'

Chubikov shook his head slowly and frowned.

'We are quite capable of sorting out our own difficult cases,' he said. 'It's not your job to meddle in matters outside your concern. Your job is to write down what's dictated to you.'

Dyukovsky flared up at this and left, banging the door behind him.

'He's a clever devil, though,' Chubikov murmured as he watched him go. 'Damned clever! If only he weren't such a hothead. I must buy him a cigar-case at the Fair.'

Next morning a young lad from Klauzovka with a large head and a hare lip was brought before the inspector. He gave his name as Danilka the cowherd and provided some very interesting evidence.

'I were drunk,' he said. 'I sat up till midnight at me auntie's. On me way home I got this drunken fancy for a bathe in the river. So I'm there bathing when I sees two people carrying something dark across the dam. "Tallyho!" I yelled at them. They took fright and beat it like hell towards the Makarevs' vegetable patch. God help me if that weren't the master they was dragging.'

Before evening on that same day Psekov and Nikolashka were arrested and conveyed under escort to the regional town. Here they were incarcerated in the gaol house.

2

Twelve days had gone by.

It was morning. At his baize-topped desk the inspector sat leafing through the file on the Klauzov case, while Dyukovsky paced up and down the room like a restless wolf in a cage.

'You're convinced that Nikolashka and Psekov are guilty,' he was saying, tugging nervously at his newly grown beard. 'So why don't you want to be convinced of Marya Ivanovna's guilt? Not enough evidence for you, is that it?'

'I'm not saying I'm not convinced. I am convinced, but somehow I can't believe it . . . There's no real evidence, just a lot of ideas, fanaticism and all that stuff . . .'

'And you've got to have an axe and blood-stained sheets! Lawyers! Right then, I'll find proof for you. I'll make you take the psychological aspects more seriously. We'll have your Marya Ivanovna in Siberia yet! I'll find proof. If ideas aren't enough for you, I've got something concrete . . . It'll show you how right my ideas are. Just let me do a spot of travelling.'

'What are you on about?'

'What I'm on about, my dear sir, is the Swedish match. You'd forgotten about that, hadn't you, but I hadn't! I shall find out who struck it in the victim's bedroom. It wasn't Nikolashka or Psekov, because we didn't find matches on either of them during the search, so it was the third person, i.e. Marya Ivanovna. And I'll prove it. Just let me do a spot of travelling round the region and make a few enquiries.'

'Yes, all right, but now sit down and let's get on with the interrogation.'

Dyukovsky sat down at his desk and buried his long nose in some papers.

'Bring in Nikolay Tetyokhov!' shouted the inspector.

Nikolashka was brought in. He was pale, thin as a rake and trembling.

'Tetyokhov,' Chubikov began, 'I understand that in 1879 you were tried for theft in No.1 district court and sentenced to imprisonment. You were tried again for theft in 1882 and again landed in prison. So we know all about you . . .'

Nikolashka's face registered astonishment. He was amazed by the inspector's omniscience. But his expression of astonishment was quickly replaced by one of extreme anguish. He started sobbing and asked permission to go out and wash his hands and calm down. He was led away.

'Bring in Psekov!' the inspector ordered.

Psekov was brought in. The young man's face had undergone a considerable change during the past few days. He looked pale, thin and hollow cheeked, and there was an apathetic look in his eyes.

'Sit down, Psekov,' Chubikov said. 'I hope you will be sensible today and not go on telling lies, as you have done previously. For the past twelve days you have denied your part in the murder of Klauzov, despite the mass of evidence piled up against you. You are being foolish. A confession will mitigate your guilt. This will be my last chat with you. If you do not confess today, tomorrow will be too late. So please tell us the whole story . . .'

'I know nothing about it . . . And I know nothing of your evidence,' Psekov whispered.

'This won't get you anywhere, you know. Well then, let me tell *you* what happened. You spent Saturday evening sitting in Klauzov's bedroom drinking beer and vodka.' (During the whole of the inspector's monologue Dyukovsky never once took his penetrating gaze off Psekov's face.) 'Nikolay was attending to your requirements. Some time after midnight Mark Ivanych announced his wish to retire for the night. He always went to bed between twelve and one. While he was taking off his boots and giving you instructions concerning the estate, you and Nikolay, at a prearranged signal, seized your inebriated master and threw him down on the bed. One of you sat on his legs, the other on his head. At that moment a woman in a black dress, who was already known to you and had agreed to be your accomplice in this criminal act, entered the room from the passage. She seized the pillow and began smothering him with it. In the ensuing struggle a candle was extinguished. The woman took a box of Swedish matches out of her pocket and re-lit it. Am I not correct? I can see

49

from your expression that what I am saying is the truth. But to continue . . . Having smothered him and made sure he wasn't breathing, you and Nikolay dragged him through the window and put him down by the burdock. Fearing he might recover, you struck him with a sharp object. Then you lifted him and put him down for a short time under the lilac. After pausing to rest and consider your next move, you picked him up again . . . You lifted him over the fence . . . Then you set out along the road . . . You'd got as far as the dam when you were scared off by a peasant. What's the matter, are you ill?'

Psekov, white as a sheet, rose unsteadily to his feet.

'I can't breathe!' he said. 'All right . . . whatever you say . . . only please let me have some air.'

Psekov was led out.

'A confession at last,' Chubikov purred. 'He's given himself away now. Fairly tripped him up, didn't I? Gave him the works . . .'

'And he's not even denying the woman in black,' Dyukovsky said gleefully. 'All the same, that Swedish match is still preying on my mind. I can't wait a moment longer. Goodbye, then, I'm off!'

Dyukovsky donned his cap and left. Chubikov proceeded to interrogate Akulka. Akulka declared she didn't know nothing about it . . .

'I never lived with no one but you,' she said.

It was after five when Dyukovsky returned. He was more excited than ever. His hands were shaking so much he couldn't even unbutton his coat. His cheeks were aflame. Evidently he had not had a wasted journey.

'*Veni, vidi, vici!*' he exclaimed, bursting into Chubikov's room and collapsing into an armchair. 'On my word of honour, I'm beginning to believe I really am a genius. Just wait till you hear what I've got to tell you, chief! You won't believe your ears! I don't know whether to laugh or cry. You've got three of them in the bag already – right? Well, I've found a fourth murderer, or rather, murderess, because this one's a woman, too! And what a woman! For one touch of her shoulders I'd give ten years of my life. Just wait till you hear . . . I drove to Klauzovka and set out from there in widening circles. I visited every shop, tavern and alehouse en route, asking for Swedish matches. The answer was always the same, we don't stock them. I've been chasing round until now. Twenty times my hopes were dashed and twenty times I raised them again. All day I drew a blank and only an hour ago

I stumbled on my quarry. Three versts from here I'm offered a pack of ten – *and there's one box missing*! "Who bought that box?" I ask. A certain lady . . . "She fancied the way they fizz." Oh, Nikolay Yermolaich, dear old friend! To think that someone who's been expelled from theological college and steeped himself in the crime novels of Gaboriau can reach such heights! I begin to respect myself from this day forth. Goodness, I'm tired though . . . Still, we must be off.'

'Off where?'

'To see her, the fourth accomplice . . . We must get a move on, otherwise I'll burn up with impatience. Do you know who it is? You'll never guess. It's Olga Petrovna, the charming young wife of Yevgraf Kuzmich, our venerable district officer. That's who it is! She's the one who bought the box of matches!'

'Are you . . . have you gone completely crazy?'

'But it all fits. First, she smokes. Second, she was head over heels in love with Klauzov. He'd rejected her love in favour of some Akulka or other. Revenge. I remember now catching them once in the kitchen behind a screen. She was swearing her love, and he was smoking her cigarette and puffing smoke in her face. But we must be off . . . If we don't hurry, it'll be dark soon . . . Come on!'

'I'm not yet so crazy that I intend disturbing a respectable virtuous woman after dark on account of some callow youth and his ideas.'

'Respectable virtuous woman? Some detective you are! I have never taken the liberty of calling you names before, but you leave me no choice. You're a bungler! An amateur! Oh, come on, chief! Please!'

The inspector gestured impatiently and spat.

'Please! I'm not asking for myself, I'm asking in the interests of justice. Look, I'm imploring you. Do me a favour just this once.'

Dyukovsky went down on his knees.

'Please, chief, please! You can call me every name under the sun if I'm wrong about this woman. And think what a case this is. Phenomenal! More like a detective novel! Your fame will spread all over Russia. They'll make you head of Special Investigations. Oh use your loaf, you ancient halfwit!'

The inspector furrowed his brow and reached tentatively for his hat.

'All right then, blast you.'

It was already dark when the inspector's gig drove up to the district officer's front porch.

'We're a couple of swine, though,' said Chubikov, reaching for the bell. 'Disturbing people like this.'

'Not to worry . . . We can say a spring has snapped on the gig.'

Chubikov and Dyukovsky were greeted on the doorstep by a tall shapely woman of about twenty-three with jet-black eyebrows and full red lips. It was Olga Petrovna herself.

'Why, this is a pleasure,' she said with a beaming smile. 'You've arrived just in time for supper. My Yevgraf Kuzmich isn't home yet, he must have stayed on at the priest's house, but we can get along without him. Come and sit down! Have you been working on the case?'

'That's right . . . And the thing is, a spring has snapped on the gig,' Chubikov began, going into the sitting-room and settling into an armchair.

'Catch her off guard!' Dyukovsky whispered. 'Do it now.'

'Er, yes . . . a spring . . . So we thought we'd drop in.'

'Now, man! She'll rumble us if you mess about.'

'Do it your way, but count me out,' Chubikov muttered, rising to his feet and moving over to the window. 'I don't fancy it. You stirred this up, you can get on with it.'

'Yes, a spring. . .' Dyukovsky began, going up to Olga Petrovna and wrinkling his long nose. 'But we didn't really call in to . . . er . . . to have supper or to see Yevgraf Kuzmich. We have come here to ask you a question, madam. Where is Mark Ivanych, the man you murdered?'

'Mark Ivanych? Whatever do you mean?' Olga Petrovna began babbling, and her large face instantly turned bright crimson. 'I . . . I don't know what you're talking about.'

'I ask in the name of the law! Where is Klauzov? We've been told all about it.'

'Who by?' Olga Petrovna said quietly, averting her eyes from Dyukovsky's gaze.

'Kindly tell us where he is!'

'But how did you find out? Who told you?'

'I said, we've been told all about it. I demand to know in the name of the law.'

Encouraged by Olga Petrovna's confusion, the inspector went up to her and said:

'If you tell us where he is, we shall go away. But otherwise. . .'

'What do you want him for?'

'Why all these questions, madam? We're asking you to tell us where he is, and here you are all shaking and confused . . . You know very well he's been murdered and murdered, moreover, by you. Your accomplices have given you away.'

Olga Petrovna turned pale.

'Follow me,' she said softly, wringing her hands. 'I've got him hidden in the bath-house. Only for God's sake don't tell my husband, I beg you! He'll never get over it.'

Olga Petrovna unhooked a large key from the wall and led her visitors through the kitchen and passageway into the yard. Outside it was dark and drizzling. Olga Petrovna led the way, followed by Chubikov and Dyukovsky. They found themselves walking through long grass, breathing in the smells of wild hemp and of garbage squelching beneath their feet. The yard was very wide. Soon they felt ploughed soil instead of garbage underfoot. Through the darkness the silhouettes of trees showed up, and amongst the trees they made out a small building with a crooked chimney.

'This is the bath-house,' said Olga Petrovna. 'But please don't tell anyone, I beg you.'

As they got nearer, Chubikov and Dyukovsky could see that the bath-house door was secured by an enormous padlock.

'Be ready with your candle and matches!' the inspector whispered to his assistant.

Olga Petrovna unfastened the padlock and showed her visitors in. Dyukovsky struck a match and lit up the outer room. In the middle of the room stood a table. On the table next to a squat little samovar stood a soup bowl with the congealed remains of some shchi and a dish containing some cold gravy.

'Nothing here!'

They moved into the inner room. Here, too, stood a table. On the table stood plates and cutlery, a large dish with a leg of ham, and an outsize bottle of vodka.

'But where is it?' asked the inspector. 'I mean, where's the body?'

Still pale and trembling, Olga Petrovna pointed to the upper bench. 'Up there,' she whispered.

Dyukovsky climbed on to the upper bench, candle in hand. There he perceived a long human body lying motionless on a thick down quilt. The body was gently snoring . . .

'Damn it, they're trying to trick us,' Dyukovsky shouted down. 'This isn't him. There's some idiot lying here who's still alive. Hey, you, who the devil do you think you are?'

The body sucked in air with a whistling sound and began

stirring. Dyukovsky dug it in the ribs. It lifted its arms in the air, stretched and raised its head.

'Who's that?' a deep hoarse bass enquired. 'Whaddya want?'

Dyukovsky raised his candle to the face of the unknown figure and let out a yell. In the purple nose, untidy tousled hair, and coal-black moustachios, one of which, rakishly twirled, was pointing impudently upwards, he recognized the features of Lieutenant Klauzov.

'It's you . . . it's Mark Ivanych?! But it can't be!'

The inspector stared up at them, transfixed . . .

'It's me all right . . . And if it isn't Dyukovsky! What on earth are you doing here? And whose mug is that I see down below? Good grief, it's the inspector! Well, I'll be blowed!'

Klauzov jumped down and embraced Chubikov. Olga Petrovna made herself scarce.

'Surprise, surprise! This calls for a drink, damn it! Pom-pa-pom-ti-ti . . . A drink! But who brought you over? How did you find out I was here? What the hell, let's have a drink on it, anyway!'

Klauzov lit the lamp and poured out three glasses of vodka.

'I just can't make it out,' said the inspector with a gesture of disbelief. 'Are you sure you know who you are?'

'Oh come *on* . . . Spare me the sermon. Let's see you knock that one back, Dyukovsky my lad! "Here we are again, Happy as can . . ." What do you keep staring at me like that for? Drink!'

'I still can't make out why you're here,' said the inspector, knocking back his vodka automatically.

'Why shouldn't I be if I like it?' said Klauzov, knocking back his drink and helping himself to some ham. 'I'm living here with Olga Petrovna, as you can see – hidden away in the back of beyond like some kind of demon lover. Go on, drink! I got sorry for the woman, you see. Took pity on her plight and here I am living in a derelict bath-house like a hermit . . . Getting fed, though. But I think I'll clear out next week. Had enough of it . . .'

'Incredible!' said Dyukovsky.

'What's so incredible about it?'

'Incredible! How on earth did your boot turn up in the garden?'

'Boot, what boot?'

'We found one of your boots in the bedroom and the other one in the garden.'

'What's that to do with you? My boots are my business . . . Oh

54

drink up for God's sake! It's the least you can do after waking a man up. Actually, it's funny you should mention that boot. You see, I didn't feel like going out to meet Olya that night. I'd had too much to drink and wasn't in the mood. Up she comes to my window and starts being abusive – you know how women are. So I took a drunken fling at her with my boot, ho-ho . . . Teach her not to call me names. Then in she climbed through the window, lit the lamp and took advantage of my drunken state to lay into me. Beat the living daylights out of me, dragged me over here and locked me in. I'm getting fed now . . . Love, vodka and a bite to eat! Hey, where are you off to? Chubikov, old chap, come back!'

The inspector made a furious spitting sound and walked out. He was followed by a crestfallen Dyukovsky. They got into the gig without saying a word and drove off. Never before had the journey seemed so long and tedious as on that night. Neither man spoke. Chubikov was seething with rage the whole way, while Dyukovsky kept his collar turned right up, as if fearing to expose the look of shame on his face to the darkness and drizzle.

On reaching home, the inspector found Doctor Tyutyuyev waiting for him. The doctor was sitting at a table leafing through a copy of the journal, *Niva*, and sighing deeply.

'I don't know what the world's coming to,' he said, greeting the inspector with a melancholy smile. 'It's Austria again, of course . . . And Gladstone's mixed up in it in some way . . .'

Chubikov hurled his hat under the table in a towering rage.

'Give it a rest, you creeping bag of bones! How many times have I told you not to come pestering me with your politics! It's no concern of ours. And as for you,' he said, shaking his fist in Dyukovsky's face, 'as for you . . . I'll not let you forget this in a hurry!'

'I'm sorry . . . but there was that Swedish match! How could I know?'

'You can choke on your Swedish match for all I care! Go away and don't annoy me, otherwise there's no knowing what I might do to you. Go on, out!'

Dyukovsky sighed, picked up his hat and left.

'Better go on the booze,' he decided on reaching the road, and wandered off sadly towards the pub.

When Olga Petrovna got back from the bath-house, she found her husband in the sitting-room.

'What was the inspector doing here?' he asked.

'He came to say that Klauzov's been found. Just imagine, he was living with someone else's wife!'

'Oh, Mark Ivanych, Mark Ivanych,' the district officer sighed, raising his eyes heavenwards. 'I told you no good ever comes from a life of dissipation. I told you, but you wouldn't heed!'

1883

Rapture

Midnight.

Wild-eyed and dishevelled, Mitya Kuldarov burst into his parents' flat and dashed into every room. His parents were about to go to bed. His sister was in bed already and had just got on to the last page of her novel. His schoolboy brothers were asleep.

'Where've you come from?' his parents exclaimed in astonishment. 'Is something wrong?'

'Oh, I don't know how to tell you! I'm staggered, absolutely staggered! It's . . . it's quite incredible!'

Mitya burst out laughing and collapsed into an armchair, overcome with happiness.

'It's incredible! You'll never believe it! Take a look at this!'

His sister jumped out of bed and came over to him, wrapping a blanket round her. The schoolboys woke up.

'Is something wrong? You look awful!'

'I'm so happy, Mum, that's why! Now everyone in Russia knows about me! Everyone! Till now only you knew of the existence of clerical officer of the fourteenth grade, Dmitry Kuldarov, but now everyone in Russia knows! O Lord, Mum!'

Mitya jumped up, ran round every room and sat down again.

'But tell us what's happened, for goodness' sake!'

'Oh, you live here like savages, you don't read the papers, you've no idea what's going on, and the papers are full of such remarkable things! As soon as anything happens, they make it all public, it's down there in black and white! O Lord, I'm so happy! Only famous people get their names in the paper, then all of a sudden – they go and print a story about me!'

'What?! Where?'

Dad turned pale. Mum looked up at the icon and crossed herself. The schoolboys jumped out of bed and ran over to their elder brother, wearing nothing but their short little nightshirts.

'They have! About *me*! Now I'm known all over Russia! You'd better keep this copy, Mum, and we can take it out now and then and read it. Look!'

Mitya pulled the newspaper out of his pocket and handed it to his father, jabbing his finger at a passage ringed with blue pencil.

'Read it out!'

Father put on his glasses.

'Go on, read it!'

Mum looked up at the icon and crossed herself. Dad cleared his throat and began:

'On December 29th at 11 p.m. clerical officer of the fourteenth grade, Dmitry Kuldarov –'

'See? See? Go on, Dad!'

'. . . clerical officer of the fourteenth grade, Dmitry Kuldarov, emerging from the public alehouse situated on the ground floor of Kozikhin's Buildings in Little Bronnaya Street and being in a state of intoxication –'

'It was me and Semyon Petrovich . . . They've got all the details! Go on! Now listen, listen to this bit!'

'. . . and being in a state of intoxication, slipped and fell in front of a cab horse belonging to Ivan Knoutoff, peasant, from the village of Bumpkino in Pnoff district, which was standing at that spot. The frightened horse, stepping across Kuldarov, dragged over him the sledge in which was seated Ivan Lukov, merchant of the Second Guild in Moscow, bolted down the street and was arrested in its flight by some yard porters. Kuldarov, being at first in a state of unconsciousness, was taken to the police station and examined by a doctor. The blow which he had received on the back of the head –'

'I did it on the shaft, Dad. Go on, read the rest!'

'. . . which he had received on the back of the head, was classified as superficial. A police report was drawn up concerning the incident. Medical assistance was rendered to the victim –'

'They dabbed the back of my head with cold water. Finished? So what do you say to that, eh?! It'll be all over Russia by now! Give it here!'

Mitya grabbed the newspaper, folded it and stuffed it into his pocket.

'Must run and show the Makarovs . . . Then on to the Ivanitskys, Nataliya Ivanovna and Anisim Vasilich . . . Can't stop! Bye!'

Mitya put on his official cap with the cockade and radiant, triumphant, ran out into the street.

1883

Vint

One nasty autumn evening Andrey Stepanovich Martinetoff was driving home from the theatre. Driving along, he mused on the beneficial influence that theatres might have if they were to put on morally uplifting plays. But as he drew near to County Hall, he forgot all about beneficial influences and began staring at the windows of the building in which, to use the language of poets and skippers, he was at the helm. Lights were blazing in two windows of the duty room.

'Surely they can't still be messing about with the accounts?' Martinetoff thought. 'There are four idiots on the job and they still haven't finished! Then people will get the idea I keep them at it day and night. I'll go in and buck their ideas up. Stop here, Gury!'

Martinetoff got out of his carriage and proceeded on foot. The front door of County Hall was locked, but the back entrance, which had only a single broken bolt, was wide open. Martinetoff made use of this and a minute later was standing outside the duty room. The door was slightly ajar and when Martinetoff peeped in, he saw an extraordinary sight. By the light of two lamps, at a table littered with large account sheets, four clerks were sitting playing cards. As they sat there motionless, concentrating, their faces green in the light from the lampshades, they looked like gnomes in a fairy tale or, heaven forbid, counterfeiters . . . The game they were playing made them even more mysterious. To judge by their demeanour and the card-playing terms they called out from time to time, it must be vint; but to judge by everything else that Martinetoff heard, it could not be called vint or any other known card game. It was more like some kind of mysterious ritual . . . Martinetoff recognized the clerks as Serafim Zvishdoolin, Stepan Fistikoff, Jeremiah Malingrin and Ivan Skribblitch.

'Why did you play that, you Dutch devil?' Zvishdoolin was demanding, glaring at his partner opposite and completely beside himself. 'Call that a lead? There was I holding Dorofeyev and one other, Shepelev and his wife and Stevie Yerlakov, and you go and

59

play Coffeekin. So we end up two down. Cabbage head! Why didn't you play Funguskin?'

'And what good would that have done?' his partner snarled. 'How could I play Funguskin when Ivan had his arms round Martinetoff?'

'Now they're mixing my name up in it,' Martinetoff shrugged his shoulders in perplexity. 'What on earth's going on?'

Skribblitch dealt again and the clerks continued.

'National Bank . . .'

'Two – Tax Office . . .'

'No trumps . . .'

'Oho, going no trumps, are you? Well then . . . County Hall – two tricks. May as well be hanged for a sheep as a lamb, dammit! I was one down on Education Office last time, this time I'll go bust on County Hall. What the hell!'

'Small slam on Education Office!'

'What on *earth* . . .' Martinetoff whispered to himself.

'I'm playing a state counsellor . . . Come on, Vanya, you'll have to chuck in some old titular or provincial.'

'See if we care! We're going to catch you with old Martinetoff!'

'And we belt your Martinetoff for you – right across the chops. We've got Rybnikov. You'll be three down this time! Out with la belle Martinetova. There's no use hiding the old bag away in your jacket.'

'Now they're bringing my wife into it,' Martinetoff said to himself. 'What the . . .'

And unable to contain his curiosity any longer, Martinetoff opened the door and entered the duty room. The appearance of the devil himself, complete with horns and a tail, could not have caused the civil servants greater astonishment and consternation than did the arrival of their chief. Had the head supplies clerk, who had died the previous year, appeared and said in sepulchral tones: 'I come to lead you, evil ones, to the place destined for rogues,' and they had felt the cold breath of the tomb from him, they could not have turned more pale than they did on recognizing Martinetoff. Malingrin got such a fright his nose started to bleed, while Fistikoff got a drumming sound in his right ear and his cravat came untied all by itself. The clerks dropped their cards, rose slowly to their feet, and after exchanging glances, gazed fixedly at the floor. Silence reigned in the duty room for a minute . . .

'I see you're making a good job of copying out the accounts,'

Martinetoff began. 'Now I understand why you're so fond of the job. What were you doing just now?'

'It was only for a minute, excellency. . .' Zvishdoolin said in a very small voice. 'We were having a look at some photos . . . while we had a break . . .'

Martinetoff went up to the table and slowly hunched his shoulders. Lying on the table were not playing cards, but photographs of normal size and shape, removed from their cardboard mounts and stuck on to playing cards. There were lots of photographs, and as Martinetoff looked at them, he recognized himself, his wife, and many of his subordinates and acquaintances.

'Ridiculous! How do you play this game anyway?'

'It wasn't us thought it up, excellency . . . God forbid . . . We just got the idea from someone else . . .'

'Come on, Zvishdoolin, explain how you were playing. I saw everything and heard you beating me with Rybnikov. What's the use of humming and hawing? I won't eat you, will I? Out with it, man!'

For a long time Zvishdoolin was too nervous and scared. Only when an angry flush came to Martinetoff's cheeks and he began to snort with impatience, did Zvishdoolin obey. Gathering up the cards, he reshuffled them, laid them out on the table and began to explain.

'Every portrait has its character . . . its value, just like every card, excellency. There are fifty-two cards and four suits just as in a normal pack. Tax Office staff are hearts, County Hall administrators are clubs, employees of the Ministry of Public Education are diamonds, and spades are personnel of the National Bank. That's the suits . . . Then for aces we've got actual state counsellors, state counsellors are kings, the wives of persons in grades 4 and 5 are queens, collegiate counsellors are knaves, court counsellors are tens, and so on. Me, for instance – here's my card – I'm a three, seeing I'm a provincial secretary . . .'

'Well, well! So I'm an ace then, am I?'

'Yes, the ace of clubs, and your excellency's good lady is the queen . . .'

'Hm. Quite an intriguing idea . . . Well then, let's have a game and see how it goes.'

Martinetoff took off his coat and sat down at the table with a cautious smile. At his behest the clerks also sat down and the game commenced . . .

It was a shock for the porter, Nazar, when he arrived at seven in the morning to sweep out the duty room. The scene that met his eyes as he entered with his broom so impressed him that he recalls it to this day, even when lying beyond recall in a drunken stupor. Martinetoff, pale, bleary eyed and dishevelled, was standing in front of Malingrin holding on to one of his coat buttons and saying:

'But don't you see, you couldn't possibly play Shepelev if you knew I was holding me and three other clubs. Zvishdoolin had Rybnikov and his wife, three grammar-school teachers and my wife, and Skribblitch had the bankers and three low cards from County Hall. So you should have led with Kaputsky! You shouldn't have paid any attention when they led with Tax Office. They've got their heads screwed on!'

'But excellency, I played a titular because I thought they had an actual state.'

'Oh gracious me, old chap, *that's* no argument! You haven't a clue! Only beginners play that way. Work it out for yourself – when Fistikoff led with the court counsellor of County Hall you should have played Ivan Ivanovich Greenlandsky, because you knew he had Natalya Dmitriyevna and two others of the same suit plus Yegor Yegorych . . . You made a mess of the whole thing! I'll show you in a moment. Sit down, gentlemen, let's have one more rubber!'

And the civil servants, having dismissed the astounded Nazar, sat down and went on with the game.

1884

On the Telephone

'How can I help you?' asks a female voice.

'Put me through to the "Slavic Bazaar".'

'Right away.'

Three minutes later my bell rings. I put the receiver to my ear and hear vague sounds, like the wind howling or a hail of dry peas. Someone's babbling something.

'Have you any private rooms?' I ask.

'There's no one at home,' a child answers in a broken voice. 'Papa and Mamma have gone to Serafima Petrovna's, and Luise Frantsovna's got flu.'

'Who's that speaking? Is that the "Slavic Bazaar"?'

'This is Seryozha speaking. My papa's a doctor. He sees patients in the mornings.'

'I don't need a doctor, thank you, Seryozha, I need the "Slavic Bazaar".'

'What bazaar? (laughter). Oh I get it, you're Pavel Andreich, aren't you? Guess what, we had a letter from Katya (laughter) and she's proposed to an officer. When are you going to buy me those paints?'

I move away from the telephone and ten minutes later ring again.

'Put me through to the "Slavic Bazaar"!' I ask.

'About time, too!' a hoarse bass replies. 'Have you got Fuchs with you?'

'Fuchs? What Fuchs? I'm trying to get the "Slavic Bazaar"!'

'You're at the "Slavic Bazaar"! Splendid, I'll be right round. We can get the whole business tied up today. I shan't be long. Be a good chap and order me a portion of sturgeon hot-pot, I've not eaten yet.'

'Good grief!' I think, moving away from the telephone. 'Maybe I don't know how to use the telephone, I'm doing something wrong. Now, what do you have to do? First twiddle this little thing round, then take this thing off and put it to your ear. Then what? Then you hang this thing on these little things and turn this little thing round three times. That seems right .. '

I ring again. No reply. I ring with such fury that the little thing's in danger of breaking off. There's a noise in the receiver like mice running over paper.

'Who's that?' I shout. 'Answer me! Speak up!'

'Timofey Vaksin Sons, Drapers' Materials.'

'I'm deeply obliged, but I don't need any drapers' materials.'

'You must be Sychov? Your calico's already been sent off.'

I hang up the receiver and start wondering again if I'm doing something wrong. I read through the book of instructions, smoke a cigarette and ring again. No reply.

'The telephone at the "Slavic Bazaar" must be out of order. I'll try the "Hermitage" instead.'

I consult the book of instructions again on how to call up the central exchange, and ring.

'Put me through to the "Hermitage"!' I shout. ' "The Her-mit-age"!!'

Five minutes pass, ten. My patience is gradually ebbing away when – hurrah! – the bell rings.

'Who's that?' I ask.

'Central exchange here.'

'What! For heaven's sake, I want the "Hermitage"!'

'The pharmacy?'

'No, the "Her-mit-age"!!'

'Right away.'

'At last,' I think, 'my torments should be over. Phew, I'm in a real sweat.'

The bell goes. I grab the receiver.

'Any private rooms?' I demand.

'Papa and Mamma have gone to Serafima Petrovna's, and Luise Frantsovna's got flu. There's no one at home.'

'Oh, it's you, is it, Seryozha?'

'Yes, it's me ... Who's that? (laughter) Pavel Andreich? Why didn't you come to see us yesterday? (laughter) Papa gave us a shadow pantomime. He put on Mamma's hat and pretended he was Avdotya Nikolayevna –'

Seryozha's voice suddenly breaks off. Silence ensues. I hang up the receiver and ring for about three minutes until my fingers ache.

'Put me through to the "Hermitage"!' I shout. 'The restaurant on Trubnaya Square! Can you hear me or can't you?'

'I can hear you perfectly, sir, only this isn't the "Hermitage",
it's the "Slavic Bazaar".'
'You're the "Slavic Bazaar"?'
'That's right, sir, the "Slavic Bazaar".'
'Oh no, it's all beyond me! Have you any private rooms?'
'I'll just find out for you, sir. . . .'
A minute passes, then another. In the receiver I can hear the
faint sound of voices. I listen hard but can't make anything out.
'Answer me: have you any private rooms?'
'How can I help you?' asks a female voice.
'Is that the "Slavic Bazaar"?'
'Central exchange here . . .'

(The sequel goes on indefinitely.)

1886

Romance with Double-Bass

Pitsikatoff was making his way on foot from town to Prince
Bibuloff's country villa where 'a musical evening with dancing'
was to take place in celebration of the engagement of the Prince's
daughter. A gigantic double-bass in a leather case reposed on
Pitsikatoff's back. He was walking along the bank of a river
whose cooling waters rolled on if not majestically, then at least
most poetically.
'How about a dip?' he thought.
In the twinkling of an eye he had taken off his clothes and
immersed his body in the cooling stream. It was a glorious
evening, and Pitsikatoff's poetic soul began to attune itself to the
harmony of its surroundings. And imagine what sweet emotions
filled his spirit when, swimming a few yards upstream, he beheld
a beautiful young woman sitting on the steep bank fishing! A
mixture of feelings welled up and made him stop and catch his
breath: memories of childhood, regret for the past, awakening
love . . . Love? But was he not convinced that for him love was no
longer possible? Once he had lost his faith in humanity (his

beloved wife having run off with his best friend, Sobarkin the bassoon), a sense of emptiness had filled his breast and he had become a misanthrope. More than once he had asked himself: 'What is life? What is it all for? Life is a myth, a dream . . . mere ventriloquy . . .'

But now, standing before this sleeping beauty (there could be no doubt she was asleep), suddenly, against his will, he felt stirring in his breast something akin to love. He stood a long time before her, devouring her with his gaze . . .

Then, sighing deeply, he said to himself: 'Enough! Farewell, sweet vision! It's time I was on my way to his Excellency's ball . . .'

He took one more look at the fair one and was just about to swim back when an idea flashed into his mind.

'I'll leave her a token!' he thought. 'I'll tie something to her line . . . It'll be a surprise – "from an unknown admirer".'

Pitsikatoff quietly swam to the bank, culled a large bouquet of wild flowers and waterlilies, bound them together with goosefoot and attached them to the end of the line.

The bouquet sank to the bottom, pulling the gaily painted float after it.

Good sense, the laws of Nature and the social station of my hero would seem to demand that the romance should come to an end at this point, but (alas!) the author's destiny is inexorable: because of circumstances beyond the author's control the romance did not end with the bouquet. In defiance of common sense and the entire natural order, our poor and plebeian Pitsikatoff was fated to play an important role in the life of a rich and beautiful young gentlewoman.

On reaching the bank, Pitsikatoff got a shock. His clothes were gone. Stolen . . . While he had been gazing in admiration at the fair one, anonymous villains had pinched everything except his double-bass and his top-hat.

'Accursed Fate!' he exclaimed. 'Oh Man, thou generation of vipers! It is not so much the deprivation of my garments that perturbs me (for clothing is but vanity), as the thought of having to go naked and thereby offending against public morality.'

He sat down on his instrument case and began to think how he was going to get out of this dreadful situation. 'I can't go to Prince Bibuloff's without any clothes,' he mused. 'There will be ladies present. What is more, the thieves have stolen not only my trousers, but also the rosin I had in my trouser pocket!'

He thought long and painfully, until his head ached.

'Aha!' – at last he'd got it – 'not far from here there's a little bridge surrounded by bushes. I can sit under there till nightfall and then make my way in the dark to the nearest cottage . . .'

And so, having adopted this plan, Pitsikatoff put on his top-hat, swung the double-bass on to his back and padded off towards the bushes. Naked, with his musical instrument slung over his shoulders, he resembled some ancient mythological demigod.

But now, gentle reader, while our hero sits moping under the bridge, let us leave him for a while and turn to the young lady who was fishing. What has become of her? When the fair creature awoke and could see no sign of her float she hurriedly tugged on the line. The line tautened, but neither float nor hook appeared. Presumably Pitsikatoff's bouquet had become water-logged and turned into a dead weight.

'Either I've caught a big fish,' thought the girl, 'or the line has got entangled.'

After another couple of tugs she decided it was the latter.

'What a pity!' she thought. 'They bite so much better towards dusk. What shall I do?'

In the twinkling of an eye the eccentric young lady had cast aside her diaphanous garments and immersed her beauteous person in the cooling stream right up to her marble-white shoulders. The line was all tangled up in the bouquet, and it was no easy matter extricating the hook, but perseverance triumphed in the end, and some fifteen minutes later our lovely heroine emerged from the water all glowing and happy, holding the hook in her hand.

But a malevolent fate had been watching out for her too: the wretches who had stolen Pitsikatoff's clothing had removed hers as well, leaving behind only her jar of bait.

'What am I to do?' she wept. 'Go home in this state? No, never! I would rather die! I shall wait until nightfall, then walk as far as old Agatha's cottage in the dark and send her to the house for some clothes . . . And in the meantime I'll go and hide under the little bridge.'

Our heroine scuttled off in that direction, bending low and keeping to where the grass was longest. She crept in under the bridge, saw a naked man there with artistic mane and hairy chest, screamed, and fell down in a swoon.

Pitsikatoff got a fright too. At first he took the girl for a naiad.

'Perhaps 'tis a water-sprite,' he thought, 'come to lure me away?', and felt flattered by the notion, since he had always had a high opinion of his appearance. 'But if it is not a sprite but a human being, how is this strange metamorphosis to be explained? What is she doing here under the bridge, and what has befallen her?'

As he pondered these questions the fair one recovered consciousness.

'Do not kill me!' she whispered. 'I am the Princess Bibuloff. I beseech you! They'll give you lots of money! I was disentangling my fishing-hook just now and some thieves stole my new dress and shoes and everything!'

'Mademoiselle,' Pitsikatoff replied plaintively, 'they've stolen my clothes too – *and* the rosin I had in my trouser pocket!'

Usually people who play the double-bass or the trombone are not very inventive, but Pitsikatoff was a pleasant exception.

'Mademoiselle,' he said after a pause, 'I see that my appearance embarrasses you. You must agree, though, that there is just as good reason for me to stay under here as for you. But I have had an idea: how would it be if you were to get into the case of my double-bass and close the lid? Then you wouldn't see me . . .'

So saying, Pitsikatoff dragged the double-bass out of its case. Just for a moment he wondered whether he might be profaning Art by using his case thus, but his hesitation did not last long. The fair one lay down in the case and curled up in a ball, while he fastened the straps with a feeling of pleasure that nature had endowed him with such intelligence.

'Now, mademoiselle, you cannot see me,' he said. 'You can lie there and relax, and when it gets dark I shall carry you to your parents' house. I can come back here for the double-bass afterwards.'

When darkness fell Pitsikatoff heaved the case with the fair one inside on to his shoulders and padded off towards Bibuloff's villa. His plan was that he should walk as he was to the nearest cottage, get some clothing there, and then go on . . .

'It's an ill wind that blows nobody good . . .' he thought, bending under his burden and stirring up the dust with his bare feet. 'No doubt Bibuloff will reward me handsomely for the deep concern that I have shown over his daughter's fate.'

'I trust you are comfortable, mademoiselle?' he enquired with a note of gallantry in his voice like that of a gentleman inviting a lady to dance a quadrille. 'Please don't stand on ceremony. Do make yourself at home in there.'

Suddenly the gallant Pitsikatoff thought he saw ahead of him two figures shrouded in darkness. Peering more closely he assured himself that it was not an optical illusion: there really were two figures walking ahead and – they were carrying bundles of some kind . . .

'The thieves!' it flashed through his mind. 'I bet that's who it is! And they're carrying something – must be our clothes!'

Pitsikatoff put the case down at the side of the road and chased after the figures.

'Stop!' he shouted. 'Stop thief!'

The figures looked round, and seeing they were pursued, took to their heels. The Princess continued to hear the sound of rapid footsteps and cries of 'Stop, stop!' for a long time, then all was quiet.

Pitsikatoff was quite carried away by the chase, and no doubt the fair one would have been lying out there at the roadside for a long time to come, had it not been for a lucky chance. It so happened that Pitsikatoff's two colleagues, Dronin the flute and Flamboisky the clarinet, were making their way along the road at that same time. Tripping over the double-bass case, they looked at each other with expressions of surprise and puzzlement.

'A double-bass!' said Dronin. 'Why, it's old Pitsikatoff's! How could it have got here?'

'Something must have happened to him,' Flamboisky decided. 'Either he's got drunk or he's been robbed . . . Anyway we can't leave his instrument lying here. Let's take it with us.'

Dronin heaved the case on to his back and the musicians walked on.

'What a ruddy weight!' the flautist kept groaning all the way. 'I wouldn't play a monster like this for all the tea in China . . . Phew!'

When they arrived at Prince Bibuloff's villa they deposited the case at the place reserved for the orchestra and went off to the buffet.

By now the chandeliers and candelabras were being lit. Princess Bibuloff's fiancé, Counsellor Sikofantoff, a nice handsome official from the Ministry of Communications, was standing in the drawing-room with his hands in his pockets, chatting to Count Tipplovitch. They were talking about music.

'You know, Count,' said Sikofantoff, 'in Naples I was personally acquainted with a violinist who could do absolute marvels.

You'll hardly believe it, but he could get the most fantastic trills out of a double-bass – an ordinary double-bass – stupendous! He could play Strauss waltzes on the thing!'

'Come now, that's scarcely –' the Count objected.

'I assure you he could. He could even play Liszt's Hungarian rhapsody! I shared a hotel room with him and to pass the time I got him to teach me Liszt's Hungarian rhapsody on the double-bass.'

'Liszt's Hungarian . . .? Come now . . . you're pulling my leg.'

'Ah, you don't believe me?' laughed Sikofantoff. 'Then I'll prove it to you straight away. Let's get an instrument!'

Bibuloff's prospective son-in-law and the Count made for the orchestra. They went over to the double-bass, quickly undid the straps and . . . oh, calamity!

But at this point, while the reader gives free rein to his imagination in picturing the outcome of this musical debate, let us return to Pitsikatoff . . . The unfortunate musician, not having caught up with the thieves, went back to the spot where he had left his case but could see no sign of his precious burden. Lost in bewilderment, he walked up and down several times in vain, and decided he must be on the wrong road . . .

'How awful!' he thought, tearing his hair and feeling his blood run cold. 'She'll suffocate in that case. I've murdered her!'

Pitsikatoff tramped the roads till midnight in search of the case and then, exhausted, retired under the bridge.

'I'll look for it in the morning,' he decided.

But his dawn search proved equally fruitless, and he decided to stay under the bridge again until nightfall . . .

'I shall find her!' he muttered, taking off his top-hat and tearing his hair. 'Even if it takes me a whole year – I'll find her!'

And to this day the peasants who live in those parts will tell you that at night near the little bridge you can sometimes see a naked man all covered in hair and wearing a top-hat . . . and occasionally from beneath the bridge you can hear the melancholy groaning of a double-bass.

1886

The Death of a Civil Servant

One fine evening, a no less fine office factotum, Ivan Dmitrich Kreepikov, was sitting in the second row of the stalls and watching *The Chimes of Normandy* through opera glasses. He watched, and felt on top of the world. But suddenly ... You often come across this 'But suddenly ...' in short stories. And authors are right: life is so full of surprises! But suddenly, then, his face puckered, his eyes rolled upwards, his breathing ceased – he lowered his opera glasses, bent forward, and ... atchoo!!! Sneezed, in other words. Now sneezing isn't prohibited to anyone or in any place. Peasants sneeze, chiefs of police sneeze, and sometimes even Number 3s in the Civil Service. Everyone sneezes. Kreepikov did not feel embarrassed at all, he simply wiped his nose with his handkerchief and, being a polite kind of person, looked about him to see if he had disturbed anyone by sneezing. But then he did have cause for embarrassment. He saw that the little old gentleman sitting in front of him, in the first row, was carefully wiping his pate and the back of his neck with his glove, and muttering something. And in the elderly gentleman Kreepikov recognized General Shpritsalov, a Number 2 in the Ministry of Communications.

'I spattered him!' thought Kreepikov. 'He's not my chief, it's true, but even so, it's awkward. I'll have to apologize.'

So he gave a cough, bent respectfully forward, and whispered in the General's ear:

'Please excuse me, Your Excellency, for spattering you ... it was quite unintentional ...'

'That's all right, that's all right ...'

'Please, please forgive me. I –I didn't mean to!'

'Oh do sit down, please, I can't hear the opera!'

Disconcerted by this, Kreepikov gave a stupid grin, sat down, and began to watch the stage again. He watched, but no longer did he feel on top of the world. He began to feel pangs of worry.

In the interval he went over to Shpritsalov, sidled along with him, and, conquering his timidity, stammered:

'I spattered you, Your Excellency . . . Please forgive me . . . I – it wasn't that –'

'Oh for goodness' sake . . . I'd already forgotten, so why keep on about it!' said the General, and twitched his lower lip impatiently.

'Hm, he says he's forgotten,' thought Kreepikov, eyeing the General mistrustfully, 'but looks as nasty as you make 'em. He won't even talk about it. I'll have to explain that I didn't want – that sneezing's a law of nature . . . Otherwise he may think I meant to *spit* at him. And if he doesn't now, he may later! . . .'

When he got home, Kreepikov told his wife about his breach of good manners. His wife, he felt, treated the incident much too lightly: at first she had quite a fright, but as soon as she learned that Shpritsalov was 'someone else's' chief, she calmed down again.

'Even so, you go along and apologize,' she said. 'Otherwise he'll think you don't know how to behave in public!'

'That's right! I did apologize to him, but he acted sort of strangely . . . I couldn't get a word of sense out of him. There wasn't time to discuss it, either.'

Next day, Kreepikov put on his new uniform, had his hair trimmed, and went to Shpritsalov to explain . . . As he entered the General's audience room, he saw a throng of people there, and in their midst the General himself, who had just begun hearing petitions. After dealing with several petitioners, the General looked up in Kreepikov's direction.

'Yesterday at the Arcadia Theatre, Your Excellency, if you recall,' the little clerk began his speech, 'I sneezed, sir, and – inadvertently spattered . . . Forg –'

'Drivel, sir! . . . You're wasting my time. Next!' said the General, turning to another petitioner.

'He won't even talk about it!' thought Kreepikov, going pale. 'He must be angry, then . . . No, I can't leave it at that . . . I must explain to him . . .'

When the General had finished interviewing the last petitioner and was on his way back to the inner recesses of the department, Kreepikov strode after him and mumbled:

'Your Excellency! If I make so bold as to bother Your Excellency, it is only from a sense of – of deep repentance, so to speak! . . . I'm not doing it on purpose, sir, you must believe me!'

The General pulled an agonized face and brushed him aside. 'Are you trying to be funny, sir?' he said, and vanished behind a door.

'Funny?' thought Kreepikov. 'Of course I'm not trying to be funny! Calls himself a general and can't understand! Well, if he's going to be so snooty about it, I'm not going to apologize any more! To hell with him! I don't mind writing him a letter, but I'm not coming all the way over here again. Oh no!'

Such were Kreepikov's thoughts as he made his way home. He did not write to the General, though. He thought and thought, but just could not think what to say. So next morning he had to go to explain in person.

'Yesterday I came and disturbed Your Excellency,' he started stammering, when the General raised his eyes questioningly at him, 'not to try and be funny, as you so kindly put it. I came to apologize for sneezing and spattering you, sir – it never occurred to me to try and be funny. How could I dare to laugh?! If we all went about laughing at people, there'd be no respect for persons, er, left in the world –'

'Clear out!!' bellowed the General suddenly, turning purple and trembling with rage.

'Wha-what?' Kreepikov asked in a whisper, swooning with terror.

'Clear out!!' the General repeated, stamping his feet.

Something snapped in Kreepikov's stomach. Without seeing anything, without hearing anything, he staggered backwards to the door, reached the street, and wandered off . . . He entered his home mechanically, without taking off his uniform lay down on the sofa, and . . . died.

1883

Overdoing It

Gleb Gavrilovich Smirnov, a land surveyor, arrived at Rotten Stumps railway station. He had been engaged to carry out a survey at an estate which lay another thirty or forty versts further on by horse. (With a sober driver and good horses it'll be thirty or less, but a full fifty if the driver's had a drop too much and the horses are worn out.)

'Can you tell me where I'll find posthorses round here?' the surveyor enquired of the station gendarme.

'Posthorses? You'll be lucky. You won't find a decent dog for a hundred versts around, let alone posthorses. Where are you going?'

'Devkino, General Haharin's estate.'

'Well, in that case,' the gendarme yawned, 'try round the back of the station, there are sometimes peasants knocking about who take passengers.'

The surveyor sighed and wandered round the back. There, after prolonged searches, conversations and waverings, he hired a hefty great peasant who had a sullen look and pockmarked face, and was wearing a torn caftan of undyed cloth and bast shoes.

'God knows what kind of a cart you've got!' the surveyor said with a frown as he climbed in. 'It's hard to tell the front from the back.'

'It's not hard at all. The front's where the horse's tail is, and where your excellency is sitting, that's the back.'

The little horse was young but skinny, with spread-out feet and ragged ears. When the driver half-rose and lashed it with his cord whip, it did no more than shake its head, when he started cursing and lashed it again, the cart squealed and shook like someone in a fever, after the third blow the cart began to rock, and after the fourth it finally moved off.

'Will the whole journey be like this?' asked the surveyor, feel-

74

ing badly jolted, and marvelling at how Russian drivers manage to combine travelling at a snail's pace with shaking you to bits.

'Never you worry, we'll get there,' said the driver. 'She's a smart young filly, once she gets going, there'll be no stopping her. Gee up there, damn you!'

It was dusk by the time the cart left the station. To the surveyor's right stretched the dark frozen plain, with no end to it. Go out there and you'd most likely finish up in the middle of nowhere. On the horizon, disappearing and merging with the sky, the cold autumn sun was lazily setting. To the left of the road mounds of some kind rose up in the darkening air: were they last year's haystacks or was it a village? What lay ahead the surveyor could not see, since his whole field of vision in that direction was blocked by the broad clumsy back of the driver. It was still, but cold and frosty.

'What a remote area!' thought the surveyor, pulling up the collar of his greatcoat in an attempt to protect his ears. 'Not a sign of life. Get attacked and robbed here, and no one's going to find out, even if you fired a cannon. And the driver's unreliable. Look at that huge back of his! A child of nature like that need only lift a finger and you've had it! And his face looks sinister, it's like a wild beast's . . .'

'Tell me, friend,' asked the surveyor, 'what's your first name?'

'Name's Klim.'

'What's it like round here, Klim? Dangerous sort of place? Many robberies?'

'No, it's all right, God's spared us . . . Who'd want to start robbing?'

'That's good news, but to be on the safe side I've brought three revolvers with me,' said the surveyor, lying. 'You don't play games with a revolver, I can tell you. It'll take care of a dozen robbers.'

It grew dark. The cart suddenly gave a creak and a squeal, began shaking and turned left as if against its will.

'Where's he taking me?' thought the surveyor. 'He was going straight on before, now suddenly he turns left. For all I know, the villain may be taking me into some den of thieves and then . . . You do hear of cases like that!'

'Listen,' he said to the driver. 'You say it's not dangerous here? Well, that's a pity, because I love tackling robbers. I know I look thin and sickly, but I've got the strength of an ox. Once I was attacked by three robbers, and what do you think happened? I beat one of them up so badly he gave up the ghost, and the other two got penal servitude in Siberia thanks to me. I don't know where my strength comes from. I can pick up a great big fellow like you with one hand and flatten him.'

Klim glanced round at the surveyor, his face twitched and he whipped up the little horse.

'Yes, brother,' the surveyor went on. 'Woe betide anyone who tangles with me. It's not just that a robber will lose an arm or a leg, he'll also have to answer before the law. The judges and police chiefs are all friends of mine. I'm a state official, they depend on me. The authorities know all about my movements, they're watching to see no harm befalls me. There are village constables and peasant auxiliaries stuck behind every bush along my route. Hey ... hang on!' the surveyor yelled suddenly. 'Where are you taking me now? Where are we?'

'You can see, can't you? In the forest!'

'Oh yes, so we are,' thought the surveyor. 'What a fright that gave me! But I mustn't let him see I'm worried. He's noticed already I'm in a funk. What's he begun looking round at me so often for? He must be up to something. He was dawdling earlier, just plodding along, now look how he's racing!'

'Listen, Klim, why are you driving the horse so hard?'

'I'm not. She got going by herself. Once she gets going, there's no way of stopping her. She'd be glad herself if her legs wouldn't do it.'

'You're lying, brother, I can see you're lying! Look, my advice to you is to slow down. Rein the horse in. Do you hear? Rein her in!'

'What for?'

'What for? Well ... it's like this. Four friends of mine are following me from the station. We must let them catch us up. They promised they'd catch me up in this forest. It'll be jollier travelling together. They're fit stocky fellows, each one's got a pistol. What do you keep looking round for, as if you were on tenterhooks? Eh? Now see here, brother, see here ... You're wasting your time looking round, there's nothing interesting about me ... Apart from my revolvers, of course ... I'll take them out and show you if you like ... Why don't I do that?'

While the surveyor pretended to be rummaging in his pockets, something happened that he could not have anticipated, being such a coward. Klim suddenly threw himself out of the cart and scuttled off on all fours towards the trees.

'Help!' he cried. 'Help! Take the horse and cart, curse you, only spare my life. Help!'

Then followed the sound of rapidly disappearing footsteps, the snapping of twigs – and silence. The surveyor, who had not expected such a reprimand, first stopped the horse, then arranged himself more comfortably in the cart and began thinking.

'He's run off . . . the fool got scared . . . So what do I do now? I can't go on alone because I don't know the road, and they'll think I've stolen his horse. What can I do? Klim! Klim!'

'Klim!' the echo replied.

The thought of having to spend the whole night sitting in the cold in a dark forest, listening only to the wolves, the echo and the snorting of the skinny mare, sent icy shivers running down the surveyor's spine.

'Klimmie!' he shouted. 'Where are you, old friend? Klimmie?'

For a couple of hours the surveyor shouted, and it was only when he had become hoarse and was reconciled to the thought of having to spend the night in the forest that he caught the sound of a moan on the faint breeze.

'Klim! Is that you, old friend? Let's go on!'

'But you'll . . . you'll kill me!'

'I was joking, old friend! So help me, I was joking! I don't have any revolvers. I lied because I was scared! Please let's go on! I'm frozen!'

Probably reckoning that a real robber would have disappeared long ago with the horse and cart, Klim came out of the forest and walked hesitantly up to his passenger.

'What did you get so scared for, you chump? I was joking and you got scared . . . Come on, get in!'

'God forgive you, master,' grumbled Klim, climbing into the cart. 'If I'd known, I wouldn't have taken you for a hundred roubles. I almost died of fright.'

Klim lashed the little horse. The cart began shaking. Klim gave another lash, and it began rocking. When, after the fourth blow, the cart had moved off, the surveyor covered his ears with his collar and fell to thinking. The road and Klim no longer seemed dangerous.

1885

Surgery

A zemstvo hospital. In the absence of the doctor, who has gone off to get married, patients are being received by his feldsher Kuryatin, a fat man of about forty, dressed in a shabby tussore jacket and frayed tricot trousers. His expression is a mixture of devotion to duty and affability. Between the index and middle fingers of his left hand he is holding an evil-smelling cigar.

Into the reception room comes Exaudimeyev the sexton, a tall heavily built old man in a brown cassock and wide leather belt. His right eye has a cataract and is half-closed, and there's a wart on his nose that looks from a distance like a large fly. Glancing round for a second in search of an icon and failing to find one, the sexton crosses himself in the direction of a large bottle of carbolic solution, then takes some communion bread out of a red cloth and places it with a bow in front of the feldsher.

'Ahh . . . my compliments!' says the feldsher, yawning. 'What brings you here?'

'May I wish you joy of the Sabbath, Sergey Kuzmich . . . I've come to see *you*, sir . . . Verily, verily doth it say in the Psalter, if you'll pardon me: "I have mingled my drink with weeping". The other day I sat down with my old woman to drink tea and no sooner had I begun to put cup to lip than it was like being at death's door . . . Each time I tried taking a tiny sip, it was too much for me! It's not just the tooth itself, it's the whole of this side – it's one big ache! And my ear, if you'll pardon me, feels as if it had a nail or something in it, there's this shooting pain all the time! Oh, I have sinned and done iniquity . . . I have darkened my soul with shameful sins and have sojourned in sloth . . . It's a punishment, Sergey Kuzmich, a punishment! After the liturgy his reverence the priest ticks me off. "Your voice has become all thick and nasal, Yefim. One can't make out a word you're singing." But, I ask you, how can you sing when you can't open your mouth and everything's all swelled up, if you'll pardon me, and you ain't

78

slept a wink all night . . .'

'Hmm . . . Sit down . . . Open wide!'

Exaudimeyev sits down and opens wide.

Kuryatin furrows his brow, looks into the sexton's mouth and espies among the teeth stained yellow by time and tobacco one that is adorned with a gaping cavity.

'His reverence the deacon told me to apply vodka and horse-radish – that was no good. Glikeriya Anisimovna, may the Lord preserve her, gave me a thread from Mount Athos to wear on my wrist and told me to rinse the tooth in warm milk, and I did wear the thread, but as for the milk, I have to admit, I didn't keep it up. It's Lent and I'm a God-fearing person . . .'

'That's superstition . . . (pause). It'll have to come out, Yefim Mikheich!'

'You know best, Sergey Kuzmich. That's what you've been trained for, to understand these matters aright, to know which tooth needs pulling out and which needs drops or whatever . . . That's why you've been appointed, may the Lord preserve you, to be our benefactors, to give us cause to pray for you by day and night, like our own fathers . . . till our dying gasp . . .'

'Nothing to it,' the feldsher says with assumed modesty, going up to the cupboard and rummaging among the instruments. 'Nothing to it, surgery . . . It's all a question of experience and a steady hand . . . Simple as kiss your foot. The other day Alexander Ivanych Egyptyanoff, the landowner, came in with a bad tooth, just like you. He's an educated man, he asks about everything and wants to know all the whys and wherefores. Shakes me by the hand, calls me Sergey Kuzmich . . . He spent seven years in St Petersburg and sniffed out all the professors . . . Had a long chat, we did . . . Sergey Kuzmich, he implores me, take this tooth out, in the name of Christ the Lord! And why not, after all? The only thing is, when you take teeth out, you've got to know what you're doing, it's no good otherwise . . . No two teeth are alike. Some you take out with ordinary forceps, some with molar forceps, others with the tooth-key. It all depends.'

The feldsher picks up a pair of molar forceps, looks at them questioningly for a minute, then puts them back and picks up a pair of ordinary forceps.

'Right, open wide,' he says, going up to the sexton with the forceps. 'We'll soon see about this . . . Simple as kiss your foot. Just cut into the gum, then vertical traction and that's it . . . (cuts into the gum) that's it.'

'You people are our benefactors ... Fools like us don't have a clue, but the Lord sent *you* enlightenment ...'

'Don't pass remarks when your mouth's wide open. This one's easy to take out, but some of them are nothing but little roots. Simple as kiss your foot, this one ... (puts on the forceps). Stop twitching like that ... Sit still ... Won't take a second (applies traction). The thing is, you must go down deep (pulling) so that the crown doesn't break off ...'

'Oh my godfathers ... Holy Mother of God ... A-a-akh ...'

'Can't you ... can't you stop ... stop *grabbing* me! Let go! (pulling) Any moment now ... Almost there, almost ... This isn't easy work, I'm telling you ...'

'Godfathers ... Patron saints ... (shouts). Heavenly angels! Oh-oh! Yank it out, I tell you! Don't spend five years pulling!'

'And I'm telling you, this is surgery ... You can't do it in one go ... Almost there, almost ...'

Exaudimeyev draws his knees up to his elbows and twiddles his fingers about, his eyes goggling and his breathing fitful. Sweat breaks out on his crimson face, his eyes fill with tears. Kuryatin is breathing heavily, shifting his weight from foot to foot in front of the sexton and pulling. Thirty agonizing seconds go by – then the forceps slip off. The sexton jumps up and pokes his fingers in his mouth. The tooth's still in the same position.

'Call that pulled!' he says in a voice that is tearful and sarcastic at the same time. 'I hope they pull *you* about like that in the next world! Much obliged! If you don't know how to take a tooth out, don't try! I can't see for pain ...'

'And why do you keep grabbing me?' the feldsher asks angrily. 'Here am I pulling and you go jogging my arm and talking rubbish ... Old woman, you!'

'Old woman, yourself!'

'You think taking a tooth out's easy, I suppose? Peasant! Just you try! It's not like you climbing into the belfry and pounding away on your bell! (mockingly) "Don't know how, don't know how!" Who are you to go laying down the law? I ask you ... I took out a tooth for Mr Egyptyanoff, Alexander Ivanych, and he didn't make a fuss and start saying things ... He's more respectable than you are, and he didn't keep grabbing me. Sit down! Sit down, I tell you!'

'I can't see straight ... Let me get my breath back ... Phew! (sits down). Only don't keep pulling, yank it out. Don't pull, yank ... Do it in one!'

'Go on, teach me my job! Lord, what uneducated people! Living with you lot is enough to send anyone round the bend. Open wide . . . (puts on the forceps). Surgery, my friend, is no laughing matter. It's not like you standing there in your choir intoning . . . (applies traction). Stop twitching . . . This tooth should have been seen to ages ago, it's got such deep roots . . . (pulls). Keep still . . . Gently does it . . . Keep still . . . Hold on . . . (there's a crunching sound). I knew it!'

Exaudimeyev sits motionless for a minute, as if unconscious. He is stunned . . . His eyes gaze blankly into space, his pale face is bathed in sweat.

'Should have used the molar forceps,' mumbles the feldsher. 'What a mess!'

On coming to, the sexton puts his fingers in his mouth and finds in place of the rotten tooth two jagged peaks.

'Why, you lousy devil,' he says. 'You're monsters, the lot of you, you've been planted on us to lead us to perdition!'

'That's right, call me names,' the feldsher mumbles, putting the forceps away in the cupboard. 'Yokel . . . A pity they didn't use the birch on you more often at the seminary . . . Mr Egyptyanoff, Alexander Ivanych, spent seven years in St Petersburg . . . educated man . . . pays a hundred roubles for a single suit . . . didn't use bad language neither. So who are you to give yourself airs? Don't worry, you won't snuff it!'

The sexton picks up his communion bread from the table and goes off home clutching his cheek.

1884

In the Dark

A medium-sized fly had found its way into the nose of deputy prosecutor (civil service, grade 7) Gagin. It may have been overcome by curiosity, perhaps it had acted on a sudden whim or got lost in the dark, but anyway, Gagin's nose refused to tolerate the presence of a foreign body and gave the signal for sneezing. Gagin sneezed, sneezed heartily, with a shrill whistle and such force that the whole bed shook and all the springs squealed in protest. Gagin's spouse, Marya Mikhaylovna, large, plump and fair, also gave a start and woke up. Peering into the darkness, she sighed and turned over. Five minutes later she turned over again and closed her eyes more tightly, but sleep had now gone for good. After sighing several more times and tossing about, she sat up, scrambled over her husband, and putting on a pair of slippers, went across to the window.

It was dark outside. Only the silhouettes of the trees and the dark roofs of the outbuildings were visible. A very faint light glimmered in the east, but that too would soon be blotted out by dark clouds. The air was silent, sleeping and shrouded in mist. Even the watchman, paid by the summer residents to disturb the nocturnal silence with his warning knocks, was quiet, and so was the corncrake, the one wild bird which did not object to living alongside datcha-dwellers from the town.

It was Marya Mikhaylovna herself who broke the silence. As she stood looking out of the window, she suddenly gave a scream. She had the impression that a dark figure was making its way from the flower garden with its gaunt clipped poplar tree towards the house. At first she thought it was a cow or a horse, but after rubbing her eyes, she began to discern quite clearly the outlines of a human being.

Then she had the impression that the dark figure went up to the kitchen window, stood there for a few moments in apparent hesitation, put one foot on the sill . . . and was swallowed up by darkness.

'Burglars!' she thought in a flash and felt her face go deathly pale.

And in a trice she conjured up in her mind's eye the picture that haunts all female datcha-dwellers: a burglar breaks into the kitchen, proceeds to the dining-room . . . finds silver in sideboard . . . the bedroom . . . an axe . . . villainous face . . . gold and valu- ables . . . Her knees went wobbly and cold shivers ran down her spine.

'Vasya!' she cried, shaking her husband. 'Basil! Vasily Prokofich! Heavens, he might as well be dead! Wake up, Basil, wake up!'

'Eh-h?' groaned the deputy prosecutor, sucking in air and making chewing noises.

'Wake up, for God's sake! There's a burglar in the kitchen. I was standing by the window just now and saw him climb in. He'll go from the kitchen to the dining-room . . . and our spoons are in the sideboard! Basil, exactly the same thing happened to Mavra Yegorovna last year.'

'What . . . what say?'

'Heavens, he's not listening! Can't you understand, you fat dummy, I've just seen someone climb into the kitchen! Pelageya will be scared stiff . . . and there's the silver in the sideboard.'

'Oh, rubbish!'

'Basil, you're impossible! I'm telling you we're in danger and all you do is go on sleeping and groaning! I suppose you want us to be robbed and murdered in our beds. Is that it?'

The deputy prosecutor sat up slowly, filling the air with his yawns.

'I don't know about you,' he muttered, 'really I don't. Can't you leave a chap alone even at night? Waking me up for nothing.'

'But, Basil, I swear to you, I saw a man climb through the window.'

'So what? Let him climb . . . It's probably Pelageya's fireman.'

'*What* did you just say?'

'I said it's Pelageya's fireman.'

'Even worse!' shrieked Marya Mikhaylovna. 'That's worse than a burglar. I will not tolerate cynicism under my roof.'

'You *are* the virtuous one. I will not tolerate cynicism . . . What do you mean, cynicism? Why go throwing foreign words like that about? All that kind of thing's as old as the hills, woman, it's hallowed by tradition. That's why he's a fireman – so that he can visit cooks at night.'

'No, Basil, I can see you just don't understand me. I simply cannot abide the thought that in my house anyone should ... that they ... Kindly go to the kitchen this instant and send him packing. This instant! And tomorrow I shall tell Pelageya not to dare let this kind of thing happen again. When I'm dead and buried, you can allow cynicism in the house if you like, but not a moment before. Off with you, now!'

'Damn it,' Gagin muttered irritably. 'Just use that tiny little female brain of yours for a moment and tell me, where's the point?'

'I'm going to faint, Basil, I am!'

Gagin snorted with disgust, put on his slippers, snorted a second time and set off for the kitchen. It was as dark as being inside a corked barrel, and the deputy prosecutor had to feel his way along. En route he managed to find the door of the nursery and woke up the nursemaid.

'Vasilisa,' he said, 'where's my dressing-gown you took to be brushed last night?'

'I gave it to Pelageya to brush, sir.'

'That's a fine way to carry on. Why wasn't it put back in the right place? Now I've got to traipse round the house without a dressing-gown.'

On reaching the kitchen, he made his way towards the spot where Cook slept on a chest underneath the saucepan shelf.

'Pelageya!' he began, feeling about for her shoulder and giving it a shake. 'Hey, Pelageya! What do you think you're playing at? I know you're not asleep. Who was that climbed through the window to you just now?'

'Well, I like that! Climbed through the window? And who would that be?'

'Now look, don't try fobbing me off ... Just tell that scoundrel of yours to get out of it double quick. Right? He's no business to be here.'

'Are you out of your mind, sir? I like that ... You picked a proper fool in me all right. Slave away the whole day long, on your feet, never a moment's peace, then at night words like that. And all for four roubles a month, supply your own tea and sugar, and never the least respect from anyone, only words ... I've worked in merchants' houses and not been treated so bad.'

'All right, all right, there's no need for the sob stuff. Just tell that ruffian of yours to clear out straight away. Right?'

'Shame on you, sir!' said Pelageya, and there were tears in her voice. 'Educated people, upper-class people, and they've just no idea, they don't understand what we have to go through . . . how much we suffer.' She burst into tears. 'Yes, you can all insult us. There's no one to take our part.'

'Look, it's all the same to me. It was the mistress sent me down. For all I care, you can let the devil himself climb through your window.'

The deputy prosecutor was left with no choice but to apologize for the cross-examination and go back to his wife.

'Pelageya,' he said before leaving, 'where did you put my dressing-gown you were going to brush?'

'Oh dear, I'm sorry, sir, I forgot to put it back on your chair. It's over there on the nail by the stove.'

Gagin groped around by the stove for his dressing-gown, put it on and quietly wended his way back to the bedroom.

On her husband's departure Marya Mikhaylovna had lain down on the bed and started to wait. For three minutes or so she was calm, but then she began to feel rather anxious.

'Why's he taking so long?' she thought. 'It's all right if it's only that . . . that cynic, but suppose it really is a burglar?'

And in her mind's eye she conjured up another picture: her husband enters the dark kitchen . . . a blow with the butt-end of an axe . . . dies without a sound . . . pool of blood . . .

Five minutes passed, five and a half, then six . . . She broke into a cold sweat.

'Basil!' she shrieked. 'Basil!'

'What's all the noise about? Here I am.' She recognized her husband's voice and footsteps. 'Being murdered, are you?'

The deputy prosecutor approached the bed and sat down on the edge.

'There's no one there,' he said. 'Silly thing, you must have imagined it. You can rest easy, your fool of a Pelageya is every bit as virtuous as her mistress. Doesn't take much to scare you, though, does it?'

And the deputy prosecutor, who now felt wide awake, began teasing his wife.

'Yes, you *do* scare easily,' he said with a laugh. 'Better pop along to the doctor tomorrow and see what he can do for hallucinations. A proper case, you are!'

'Can you smell tar?' asked his wife. 'Tar or . . . maybe onion . . . or shchi.'

'You're right, there is something in the air. I don't feel sleepy, so I'll just light a candle. Where are the matches? And I can show you that photograph of the public prosecutor. It was his farewell yesterday and he gave us all photographs. Signed ones, too.'

Gagin struck a match on the wall and lit the candle. But he had not taken a single step from the bed on his way to fetch the photograph before a piercing, soul-searing scream rang out behind him. Glancing round, he saw his wife staring at him with a wide-eyed expression that was full of surprise, horror and anger.

'Did you take your dressing-gown off in the kitchen?' she asked, turning pale.

'What do you mean?'

'Well, have a look at yourself!'

The deputy prosecutor looked at himself and gasped. Instead of a dressing-gown a fireman's greatcoat was hanging down loosely from his shoulders. How had it got there? While he was working out the answer, his wife was conjuring up in her mind's eye yet another picture: a dreadful, unbelievable picture of darkness, silence, whispering, etcetera, etcetera . . .

1886

Kashtanka

A Tale

1
Behaving Badly

A young ginger-coloured bitch – a mixture of dachshund and mongrel, with a muzzle very reminiscent of a fox – was running up and down the pavement, throwing anxious glances to either side. Every so often she would stop, and whimpering, half-raise one frozen paw and then the other, trying to work out how she could possibly have managed to lose herself.

She remembered very clearly how she had spent the day, and how she had ended up on this unfamiliar pavement.

It began when her master, the joiner Luka Aleksandrych, put on his cap, placed some kind of wooden object, wrapped in a red cloth, under his arm, and shouted:

'Come on, Kashtanka!'

Hearing her name, the mixture of dachshund and mongrel came out from her sleeping place on the shavings under the bench, had a nice stretch and ran after her master. Luka Aleksandrych's customers lived so terribly far away that before calling on each of them, he needed to drop into several pubs to build up his strength. Kashtanka remembered that her behaviour on the way had been extremely improper. In her joy at being taken for a walk, she had pranced around, rushed out barking at the horse-drawn trams, dashed into courtyards and chased after dogs. The joiner was forever losing sight of her, stopping and shouting at her angrily. Once, with a voracious expression on his face, he had even got hold of her fox-like ear in his fist, pulled it and said very deliberately:

'Why don't you . . . just drop dead!'

After visiting his customers, Luka Aleksandrych called in briefly at his sister's, where he had a drink and something to eat, went on from his sister's to a bookbinder friend, from the bookbinder to the pub, from the pub to his old crony, and so on – with the result that by the time Kashtanka found herself on the unfamiliar pavement, evening was approaching and the joiner was as drunk as a lord. He was waving his arms about, sighing deeply and muttering:

'In her sins did my mother conceive me in my womb! Oh, sinner that I am! Here we are walking along the street looking at these little lamps, but once we die, we shall all burn in fiery Hyena . . .'

Or else he would assume a genial manner, call Kashtanka over and say:

'You, Kashtanka, are a little insect creature, nothing more. You fall as far short of a man as a carpenter does of a joiner . . .'

While he was talking to her like this, there suddenly came the sound of loud music. Kashtanka looked round and saw a regiment of soldiers advancing straight towards her. She could not bear music, as it set her nerves on edge, and started rushing about and howling. Much to her astonishment, the joiner, instead of taking fright, yelping and barking, smiled broadly, drew himself up to attention and gave a full salute. Seeing that her master was making no protest, Kashtanka began howling all the louder, and rushed distractedly across the road to the opposite pavement.

By the time she had collected herself, the music was no longer playing and the regiment had gone. She ran across the road to the spot where she had left her master, but alas! – the joiner was no longer there. She rushed this way and that, crossed the road again, but the joiner seemed to have disappeared from the face of the earth ... Kashtanka began sniffing the pavement, hoping to find her master from the smell of his footprints, but some wretch had gone by earlier wearing new rubber galoshes, and now all the finer smells were mixed up with the pungent stench of rubber, so that it was impossible to make anything out.

While Kashtanka was running up and down looking in vain for her master, it grew dark. The lamps were lit on both sides of the street, and lights appeared in the windows of buildings. Large fluffy snowflakes were falling, making the roadway, the horses' backs and the coachmen's caps white, and the darker the atmosphere became, the whiter every object appeared. Unfamiliar customers were walking up and down past Kashtanka in a continuous stream, obscuring her field of vision and bumping into her. (Kashtanka divided the human race into two very unequal classes, masters and customers; between the two classes there was an essential difference: the former had the right to beat her, whereas she herself had the right to seize the latter by the calves.) The customers were hurrying somewhere and paid her no attention.

When it became completely dark, Kashtanka was overcome by a feeling of terror and despair. She huddled into a doorway and began crying bitterly. The day-long expedition with Luka Aleksandrych had worn her out, her ears and paws were frozen, and on top of that she was dreadfully hungry. During the whole day she had eaten only twice: at the bookbinder's she had had a little paste, and in one of the pubs she had found a sausage-skin near the counter – that was all. Had she been a human being, she would no doubt have thought to herself;

'No, life is intolerable, I must shoot myself!'

2

The Mysterious Stranger

But she was not thinking of anything at all, only crying. When her head and back were completely covered by the soft fluffy snow and she had sunk into a heavy drowsiness from exhaustion, suddenly the entrance door gave a click, creaked and struck her on the side. She jumped up. Through the open door came a man belonging to the customer class. Since Kashtanka had squealed and got under his feet, he could not fail to notice her. He bent down and asked:

'Where are you from, doggie? Did I hurt you? Poor little thing ... Calm down now, calm down ... It was my mistake.'

Kashtanka looked at the stranger through the snowflakes hanging on her eyelashes and saw in front of her a short fat little man with a plump clean-shaven face. He was wearing a top-hat and his fur coat was unbuttoned.

'What are you whining for?' he went on, knocking the snow off her back with his finger. 'Where's your master? You're lost, I suppose? Poor little doggie! What are we going to do with you then?'

Detecting a note of warmth and sincerity in the stranger's voice, Kashtanka licked his hand and began whining even more piteously.

'You're nice,' the stranger said, 'and comic, too. A proper little fox! Well, nothing else for it, you'll have to come along with me. Maybe you'll be good for something ... Off we go, then!'

He smacked his lips and gestured to Kashtanka in a way that could mean one thing only: 'Let's go!' Kashtanka went.

Less than half an hour later she was sitting on the floor in a large bright room, head cocked to one side, gazing at the stranger with curiosity and a feeling of tenderness. He was sitting at a table having supper, and as he ate, he threw her scraps ... First he gave her some bread and a green cheese-rind, then a piece of meat, half a pie, some chicken bones – but in her hunger she ate everything so fast she did not distinguish one taste from the next. The more she ate, the hungrier she felt.

'Your owners don't feed you much, do they?' said the stranger, observing the fierce greed with which she swallowed unchewed bits of food. 'And how thin you are! Just skin and bones ...'

Kashtanka ate a great deal but was not satisfied, merely intoxicated by food. After supper she lay down in the middle of the room with her legs stretched out, and feeling a pleasant languor throughout her body, began wagging her tail. While her new master sprawled in an armchair smoking a cigar, she wagged her tail and tried to make up her mind which place was better: the stranger's or the joiner's? The stranger's set-up was poor and unattractive: apart from armchairs, a sofa, a lamp and carpets, he had nothing and his room seemed empty; whereas the whole of the joiner's lodging was chock-full of things: he had a table, a bench, a pile of shavings, planes, chisels, saws, a siskin in a cage, a tub ... At the stranger's there were no smells at all, whereas at the joiner's the air was always thick and there was a wonderful smell of glue, varnish and shavings. But the stranger did have one very important advantage: he gave you plenty to eat, and to give him his full due, when Kashtanka was sitting in front of the table gazing at him tenderly, he did not once strike her, stamp his feet or shout: 'Clear off, damn you!'

After finishing his cigar, her new master went out and came back a minute later, carrying a small mattress.

'Hey, dog, come over here!' he said, putting the mattress down in a corner near the sofa. 'Lie down and go to sleep!'

Then he extinguished the lamp and left the room. Kashtanka stretched herself out on the mattress and closed her eyes. She heard barking from the street and was about to reply, when suddenly she was overcome by an unexpected feeling of sadness. She remembered Luka Aleksandrych, his son Fedyushka, her cosy little place under the bench ... She remembered how on long winter evenings, when the joiner was planing wood or reading the paper out loud, Fedyushka was in the habit of playing with her ... He would drag her by the hind legs from under the bench and play such tricks on her that everything went green before her eyes and all her joints ached. He made her walk on her hind legs, pretended she was a bell, i.e., tugged her so hard by the tail that she squealed and barked, gave her snuff to sniff ... One trick was a special torture: Fedyushka would tie a piece of meat on a thread and give it to Kashtanka, then, when she had swallowed it, he would pull it back out of her stomach, laughing loudly. The more vivid her memories, the louder and more plaintively Kashtanka whined.

But soon warmth and exhaustion prevailed over sadness and she began to drop off. She could see dogs running about. One shaggy old poodle she had seen in the street earlier that day, with a cataract on its eye and tufts of fur round its nose, ran past. Fedyushka, holding a chisel, chased after the poodle, then suddenly he himself was covered in shaggy fur, began barking merrily and was standing next to Kashtanka. He and Kashtanka sniffed each other's noses good-naturedly and ran into the street ...

3
A New and Very Pleasant Circle of Acquaintance

When Kashtanka woke up, it was already light, and the noise from the street was such that it could only be daytime. There wasn't a soul in the room. Kashtanka stretched and yawned, and began walking round the room in an angry, sullen mood. She sniffed the corners and the furniture, glanced into the hall and found nothing of interest. Apart from the one into the hall there was another door, and after some deliberation Kashtanka scratched with both paws, opened it, and went into the next room. Here a customer, whom she recognized as the stranger of yesterday, lay on a bed asleep, covered by a woollen blanket.

'Rrrr. . .' she began to growl, but remembering yesterday's supper, wagged her tail and began sniffing.

On sniffing the stranger's clothing and boots, she discovered that they smelt strongly of horse. Another door, also closed, led off somewhere from the bedroom. By scratching and leaning her chest against it, Kashtanka opened this door and immediately became aware of a strange and very suspicious smell. Anticipating an unpleasant encounter, growling and looking round, Kashtanka entered a little room with dingy wallpaper, and started back in fright. Something unexpected and terrifying had met her eyes. A grey goose was advancing straight towards her, bending its neck and head towards the ground, spreading its wings wide and hissing. A little to one side of the goose a white cat lay on a small mattress. On seeing Kashtanka, it jumped up, arching its back, and with its tail sticking in the air and its fur standing on end, also began hissing. The dog was thoroughly scared, but in order not to betray her fear began barking loudly and rushed towards the cat . . . The cat arched its back even more, hissed and struck Kashtanka on the head with its paw. Kashtanka jumped back and crouching on all fours, stretched her muzzle out towards the cat and broke into a loud shrill bark. At the same time the goose came up from behind and gave her a painful peck on the back. Kashtanka jumped up and rushed at the goose . . .

'What's going on?' a loud angry voice enquired, and the stranger came into the room in his dressing-gown, smoking a cigar. 'What's all this about? To your places!'

He went up to the cat, tapped him on his arched back and said:

'Fyodor Timofeich, what have you been up to? Starting a fight? You old rascal, you! Lie down!'

Turning to the goose, he shouted:

'Ivan Ivanych, to your place!'

The cat lay down obediently on his mattress and closed his eyes. Judging by the expression of his face and whiskers, he was annoyed with himself for losing his temper and getting into a fight. Kashtanka began whining with an offended air, while the goose stretched out his neck and began talking about something: he spoke rapidly, passionately and articulately, but was quite impossible to understand.

'All right, all right!' said the owner, yawning. 'You must all live in peace and harmony.' He stroked Kashtanka and went on: 'No need to be scared, ginger . . . They're a good crowd, they won't harm you. Hang on, what are we going to call you? We can none of us do without a name.'

The stranger thought for a moment and said:

'I know . . . You'll be Auntie . . . Got it? Auntie!'

After repeating the word 'Auntie' several times, he went out. Kashtanka sat down and began to watch. The cat was sitting quite still on his mattress, pretending to be asleep. The goose continued to speak rapidly and passionately about something, stretching out his neck and marking time. He was evidently a very clever goose: after each long tirade he would step back in astonishment, pretending to admire his own speech . . . After listening to him and responding with a growl, Kashtanka set about sniffing the corners. In one of them stood a small trough containing soaked peas and soggy breadcrusts. She tried the peas but didn't like them, so she tried the crusts and began eating. The goose wasn't in the least offended that a strange dog should be eating his food, on the contrary, he began talking even more passionately and as a mark of confidence went up to the trough himself and ate a few peas.

4
Wonders Will Never Cease

Not long afterwards, the stranger came in again carrying a curious object, crudely knocked together out of wood and resembling a gate or frame. On its crossbar hung a bell and a pistol was fastened; strings stretched down from the tongue of the bell and the trigger of the pistol. The stranger stood the frame in the middle of the room, spent a long time untying and tying something, then looked at the goose and said:

'Ivan Ivanych, if you please!'

The goose went up to him and stood there in an expectant pose.

'Right then,' said the stranger, 'let's start from the very beginning. First do your bow and curtsy. Quick!'

Ivan Ivanych stretched out his neck, nodded all round and scraped his foot.

'Well done ... Now die!'

The goose lay on his back and stuck his feet in the air. After going through several other minor tricks of this kind, the stranger suddenly seized hold of his head, looking horror-struck, and shouted:

'Help! Fire! We're ablaze!'

Ivan Ivanych ran up to the frame, took the string in his beak and rang the bell.

The stranger was delighted by this. He stroked the goose on the neck and said:

'Well done, Ivan Ivanych! Now imagine you're a jeweller dealing in gold and diamonds. Imagine you arrive at your shop one day and disturb some thieves. How would you react in such a situation?'

Taking the other string in his beak, the goose pulled it and at once a deafening shot rang out. Kashtanka had loved the sound of the bell, but now the shot sent her into such transports of delight that she started running round the frame barking.

'Auntie, to your place!' the stranger shouted at her. 'Silence!'

Firing the pistol was not the end of Ivan Ivanych's work. For the next hour the stranger made him run round on a rope and cracked his whip, whereupon the goose had to jump over a hurdle and through a hoop, or rear, i.e., sit on his tail and wave his feet. Kashtanka, who could not take her eyes off Ivan Ivanych, howled with delight and on several occasions began running after him with a cheerful bark. Having exhausted the goose and himself, the stranger wiped the sweat off his brow and shouted:

'Marya, ask Piggie Ivanovna to step in, would you?'

A minute later grunting was heard ... Kashtanka growled, put on a very brave face, and edged closer to the stranger to be on the safe side. The door opened and an old woman looked in, made some remark and ushered in a very ugly black pig. Ignoring Kashtanka's growls, the pig raised its little snout and grunted merrily. She was evidently very pleased to see her master, the cat and Ivan Ivanych. When she went up to the cat and gave him a little nudge in the stomach with her snout, and then began talking about something to the goose, you could tell from her movements, her voice and the way her little tail quivered that she was very good-natured. Kashtanka realized at once that there was no point in growling and barking at characters like that.

The master put away the frame and shouted:

'Fyodor Timofeich, if you please!'

The cat stood up, stretched lazily and walked over to the pig reluctantly, as if bestowing a favour.

'Right then, let's start with the Egyptian pyramid,' began the master.

He spent a long time explaining something, then gave the command: 'One . . . two . . . three!' At the word 'three' Ivan Ivanych flapped his wings and jumped on to the pig's back . . . Once the goose was firmly settled on the pig's bristly back, balancing himself with his wings and neck, Fyodor Timofeich, looking openly contemptuous, as if he despised his art and thought it not worth a kopeck, climbed with lazy half-heartedness on to the pig's back, from there clambered reluctantly on to the goose and stood on his hind legs. The result was what the stranger called the Egyptian pyramid. Kashtanka squealed with delight, but at that moment the old cat yawned, lost his balance and fell off the goose. Ivan Ivanych wobbled and also fell off. The stranger shouted, waved his arms and began another explanation. After spending a whole hour on the pyramid, the tireless master started teaching Ivan Ivanych to ride on top of the cat, then began teaching the cat to smoke, and so on.

Teaching ended when the stranger wiped the sweat off his brow and went out. Fyodor Timofeich gave a disdainful sniff, lay down on his mattress and closed his eyes, Ivan Ivanych went over to the trough, and the pig was led away by the old woman. Thanks to the mass of new impressions, Kashtanka had not noticed the day slip by, and that evening she and her mattress were already installed in the little room with the dingy wallpaper, where she spent the night in the company of Fyodor Timofeich and the goose.

5

You've Got Talent!

A month had gone by.

Kashtanka was now used to receiving a nice meal every evening and being called Auntie. She had become used both to the stranger and her new fellow-residents. Life was running very smoothly.

Kashtanka

Every day began the same way. Ivan Ivanych usually woke up first and went straight over to Auntie or the cat, arched his neck and began talking about something with passionate conviction, but as unintelligibly as ever. Sometimes he would raise his head and deliver long monologues. In the first days of their acquaintance Kashtanka imagined he talked so much because he was very clever, but within a short time she lost all respect for him; now when he came up to her with his long speeches, she no longer wagged her tail but dismissed him as a garrulous old bore preventing others from sleeping, and responded with an unceremonious growl.

Fyodor Timofeich, on the other hand, was a gentleman of a very different kind. This individual, on waking, did not utter a sound, did not stir, and did not even open his eyes. He would gladly not have woken up at all, for he was evidently not overfond of life. Nothing was of interest to him, he responded to everything with half-hearted indifference or contempt, and he even sniffed disdainfully when eating his nice supper.

Kashtanka, on waking, began walking round the rooms and sniffing the corners. Only she and the cat were allowed the run of the whole apartment, whereas the goose was not entitled to cross the threshold of the little room with the dingy wallpaper, and Piggie Ivanovna lived in a small shed outside somewhere and appeared only at lesson-time. The master woke up late, drank tea, and at once began working on his tricks. Every day the frame, the whip and the hoops were carried into the little room, and every day they went through almost the same routine. Teaching lasted three or four hours, so that sometimes Fyodor Timofeich in his exhaustion would be reeling about like a drunk, Ivan Ivanych panting with his beak wide open, and the master turning red in the face and forever wiping the sweat off his brow.

The days were made very interesting by the teaching and the meal, but evenings were rather tedious. Most evenings the master went out somewhere, taking the goose and the cat with him. Left on her own, Auntie lay down on her mattress and began to feel sad ... This sadness crept up on her in an imperceptible kind of way and took possession of her gradually, as darkness did the room. It started with the dog losing all desire to bark, eat, run round the rooms and even look at things, then in her imagination two dim figures would appear, not quite dog, not quite human, with expressions that were kind and sympathetic, but hazy. Auntie wagged her tail when they appeared and felt she had seen them somewhere before and loved them . . . and each time as she fell asleep, she had the feeling that these figures smelt of glue, shavings and varnish.

When she was fully accustomed to her new life and had changed from a thin bony mongrel into a sleek well-fed dog, the master stroked her one day before teaching and said:

'Time you and I got down to business, Auntie. You've been kicking your heels long enough. I want to make an artist of you . . . Do you want to be an artist?'

And he began giving her various kinds of instruction. In the first lesson she learned to stand and walk on her hind legs, which gave her enormous pleasure. In the second lesson she had to jump on her hind legs for a piece of sugar held high above her head by the teacher. In subsequent lessons she danced, ran round on the end of the rope, howled to music, rang the bell and fired the pistol, and within a month she could already successfully replace Fyodor Timofeich in the Egyptian pyramid. She learned very eagerly and was pleased by her successes; running round on the rope with her tongue sticking out, jumping through the hoop and riding on old Fyodor Timofeich afforded her the greatest enjoyment. She would accompany each trick she mastered with a ringing, delighted bark, while her teacher would be amazed and delighted, too.

'You've got talent, talent!' he would say, rubbing his hands. 'Most definitely, talent! You're going to be a success all right!'

And Auntie became so used to the word 'talent' that each time the master said it, she would jump up and look round, as if it were her nickname.

6

A Troubled Night

Auntie had been having a dog's dream, in which the porter was chasing her with a broom, and woke up in a fright.

It was quiet, dark and very airless in the little room. The fleas were biting. Auntie had never been afraid of the dark before, but now for some reason she felt scared and wanted to bark. In the next room the master gave a deep sigh, a little later the pig grunted in her shed, then all was silent again. The thought of food lightens the heart, and Auntie began thinking of the chicken-leg she had stolen that day from Fyodor Timofeich and hidden in the sitting-room, in the space full of dust and cobwebs between the cupboard and the wall. It mightn't be a bad idea to go and see if it was still intact; very possibly the master had found it by now and eaten it. But the rule was that you mustn't leave the little room before morning. Auntie closed her eyes so as to fall asleep quickly, knowing from experience that the sooner you go to sleep, the sooner morning arrives. But suddenly an odd shriek rang out close by that made her start and jump to her feet. It was Ivan Ivanych, and this was not his usual earnest chatter, but a wild, piercing, unnatural shriek, like that of a creaking gate being opened. Unable to make out or understand anything in the dark, Auntie felt even more scared and growled:

'Rrrrr . . .'

A brief period elapsed, long enough to gnaw a good bone in, and the shriek was not repeated. Auntie gradually calmed down and dozed off. She had a dream about two large black dogs with tufts of last year's hair on their flanks and haunches; they were at a large tub greedily eating slops, which gave off a white steam and a very appetizing smell, and every so often they would look round at Auntie, bare their teeth and growl: 'Don't think you're getting any!' But a peasant in a fur coat ran out of the house and chased them away with a whip; then Auntie went up to the tub and began eating, but no sooner had the peasant gone back through the gate than the two black dogs hurled themselves on her with growls, and suddenly the piercing shriek rang out again.

'Geek! G-g-geek!' cried Ivan Ivanych.

Auntie jumped up fully awake, and without leaving her mattress, broke into a howling bark. It was not Ivan Ivanych shrieking, she now felt, but someone else, an outsider. And for some reason the pig grunted once more in her shed.

But then came the shuffle of slippers, and the master entered the room in his dressing-gown, holding a candle. The flickering light danced over the dingy wallpaper and the ceiling, and chased the darkness away. Auntie could see that there was no one else in the room. Ivan Ivanych was sitting on the floor awake. His wings were spread wide and his beak was open, and he had a very exhausted, thirsty kind of look. Old Fyodor Timofeich was also awake. He, too, must have been woken by the shriek.

'Ivan Ivanych, what's the matter?' the master asked the goose. 'What are you shrieking for? Are you ill?'

The goose did not reply. The master touched his neck, stroked his back and said:

'You're a funny one. You can't sleep yourself, so you won't let anyone else.'

The master went out taking the light with him, and darkness returned. Auntie was terrified. The goose was not shrieking, but Auntie felt once again that a stranger was standing there in the darkness. What terrified her most was that this stranger could not be bitten, because he was invisible and had no shape. And for some reason she imagined that something very dreadful was bound to happen that night. Fyodor Timofeich was restless, too. Auntie could hear him fidgeting about on his mattress, yawning and shaking his head.

From outside came the sound of knocking on a gate, and in her shed the pig grunted. Auntie began whining, stretching out her front paws and resting her head on them. The knocking on the gate, the grunting of the pig (why was she not asleep?), the darkness and the silence, seemed to her as melancholy and terrifying as Ivan Ivanych's shriek. Everything was in a state of anxiety and unrest, but why? Who was this invisible stranger? Then for a moment two dim little green sparks showed up by Auntie. It was the first time in their whole acquaintance that Fyodor Timofeich had come up to her. What did he want? Auntie licked his paw and without asking what he had come for, began howling softly and on various notes.

'Geek!' cried Ivan Ivanych. 'G-g-geek!'

The door opened again, and the master came in with his candle. The goose was sitting in his previous position, his beak open and his wings outspread. His eyes were closed.

'Ivan Ivanych!' called the master.

The goose did not stir. The master sat down on the floor in front of him, looked at him for a minute in silence and said:

'Ivan Ivanych! Whatever's the matter? Are you dying, is that it? Of course, I remember now!' he shouted, seizing his head in his hands. 'That's the explanation – the horse that trod on you today! Oh my God!'

Auntie did not know what the master was talking about, but could tell from his face that he, too, was expecting something terrible to happen. She stretched out her muzzle towards the dark window, through which she felt the stranger was looking, and howled.

'He's dying, Auntie!' said the master, with a gesture of despair. 'Dying! Death has visited your room. What are we going to do?'

Pale and agitated, the master returned to his bedroom, sighing

and shaking his head. Scared of being left in the dark, Auntie followed him. He sat down on his bed and repeated several times:
'My God, what are we going to do?'
Auntie hovered round his legs. Not understanding why she felt so miserable and why everyone was so anxious, and trying to do so, she followed his every movement. Fyodor Timofeich, who rarely left his mattress, had also come into the master's bedroom and started rubbing against his legs. The cat was shaking his head, as if wanting to shake the gloomy thoughts out of it, and glancing suspiciously under the bed.

The master took a saucer, poured some water into it from the wash-basin and went back to the goose.

'Drink up, Ivan Ivanych!' he said gently, placing the saucer in front of him. 'Drink up, dear.'

But Ivan Ivanych did not stir and did not open his eyes. The master lowered the goose's head to the saucer and dipped his beak in the water, but he did not drink, only spread his wings still wider, while his head went on lying where it was.

'No, there's nothing more we can do!' sighed the master. 'It's all over. Ivan Ivanych is done for!'

And shining droplets trickled down his cheeks, like raindrops on a window-pane. Not understanding his feelings, Auntie and Fyodor Timofeich pressed close to him and looked at the goose in horror.

'Poor Ivan Ivanych!' said the master, sighing mournfully. 'And there was I dreaming we'd go to the datcha this spring and I'd take you for walks in the green grass. Dear creature, we worked so well together, and now you're no more! How ever am I going to manage without you?'

Auntie had the feeling that the same thing would happen to her, that for no apparent reason she, too, would close her eyes, stretch out her paws, open her mouth wide, and everyone would look at her in horror. The same thoughts were evidently passing through Fyodor Timofeich's mind. Never before had the old cat been so gloomy and sullen.

Dawn was breaking, and the invisible stranger who had frightened Auntie so much was no longer in the room. When it was completely light, the porter arrived, picked the goose up by the feet and took him off somewhere. Shortly afterwards, the old woman appeared and carried out the trough.

Auntie went into the sitting-room and looked behind the cupboard: the master hadn't eaten the chicken-leg, it was lying in the same place among the dust and cobwebs. But Auntie felt sad and miserable and wanted to cry. She didn't even sniff the leg, but settled herself under the sofa and began whining softly, in a thin little voice:

'Ooh-ooh-ooh . . .'

7

An Unsuccessful Debut

One fine evening the master came into the little room with the dingy wallpaper, rubbed his hands and said:

'Right then . . .'

He was going to say more, but stopped and went out again. Auntie, who had studied his face and intonation very closely during lessons, decided that he was nervous and worried, and seemed to be cross. Shortly after, he came back and said:

'Today I'm taking Auntie and Fyodor Timofeich with me. Auntie, you'll take the place today of the late Ivan Ivanych in the Egyptian pyramid. What a mess! Nothing's ready, nothing's been learnt properly, we've had too few rehearsals! We'll disgrace ourselves, we'll be a flop!'

Then he went out again and returned a minute later in his fur coat and top-hat. Going up to the cat and taking hold of his front paw, he lifted him up and tucked him under his coat against his chest. Fyodor Timofeich responded with complete indifference and did not even bother to open his eyes. It evidently made absolutely no difference to him whether he was lying down, being lifted up, lolling on his mattress, or resting on his master's chest under the fur coat . . .

'Come on, Auntie,' said the master.

Not knowing what was going on and wagging her tail, Auntie followed him, and a minute later was sitting at his feet in a sledge. The master was hugging himself with cold and nervousness, and mumbling:

'We'll disgrace ourselves! We'll be a flop!'

The sledge stopped outside a strange big building like an inverted soup tureen. Its wide entrance had three glass doors and was lit by a dozen bright lamps. The doors opened with a clang and looked like mouths, gobbling up the crowds of people who bustled round the entrance. Horses, too, frequently galloped up to the entrance, but no dogs were to be seen.

The master picked Auntie up and put her under his coat against his chest with Fyodor Timofeich. It was dark and airless there, but warm. Two dim little green sparks showed up for a moment – the cat, disturbed by his neighbour's cold hard paws, had opened his eyes. Auntie licked his ear, and wanting to find the most comfortable position, shifted about restlessly, ruffled the cat's fur under her with her cold paws, and inadvertently poked her head out from under the coat, only to give an angry growl and dive back again immediately. She had seen what looked like a huge, badly lit room full of monsters; from behind the partitions and gratings which stretched along both sides of the room, terrifying faces looked out: horse faces, faces with horns or long ears, and one enormous fat face with a tail instead of a nose and two long bones, picked clean, sticking out of its mouth.

The cat mewed hoarsely under Auntie's paws, but at that moment the coat was flung open, the master said 'hop!' and Fyodor Timofeich and Auntie jumped to the ground. They were now in a small room with grey plank walls; it contained no furniture apart from a small table with a mirror, a stool and some rags hanging in the corners, and instead of a lamp or candle a bright fan-shaped light was burning, attached to a small pipe fixed to the wall. Fyodor Timofeich licked the fur that Auntie had ruffled, and went to lie down under the stool. The master, still rubbing his hands nervously, began undressing . . . He undressed just as he did at home before lying down under his woollen blanket, that is, he took everything off except his underwear, then he sat down on the stool, looked in the mirror, and began doing the most astonishing things to himself. To begin with, he put a wig on his head with a parting and two tufts like horns, then he put a thick layer of something white on his face, and on top of the white drew in eyebrows, a moustache and red cheeks. But that wasn't the end of the business. After daubing his face and neck, he began to array himself in a strange, totally absurd outfit, the like of which Auntie had never seen before either indoors or out. Imagine very baggy trousers, made from the kind of crudely patterned floral chintz used in bourgeois homes for curtains and upholstery, and buttoning up right under the armpits, with one leg coloured brown and the other bright yellow. Swamped by these, the master then added a short chintz jacket with a large scalloped collar and a gold star on the back, different-coloured stockings and green shoes . . .

Auntie was dazzled and bewildered by the variety of colours.

The white-faced, sack-like figure smelt of the master, it had the master's familiar voice, but there were moments of agonizing doubt when Auntie was quite ready to run away from this colourful figure and bark. The new surroundings, the fan-shaped light, the smell, the master's transformation – all this evoked a vague dread and a feeling that she was bound to bump into some horror like the fat face with a tail instead of a nose. On top of this, somewhere in the distance hateful music was playing, and every so often there came an unintelligible roar. One thing alone helped to calm her, and that was the imperturbability of Fyodor Timofeich. He was dozing very quietly under the stool and didn't even open his eyes when the stool was moved.

A man in tails and a white waistcoat glanced into the room and said:

'Miss Arabella's on. You're next.'

The master made no reply. He pulled a small suitcase out from under the table, and sat down to wait. Auntie saw from his lips and hands that he was nervous, and she could hear his uneven breathing.

'M. Georges, if you please!' someone outside shouted.

The master stood up and crossed himself three times, then got the cat out from under the stool and put him in the suitcase.

'Come here, Auntie!' he said quietly, holding out his hands.

Not knowing what was going on, Auntie went up to him. Kissing her on the head, he put her next to Fyodor Timofeich. Then darkness descended ... Too terrified to utter a sound, Auntie trampled on the cat and scratched the sides of the suitcase, which rocked about like a boat and shuddered ...

'It's me!' the master gave a loud shout. 'It's me!'

After this shout Auntie felt the suitcase strike something hard and stop rocking. Then came a loud deep-throated roar: someone was being clapped, and this someone, probably the character with a tail instead of a nose, was roaring and laughing so loudly that it made the locks on the suitcase shake. In response to the roar the master gave a shrill, piercing laugh such as he never did at home.

'What ho!' he shouted, trying to make himself heard above the roar. 'Ladies and gentlemen, your humble servant! I've just come from the station! Grannie's kicked the bucket and left me a legacy! This suitcase feels very heavy – must be gold ... Ho-ho! What if there's a million inside? Let's open it and have a look ...'

The lock on the suitcase clicked. A brilliant light struck Auntie in the eyes; she sprang from the suitcase and deafened by the roar, began racing at full speed round her master with ringing barks.

'Oh-ho!' shouted the master. 'If it isn't old Uncle Fyodor Timofeich! And dear old Auntie! My charming little relatives, blast you!'

He flopped down on the sand, grabbed hold of the cat and Auntie, and began hugging them. While she was being squeezed in his arms, Auntie caught a brief glimpse of the world to which fate had brought her, and was so struck by its magnificence that for a moment she was transfixed with delight and astonishment; then she broke free from her master's embrace and began spinning on the spot like a top, so vivid was the impression. This new world was vast and full of brilliant light; wherever you looked, everywhere, from floor to ceiling, all you could see were faces, more faces, and nothing but faces.

'Auntie, sit down, please!' shouted the master.

Remembering what that meant, Auntie jumped on to a chair and sat down. She looked at the master. His eyes had their usual kind, serious expression, but his face, especially his mouth and teeth, was distorted by a wide fixed grin. He himself was laughing, prancing about and twitching his shoulders, as if being in the presence of thousands of people made him feel very jolly. Believing in his jolly mood, Auntie suddenly had a feeling all over that these thousands of people were looking at her, and lifting up her fox-like muzzle, she began howling with joy.

'Stay there, Auntie,' the master said to her, 'while Uncle and I dance the Kamarinskaya.'

Fyodor Timofeich was looking round him with indifference, as he stood waiting to be made to do something silly. He danced in a languid, off-hand, gloomy way, and you could tell from his movements, his tail and his whiskers that he was deeply contemptuous of the crowd, the brilliant light, his master and himself . . . Having done his share of dancing, he yawned and sat down.

'Right then, Auntie,' said the master, 'first you and I are going to sing and then we'll do some dancing. All right?'

Taking a small pipe out of his pocket, he started playing. Auntie, who could not bear music, moved about restlessly on her chair and began to howl. There was a roar of applause on all sides. The master took a bow, waited until the noise had subsided, and went on playing . . . He had just reached a very high note when someone way up in the gods uttered a loud gasp.

'Dad!' a child's voice shouted. 'Dad, it's Kashtanka!'

'You're right,' rasped a drunken tenor. 'It *is* Kashtanka! So help me, Fedyushka, that's Kashtanka! Here!'

Someone in the gallery whistled, and two voices, a child's and a man's, called out loudly:

'Kashtanka! Kashtanka!'

Auntie gave a start and looked in the direction of the shouts. Two faces – one hairy, drunken and grinning, the other chubby, rosy-cheeked and startled – struck her in the eyes, just as the brilliant light had done earlier . . . It all came back, she tumbled off the chair and dived into the sand, then jumped up and rushed towards the faces, squealing joyfully. The deafening roar that followed was penetrated by catcalls and the piercing cry of a child:

'Kashtanka! Kashtanka!'

Auntie leapt over the barrier, and then via someone's shoulder found herself in a box. To reach the next tier, she had to surmount a high wall. She took a leap, didn't make it, and slid back down. Then she was passed from hand to hand, licking people's hands and faces as she went, ascending higher and higher until finally she reached the gallery . . .

Half an hour later Kashtanka was walking along the street behind the people who smelt of glue and varnish. As he lurched along, Luka Aleksandrych tried instinctively, as experience had taught him, to keep a good distance between himself and the gutter.

'In the abyss of sin they wallow in my womb,' he mumbled. 'And you, Kashtanka, are a puzzlement. You fall as far short of a man as a carpenter does of a joiner.'

Fedyushka was striding alongside, wearing one of his father's old caps. Gazing at their backs, Kashtanka felt as if she had been following this pair for ages and was glad that her life had not been interrupted for a moment.

She still recalled the little room with the dingy wallpaper, the goose, Fyodor Timofeich, her nice meals, the lessons and the circus, but now it all seemed to her like a long, confusing, painful dream . . .

1887

Grisha

Grisha, a chubby little boy born two years and eight months ago, is out for a walk in the park with his nanny. He is wearing a long felt pelisse, a scarf, a big cap with a fur bobble, and warm overshoes. He feels hot and stuffy, and to make matters worse the April sun is shining with cheerful abandon straight into his eyes and making his eyelids smart.

Everything about Grisha's ungainly appearance and timid, uncertain steps, expresses extreme bewilderment.

Hitherto the only world known to Grisha has been a rectangular one, with his bed in one corner, Nanny's trunk in another, the table in the third and the icon-lamp burning in the fourth. If you look under the bed, you can see a doll with one arm missing, and a drum, and if you look behind the trunk, you can see all sorts of different things: cotton-reels, pieces of paper, a box without a lid, and a broken toy clown. Apart from Nanny and Grisha, Mamma and the cat often appear in this world. Mamma looks like a doll, and the cat looks like Papa's fur coat, only the fur coat doesn't have eyes and a tail. From this world, which is called the nursery, a door leads to the space where they eat and drink tea. Here Grisha's high chair stands and on the wall hangs the clock, whose sole purpose is to swing its pendulum and strike. From the dining-room you can go through into a room with red armchairs. There is a dark stain here on the carpet which they still point to and wag their fingers at Grisha. Beyond this room is another one, which Grisha must not enter, and where Papa is sometimes to be seen – a most mysterious kind of person! Nanny and Mamma are easy to understand: they are there to dress Grisha, to feed him and put him to bed, but what Papa is there for – Grisha has no idea. Then there's another mysterious person, and that is Auntie, who gave Grisha the drum. Sometimes she's there, sometimes she's not. Where does she disappear to? Grisha has looked several times under the bed, behind the trunk and under the settee, but she was never there . . .

In this new world, though, where the sun hurts your eyes, there are so many Papas, Mammas and Aunties that you don't know which one to run up to. But the oddest, funniest thing of all are the horses. Grisha looks at the way their legs move and is completely baffled. He looks at Nanny to see if she is going to explain it for him, but Nanny says nothing.

Suddenly he hears a terrible tramping sound ... A crowd of soldiers is bearing straight down upon him, marching in step through the park. Their faces are red from the steam baths and under their arms they are carrying bundles of birch twigs. Grisha turns cold with horror and looks enquiringly at Nanny to see if they are dangerous. But Nanny doesn't run away or burst into tears, so they can't be dangerous after all. Grisha watches the soldiers go past and starts marching along in time with them.

Two big cats with pointed faces dash across the path, their tongues lolling out and their tails curling upwards. Grisha thinks he must start running, too, and hurries after them.

'Hey!' shouts Nanny, grabbing hold of him roughly by the shoulders. 'Where do you think you're going? Just you behave yourself!'

By the path another nanny is sitting with a little tub of oranges on her knees. As he walks past, Grisha quietly helps himself to one.

'What do you think you're up to?' shouts his companion, smacking him on the fingers and snatching away the orange. 'Stupid child!'

Grisha would love to pick up that piece of glass which he now sees lying at his feet and gleaming like the lamp in the corner of the room, but he's afraid of getting another smack on the fingers.

'My humble respects!' he suddenly hears a loud, deep voice say almost above his ear, and sees a tall man with bright buttons. Much to Grisha's joy, this man offers Nanny his hand and stands there talking to her. The brilliant light of the sun, the noise of the carriages, the horses, the bright buttons – all this is so astonishingly new and unfrightening that Grisha's whole being fills with delight and he starts chuckling.

'Come on! Come on!' he shouts at the man with the bright buttons, tugging at his coat-tails.

'Come on where?' the man asks.

'Come on!' Grisha insists. What he wants to say is that it would be nice to take Papa, Mamma and the cat along with them as well; but his tongue says something completely different.

After a while Nanny leaves the park and takes Grisha into a large courtyard, where there is still snow lying about. The man with the bright buttons follows, too. Carefully they pick their way round the blocks of snow and the puddles, then they go down a dark, dirty staircase and enter a room. It's very smoky inside, there's a strong smell of cooking, and a woman is standing by the stove frying some chops. The cook and Nanny kiss each other, then they and the man sit down on a bench and start talking quietly. Wrapped up in his warm clothes, Grisha begins to feel unbearably hot and stuffy.

'What's all this for?' he thinks, as he looks round.

He sees a dark ceiling, an oven-prong with curly horns, and a stove which looks like a big black hole . . .

'Ma-a-ma!' he wails.

'Now stop that!' shouts Nanny. 'You'll just have to wait!'

The cook places on the table a bottle, three glasses and a pie. The two women and the man with bright buttons clink their glasses and drink several times, and the man keeps embracing first Nanny, then the cook. And then all three of them start singing quietly.

Grisha stretches his hand out towards the pie and is given a small piece. As he eats it, he watches Nanny drinking . . . He feels like a drink, too.

'Me, Nanny, me!' he pleads.

The cook lets him have a sip from her glass. His eyes start, he frowns, coughs and for a long time afterwards waves his arms about, while the cook looks at him and laughs.

Back home again, Grisha starts telling Mamma, the walls and his bed about where he has been today and what he's seen. He talks more with his face and hands than with his tongue. He shows them the sun shining brightly and the horses trotting along, the horrible stove and the cook drinking.

That evening he just can't get to sleep. The soldiers with their birch twigs, the big cats, the horses, the piece of glass, the tub of oranges, the bright buttons – all these are rolled into one and press on his brain. He turns from side to side, babbles away and eventually, unable to bear his state of excitement any longer, starts to cry.

'You've got a temperature,' says Mamma, placing the palm of her hand on his forehead. 'I wonder how that came about?'

'Stove!' howls Grisha. 'Go away, horrid stove!'

'It's probably something he's eaten . . .' Mamma decides.

And so Grisha, bursting with impressions of the new life he has just discovered, is given a teaspoonful of castor-oil by his Mamma.

1886

Fat and Thin

Two friends bumped into each other at the Nikolayevsky railway station: one was fat, the other thin. The fat man had just dined in the station restaurant and his lips were still coated with grease and gleamed like ripe cherries. He smelt of sherry and *fleurs d'or-anger*. The thin man had just got out of a carriage and was loaded down with suitcases, bundles and band-boxes. He smelt of boiled ham and coffee-grounds. Peeping out from behind his back was a lean woman with a long chin – his wife, and a lanky schoolboy with a drooping eyelid – his son.

'Porfiry!' exclaimed the fat man, on seeing the thin. 'Is it you? My dear chap! I haven't seen you for ages!'

'Good Lord!' cried the thin in astonishment. 'It's Misha! My old schoolmate! Fancy meeting you here!'

The two friends kissed and hugged three times and stood gazing at each other with tears in their eyes. It was a pleasant shock for both of them.

'My dear old chap!' began Thin after they had finished kissing. 'Who would have guessed! Well what a surprise! Let's have a good look at you! Yes, as smart and handsome as ever! You always were a bit of a dandy, a bit of a lad, eh? Well I never! And how are you? Rich? Married? I'm married, as you see . . . This is my wife Luise, née Wanzenbach . . . er, of the Lutheran persuasion . . . And this is my son Nathaniel – he's in the third form. Misha was my childhood companion, Nat! We were at grammar school together!'

Nathaniel thought for a moment, then removed his cap.

'Yes, we were at grammar school together!' Thin continued. 'Remember how we used to tease you and call you "Herostratos", because you once burned a hole in your school text-book with a cigarette? And they called me "Ephialtes", because I was always sneaking on people. Ho-ho . . . What lads we were! Don't be shy,

Nat! Come a bit closer ... And this is my wife, née Wanzenbach ... er, Lutheran.'

Nathaniel thought for a moment, then took refuge behind his father's back.

'Well, how are you doing, old chap?' asked Fat, looking at his friend quite enraptured. 'In the Service, are you? On your way up?'

'Yes, old boy, I've had my grade 8 two years now – and I've got my St Stanislas. The pay's bad, but, well, so what! The wife gives music lessons and I make wooden cigarette-cases on the side – good ones, too! I sell them at a rouble a time, and if you buy ten or more then I give a discount. We manage. First, you know, I worked in one of the Ministry's departments, now I've been transferred here as head of a sub-office ... So I'll be working here. And what about yourself? You must be a 5 now, eh?'

'No, try a bit higher, old chap,' said Fat. 'Actually I'm a Number 3 ... I've got my two stars.'

Thin suddenly went pale, turned to stone; but then his whole face twisted itself into an enormous grin, and sparks seemed to shoot from his eyes and face. He himself shrank, bent double, grew even thinner ... And all his cases, bundles and band-boxes shrank and shrivelled, too ... His wife's long chin grew even longer, Nathaniel sprang to attention and did up all the buttons on his uniform ...

'Your Excellency, I – This is indeed an honour! The companion, so to speak, of my childhood, and all of a sudden become such an important personage! Hee-hee-hee...'

'Come now, Porfiry!' frowned Fat. 'Why this change of tone? You and I have known each other since we were children – rank has no place between us!'

'But sir ... How can you –' giggled Thin, shrinking even smaller. 'The gracious attention of Your Excellency is as – as manna from on high to ... This, Your Excellency, is my son Nathaniel ... and this is my wife Luise, Lutheran so to speak ...'

Fat was about to object, but such awe, such unction and such abject servility were written on Thin's face that the Number 3's stomach heaved. He took a step back and offered Thin his hand.

Thin took his middle three fingers, bent double over them and giggled 'Hee-hee-hee' like a Chinaman. His wife beamed. Nathaniel clicked his heels and dropped his cap. It was a pleasant shock for all three of them.

1883

The Objet d'Art

Holding under his arm an object carefully wrapped up in No.223 of the *Stock Exchange Gazette*, Sasha Smirnoff (an only son) pulled a long face and walked into Doctor Florinsky's consulting room.

'Ah, my young friend!' the doctor greeted him. 'And how are we today? Everything well, I trust?'

Sasha blinked his eyes, pressed his hand to his heart and said in a voice trembling with emotion:

'Mum sends her regards, Doctor, and told me to thank you . . . I'm a mother's only son and you saved my life – cured me of a dangerous illness . . . and Mum and me simply don't know how to thank you.'

'Nonsense, lad,' interrupted the doctor, simpering with delight. 'Anyone else would have done the same in my place.'

'I'm a mother's only son . . . We're poor folk, Mum and me, and of course we can't pay you for your services . . . and we feel very bad about it, Doctor, but all the same, we – Mum and me, that is, her one and only – we do beg you most earnestly to accept as a token of our gratitude this . . . this object here, which . . . It's a very valuable antique bronze – an exceptional work of art.'

'No, really,' said the doctor, frowning. 'I couldn't possibly.'

'Yes, yes, you simply must accept it!' Sasha mumbled away as he unwrapped the parcel. 'If you refuse, we'll be offended, Mum and me . . . It's a very fine piece . . . an antique bronze . . . It came to us when Dad died and we've kept it as a precious memento . . . Dad used to buy up antique bronzes and sell them to collectors . . . Now Mum and me are running the business . . .'

Sasha finished unwrapping the object and placed it triumphantly on the table. It was a small, finely modelled old bronze candelabrum. On its pedestal two female figures were standing in a state of nature and in poses that I am neither bold nor hot-blooded enough to describe. The figures were smiling coquettishly, and altogether seemed to suggest that but for the need to go on supporting the candlestick, they would leap off the pedestal and turn the room into a scene of such wild debauch that the mere thought of it, gentle reader, would bring a blush to your cheek.

After glancing at the present, the doctor slowly scratched the back of his ear, cleared his throat and blew his nose uncertainly.

'Yes, it's a beautiful object all right,' he mumbled, 'but, well, how shall I put it? . . . You couldn't say it was exactly tasteful . . . I mean, décolleté's one thing, but this is really going too far . . .'

'How do you mean, going too far?'

'The Arch-tempter himself couldn't have thought up anything more vile. Why, if I were to put a fandangle like that on the table, I'd feel I was polluting the whole house!'

'What a strange view of art you have, Doctor!' said Sasha, sounding hurt. 'Why, this is a work of inspiration! Look at all that beauty and elegance – doesn't it fill you with awe and bring a lump to your throat? You forget all about worldly things when you contemplate beauty like that . . . Why, look at the movement there, Doctor, look at all the air and *expression!*'

'I appreciate that only too well, my friend,' interrupted the doctor, 'but you're forgetting, I'm a family man – think of my small children running about, think of the ladies.'

'Of course, if you're going to look at it through the eyes of the masses,' said Sasha, 'then of course this highly artistic creation does appear in a different light . . . But you must raise yourself above the masses, Doctor, especially as Mum and me'll be deeply offended if you refuse. I'm a mother's only son – you saved my life . . . We're giving you our most treasured possession . . . and my only regret is that we don't have another one to make the pair . . .'

'Thank you, dear boy, I'm very grateful . . . Give Mum my regards, but just put yourself in my place – think of the children running about, think of the ladies . . . Oh, all right then, let it stay! I can see I'm not going to convince you.'

'There's nothing to convince me of,' Sasha replied joyfully. 'You must stand the candelabrum here, next to this vase. What a pity there isn't the pair! What a pity! Goodbye, then, Doctor!'

When Sasha had left, the doctor spent a long time gazing at the candelabrum, scratching the back of his ear and pondering.

'It's a superb thing, no two ways about that,' he thought, 'and it's a shame to let it go . . . But there's no question of keeping it here . . . Hmm, quite a problem! Who can I give it to or unload it on?'

After lengthy consideration he thought of his good friend Harkin the solicitor, to whom he was indebted for professional services.

'Yes, that's the answer,' the doctor decided. 'As a friend it's awkward for him to accept money from me, but if I make him a present of this object, that'll be very *comme il faut*. Yes, I'll take this diabolical creation round to him – after all, he's a bachelor, doesn't take life seriously . . .'

Without further ado, the doctor put on his coat, picked up the candelabrum and set off for Harkin's.

'Greetings!' he said, finding the solicitor at home. 'I've come to thank you, old man, for all that help you gave me – I know you don't like taking money, but perhaps you'd be willing to accept this little trifle . . . here you are, my dear chap – it's really rather special!'

When he saw the little trifle, the solicitor went into transports of delight.

'Oh, my word, yes!' he roared. 'How do they think such things up? Superb! Entrancing! Wherever did you get hold of such a gem?'

Having exhausted his expressions of delight, the solicitor glanced round nervously at the door and said:

'Only be a good chap and take it back, will you? I can't accept it . . .'

'Why ever not?' said the doctor in alarm.

'Obvious reasons . . . Think of my mother coming in, think of my clients . . . And how could I look the servants in the face?'

'No, no, no, don't you dare refuse!' said the doctor, waving his arms at him. 'You're being a boor! This is a work of inspiration – look at the movement there . . . the *expression* . . . Any more fuss and I shall be offended!'

'If only it was daubed over or had some fig leaves stuck on . . .'

But the doctor waved his arms at him even more vigorously, nipped smartly out of the apartment and returned home, highly pleased that he'd managed to get the present off his hands . . .

When his friend had gone, Harkin studied the candelabrum closely, kept touching it all over, and like the doctor, racked his brains for a long time wondering what was to be done with it.

'It's a fine piece of work,' he reflected, 'and it'd be a shame to let it go, but keeping it here would be most improper. The best thing would be to give it to someone . . . Yes, I know – there's a benefit performance tonight for Shashkin, the comic actor. I'll take the candelabrum round to him as a present – after all, the old rascal loves that kind of thing . . .'

No sooner said than done. That evening the candelabrum, painstakingly wrapped, was presented to the comic actor Shashkin. The whole evening the actor's dressing-room was besieged by male visitors coming to admire the present; all evening the dressing-room was filled with a hubbub of rapturous exclamations and laughter like the whinnying of a horse. Whenever one of the actresses knocked on the door and asked if she could come in, the actor's husky voice would immediately reply:

'Not just now, darling, I'm changing.'

After the show the actor hunched his shoulders, threw up his hands in perplexity and said:

'Where the hell can I put this obscenity? After all, I live in a private apartment – think of the actresses who come to see me! It's not like a photograph, you can't shove it into a desk drawer!'

'Why not sell it, sir?' advised the wig-maker who was helping him off with his costume. 'There's an old woman in this area who buys up bronzes like that . . . Just ask for Mrs Smirnoff – everyone knows her.'

The comic actor took his advice . . .

Two days later Doctor Florinsky was sitting in his consulting room with one finger pressed to his forehead, and was thinking about the acids of the bile. Suddenly the door flew open and in rushed Sasha Smirnoff. He was smiling, beaming, and his whole figure radiated happiness . . . In his hands he was holding something wrapped up in newspaper.

'Doctor!' he began, gasping for breath. 'I'm so delighted! You won't believe your luck – we've managed to find another candelabrum to make your pair! . . . Mum's thrilled to bits . . . I'm a mother's only son – you saved my life . . .'

And Sasha, all aquiver with gratitude, placed the candelabrum in front of the doctor. The doctor's mouth dropped, he tried to say something but nothing came out: he was speechless.

1886

A Horsy Name

Major-General Buldeyev, retired, was suffering from toothache. He tried rinsing his mouth out with vodka and with brandy, applied tobacco-ash, opium, turpentine and paraffin to the sore tooth, rubbed iodine inside his cheek and stuffed his ears with cotton-wool soaked in alcohol, but all this either did no good or made him feel sick. The doctor called, poked around a bit inside the tooth and prescribed quinine, but that did no good either. As for having the tooth pulled out, the General turned down the suggestion. All the members of the household – his wife and children, the servants, even little Petya the kitchen-boy – each put forward their own remedy. It was his steward, Ivan Yevseich, who came to him and recommended having the toothache cured by a magic spell.

'About ten years ago, excellency,' he said, 'there was this exciseman in our district called Yakov Vasilich. A top-class man he was for charming away toothache. He'd turn towards the window, whisper something, spit a few times and it'd be gone! He had this gift . . .'

'Where is he now?'

'He was sacked from the excise and went to live with his mother-in-law in Saratov. Lives off teeth only now. Anyone who gets toothache just goes along and he helps them. Saratov folk he treats at his place, anyone from outside he does by telegram. Why not send him a wire, excellency, saying, it's like this, God's servant Alexis has got toothache and will you please cure it? You can send the money for the cure on by post.'

'What rubbish! Pure quackery!'

'Why not give it a try, excellency? He's a great drinker and swearer, the woman he's living with isn't his wife but a German, but you can really call that man a miracle-worker!'

'Go on, Alyosha!' the General's wife beseeched him. 'You may not believe in spells, but I know they work from personal experi-

114

ence. Even if you don't believe, why not send off? What possible harm can it do you?'

'Oh all right,' the General agreed. 'In my state I'd send a wire to the devil, never mind an exciseman. Ouch, I can't bear it! Where does he live, this exciseman of yours? How should I address him?'

The General sat down at his desk and picked up a pen.

'Every dog in Saratov knows him,' said the steward. 'May I suggest, then, excellency, that you write: "Saratov. To his honour Yakov Vasilich ... Vasilich ..." '

'Yes?'

'Vasilich ... Yakov Vasilich ... and his surname's ... Now I've forgotten the surname! Vasilich ... Hell, what's his surname? I remembered it just now coming over. One moment ...'

Ivan Yevseich stared up at the ceiling and began moving his lips about. Buldeyev and his wife waited impatiently.

'Well come on, out with it!'

'Just a tick ... Vasilich ... Yakov Vasilich ... No, it's gone! And it's such an ordinary name, too, something to do with horses. Cobb? No, it's not Cobb. Hang on ... Was it Hunt? No, not Hunt either. It's a horsy name, I remember that, but what? My mind's gone blank.'

'Chase?'

'No sir. Hang on ... Hunter ... Hacker ... Pointer ...'

'That's not horsy, that's doggy. Hackforth?'

'No, it's not Hackforth ... Hackney ... Hansom ... Trapp ... No, it's none of them.'

'How on earth am I going to write to him, then? Think, man!'

'Just a moment. Trotter ... Boulter ... Boulting ...'

'Trotwood?' asked the General's wife.

'No madam. Stables ... No, that's not right. It's gone!'

'So why the hell come creeping to me with your advice if you can't remember?' the General exploded. 'Get out of here!'

Ivan Yevseich slowly made his way out, while the General slapped his hand to his cheek and began pacing round the house.

'Oh ye gods!' he wailed. 'Ye gods and goddesses! Ouch! The pain's blinding me!'

The steward went into the garden and stood gazing up at the sky, trying to recall the name of the exciseman.

'Smith ... Smithers ... Smithson ... No, none of them! Naismith ... Carter ... Cartwright ... Spurr ...'

After a while he was summoned to the house.

'Got it?' asked the General.

'Afraid not, excellency.'

'Not Gamble or Betts by any chance? No?'

In the house they all began vying with each other to think up names. They went through every possible age, sex and breed of horse, they tried manes, hooves and harness. People were pacing up and down the house, the garden, the kitchen and the servants' quarters, scratching their heads trying to think of the right name . . .

Every so often the steward was called in.

'Is it Studd?' he was asked. 'Mount? Steed?'

'Afraid not,' Ivan Yevseich would reply, gazing up at the sky and continuing to think aloud: 'Gallop . . . Ryder . . . Rayner . . . Sadler . . .'

'Papa!' came a cry from the nursery. 'Dobbin! Troikin!'

The whole estate was in turmoil. Impatient, exhausted, the General offered five roubles to the person finding the right name. Hordes of people began following Ivan Yevseich around, calling out: 'Bridle? Ostler? Shanks?'

But evening came, the name still hadn't been found, and they went to bed with the telegram unsent. The General spent a sleepless night, pacing up and down groaning. Some time after two he went out and roused the steward by knocking on his window.

'It's not Shoesmith, is it?' he asked plaintively.

'No, it's not Shoesmith, excellency,' Ivan Yevseich replied with an apologetic sigh.

'Maybe it's not a horsy name at all, but some other kind of name?'

'On my word of honour, excellency, it's horsy, I remember that most distinctly.'

'What a lousy memory you've got, man! That name's more precious to me now than anything else in the world. I'm a complete wreck!'

Next morning the General sent for the doctor again.

'Let him pull it out!' he decided. 'I can't take any more of this.'

The doctor came and pulled out the tooth. The pain subsided right away and the General relaxed. Having done his job and been duly rewarded for his labours, the doctor got into his trap and set off home. In the field outside the gates he met Ivan Yevseich. The steward was standing by the side of the road staring fixedly at the ground, lost in thought. Judging by his furrowed brow and the look in his eyes, he was racking his brains painfully . . .

'Furlong ... Withers ...' he was muttering. 'Palfrey ... Palfreyman ...'

'Ivan Yevseich!' the doctor addressed him. 'I wonder if you'd be a good chap and sell me five quarters of oats? The stuff I buy from the local peasants is such poor quality ...'

Ivan Yevseich stared blankly at the doctor, gave a queer kind of smile, and without a word of reply, threw up his arms and raced off to the house as if a mad dog were after him.

'Got it, excellency!' he shouted joyfully, bursting into the General's study, his voice breaking with emotion. 'I've got it, thanks to the doctor, God bless him! Oates! Oates is the man's name! Oates, excellency! Send the wire to Oates!'

'*That* to you!' said the General scornfully, thrusting his thumb between two fingers under the steward's nose. 'You can keep your horsy name now! *That* to you!'

1885

At the Bath-house

'Hey, you over there!' shouted a fat white gentleman, espying through the haze a tall scraggy fellow with a wispy beard and a large copper cross on his chest. 'How about some more steam, then?'

'I'm the barber, your excellency, not the bath-attendant. Steam's not my job. Would you like me to cup you instead, sir?'

The fat gentleman stroked his bright red thighs, thought for a moment and said:

'Cup me? Yes, why not? I'm in no hurry.'

The barber hastened off to the changing-room for his instrument, and some five minutes later there were already ten dark cupping-glasses on the fat man's back and chest.

'I remember you, your honour,' began the barber, as he applied the eleventh glass. 'You were kind enough to take a bath with us last Saturday and I also cut your corns for you. I'm the barber, Mikhaylo, if you recall, sir. And you were also kindly enquiring if I knew of any marriageable young ladies.'

'Oh was I? . . . Anything doing, then?'

'Afraid not, sir. I'm fasting now and it's a sin to pass judgement, your honour, but I can't help speaking out plain. May God forgive me for my judgements, but your modern girls are a good-for-nothing, feather-brained lot. In the past a girl wanted to marry a man what was strict and respectable and had some money behind him, a man what had fixed views and went to church regular, but all your modern girl's after is education. What she wants is an educated type, so you needn't bother with your merchants or civil service gentlemen – she'll just laugh at 'em! Well, there's education and education . . . Some educated types, of course, go right to the top, but others spend all their lives scribbling away at a desk and don't save enough for their own funeral. And what a lot of them you see around these days! There's an educated type comes in 'ere. He's a telegraphist, he's studied everything and knows how to compose telegrams, but he washes without soap. It's pitiful to look at!'

'Poor but honest!' came the sound of a deep husky voice from an upper bench. 'We should be proud of such people. Education that goes hand in hand with poverty bears testimony to a loftiness of spirit. Oaf, you!'

Mikhaylo stole a quick glance at the upper bench. The scraggy individual sitting there beating his stomach with birch twigs had bones sticking out all over him, and appeared to consist of nothing but ribs and skin. His face could not be seen, since it was completely covered by long overhanging hair. Only his two eyes were visible, gazing fixedly at Mikhaylo and full of malice and contempt.

'It's one of *them* – one of your long-haired types!' whispered Mikhaylo, winking at the fat gentleman. 'Full of ideas . . . What an awful lot of that kind you see around these days! There's no keeping 'em down. Puts you in mind of a wet floor-mop, he does! Can't bear listening to a decent Christian conversation, any more than the devil can stand incense. And then starts sticking up for education! He's the type your modern girl falls for, exactly the type, your excellency! Don't it make you sick? Last autumn I was called in by a priest's daughter. "Oh, Michel," she says – I'm called Michel at their homes, 'cos I does the ladies' hair – "oh, Michel," she says, "do find me a husband what's a writer." Well, she was in luck, 'cos I had one. He used to go to Porfiry Yemelyanich's pub and was always threatening to expose people in the newspapers. If the waiter came up to him and asked him to

118

pay for his vodka, he'd box him smartly on the ears and say: "What? You expect me to pay? Don't you know who I am? Don't you realize I could tell the whole world what you've got on your conscience?" A scruffy, down-at-heel type. Anyway, I tempts him with the priest's money, shows him the young lady's picture and round we go. Even hired a suit for him. But the young lady didn't fall. "It's his face," she says, "it's not melancholy enough." Who the 'ell does she want, I'd like to know!'

'That's a slander against the press,' said the deep husky voice from the same bench. 'Scoundrel!'

'So I'm a scoundrel, am I? I see . . . You can be grateful, mister, that I'm fasting this week, or I wouldn't let you get away with that one. You'll be another of them writers, I suppose?'

'I may not be a writer, but don't you dare talk about things you don't understand. Many are the writers who have been of benefit to Russia. They have brought light to our country, and it behoves us to honour them, not to abuse them. And I am speaking of secular writers no less than of religious ones.'

'Religious people wouldn't get mixed up in that kind of thing.'

'You're too dim to understand. Saint Dimitry of Rostov, Innocent of Kherson, Filaret of Moscow and the various other luminaries of the church have made a significant contribution to the cause of enlightenment.'

Mikhaylo took a sidelong glance at his adversary, shook his head disapprovingly and grunted.

'Yes, well, mister,' he muttered, scratching the back of his head, 'well, of course, if you're going to talk clever . . . But we know all about you long-haired types, don't you worry! We know what you're up to and we shan't let you get away with it. If you've no objection, your honour, I'll leave the cupping-glasses on you for a moment while I . . . I'll be right back.'

Hitching up his wet trousers as he walked and making a loud slapping noise with his bare feet, Mikhaylo went off to the changing-room.

'There'll be a long-haired type coming out any moment,' he said to the young fellow standing behind the counter selling soap, 'so take a good look at him. He's an agitator . . . Full of ideas . . . Someone better fetch Nazar Zakharych the constable.'

'Tell the boys to.'

'There's a long-haired type coming out any moment,' Mikhaylo whispered to the boys standing near the customers' clothes. 'He's an agitator. Take a good look at him, then run and tell the mistress to fetch Nazar Zakharych so's he can draw up a report. The man's making all kinds of remarks ... He's full of ideas.'

'A long-haired type? What long-haired type?' the boys asked in alarm. 'No one like that's been in. We've had six altogether – a couple of Tartars over there, a gent in that corner, two merchants here and the priest ... that's the lot. You didn't go and take the priest for a long-haired type?'

'Good God, as if I'd be such a fool!'

Mikhaylo glanced at the priest's robes, reached out to feel the cassock and hunched his shoulders. His face was a study in complete bewilderment.

'What's he look like, this priest of yours?'

'He's a thin little chap with very fair hair ... Just a bit of a beard ... And he coughs all the time.'

'Oh Lord,' Mikhaylo mumbled, 'I done it now! A priest ... and there was I howling abuse at him. What a right old mess! I sinned proper this time, lads – and me what's supposed to be fasting. How can I attend confession now I've insulted a man of the church? Oh, Lord have mercy on me, Lord have mercy! I'll go and ask his forgiveness.'

Mikhaylo scratched the back of his head, pulled a sorrowful face and returned to the steam-room. The priest was no longer on the upper bench. With legs wide apart, he was standing down below by the taps, filling his tub with water.

'Father!' Mikhaylo addressed the priest in a tearful voice. 'For Christ's sake forgive me, miserable sinner that I am.'

'Forgive you for what?'

With a profound sigh Mikhaylo prostrated himself at the priest's feet.

'For thinking you had ideas in your head, Father!'

1885

The Chameleon

Across the market square comes Police Inspector Moronoff. He is wearing a new greatcoat and carrying a small package. Behind him strides a ginger-headed constable bearing a sieve filled to the brim with confiscated gooseberries. There is silence all around . . . Not a soul in the square . . . The wide-open doors of the shops and taverns look out dolefully on the world, like hungry jaws; even their beggars have vanished.

'Bite me, would you, you little devil?' Moronoff suddenly hears. 'Catch him, lads, catch him! Biting's against the law now! Grab him! Ouch!'

A dog squeals. Moronoff looks round – and sees a dog run out of merchant Spatchkin's woodyard, hopping along on three legs and glancing backwards. A man in a starched calico shirt and unbuttoned waistcoat comes chasing out after it. He runs behind, bends down right over it, and tumbles to the ground catching the dog by the hind legs. There is another squeal and a shout: 'Hold him, lads!' Sleepy countenances thrust themselves out of the shop windows and soon a crowd has sprung up from nowhere by the woodyard.

'Looks like trouble, your honour!' says the constable.

Moronoff executes a half-turn to his left and marches towards the throng. He sees that the aforementioned man in the unbuttoned shirt is standing at the yard gates and with his right hand raised high in the air is showing the crowd a bloodstained finger. His half-sozzled face seems to be saying 'You'll pay for this, you scoundrel!' and his very finger has the air of a victory banner. Moronoff recognizes the man as Grunkin the goldsmith. On the ground in the midst of the crowd, its front legs splayed out and its whole body trembling, sits the actual cause of the commotion: a white borzoi puppy with a pointed muzzle and a yellow patch on its back. The expression in its watering eyes is one of terror and despair.

'What's all this about?' asks Moronoff, cutting through the

crowd. 'Why are you lot here? What's your finger –? Who shouted just now?'

'I was walking along, your honour, minding me own business . . .' Grunkin begins, giving a slight cough, 'on my way to see Mitry Mitrich about some firewood – when all of a sudden, for no reason, this little tyke goes for my finger . . . Beg pardon, sir, but I'm a man what's working . . . My work's delicate work. I want compensation for this – after all, I may not be able to lift this finger for a week now . . . There's nothing in the law even that says we have to put up with that from beasts, is there your honour? If we all went round biting, we might as well be dead . . .'

'Hm! All right . . .' says Moronoff sternly, clearing his throat and knitting his brows. 'Right . . . Who owns this dog? I shall not let this matter rest. I'll teach you to let dogs run loose! It's time we took a closer look at these people who won't obey regulations! A good fat fine'll teach the blighter what I think of dogs and such-like vagrant cattle! I'll take him down a peg! Dildin,' says the inspector, turning to the constable, 'find out who owns this dog, and take a statement! And the dog must be put down. Forthwith! It's probably mad anyway . . . Come on then, who's the owner?'

'Looks like General Tartaroff's!' says a voice from the crowd.

'General Tartaroff's? Hm . . . Dildin, remove my coat for me, will you? . . . Phew it's hot! We must be in for rain . . . What I don't understand, though, is this: how did it manage to bite you?' says Moronoff, turning to Grunkin. 'How could it reach up to your finger? A little dog like that, and a hulking great bloke like you! I expect what happened was, you skinned your finger on a nail, then had the bright idea of making some money out of it. I know you lot! You devils don't fool me!'

'He shoved a fag in its mug for a lark, your honour, but she weren't having any and went for him . . . He's always stirring up trouble, your honour!'

'Don't lie, Boss-eye! You couldn't see, so why tell lies? His honour here's a clever gent, he knows who's lying and who's telling the gospel truth . . . And if he thinks I'm lying, then let the justice decide. He's got it all written down there in the law . . . We're all equal now . . . I've got a brother myself who's in the po-lice . . . you may like to know –'

'Stop arguing!'

'No, it's not the General's . . .' the constable observes profoundly. 'The General ain't got any like this. His are more setters . . .'

122

'Are you sure of that?'

'Quite sure, your honour –'

'Well of course I know that, too. The General has dogs that are worth something, thoroughbreds, but this is goodness knows what! It's got no coat, it's nothing to look at – just a load of rubbish . . . Do you seriously think he'd keep a dog like that?! Use your brains. You know what'd happen if a dog like that turned up in Petersburg or Moscow? They wouldn't bother looking in the law books, they'd dispatch him – double quick! You've got a grievance, Grunkin, and you mustn't let the matter rest . . . Teach 'em a lesson! It's high time . . .'

'Could be the General's, though . . .' muses the constable aloud. 'It ain't written on its snout . . . I did see one like that in his yard the other day.'

'Course it's the General's!' says a voice from the crowd.

'Hm . . . Help me on with my coat, Dildin old chap . . . There's a bit of a breeze got up . . . It's quite chilly . . . Right, take this dog to the General's and ask them there. Say I found it and am sending it back. And tell them not to let it out on the street in future. It may be worth a lot, and if every swine is going to poke cigarettes up its nose, it won't be for much longer. A dog's a delicate creature . . . And you put your hand down, you oaf! Stop showing your stupid finger off! It was all your own fault!'

'Here comes the General's cook, let's ask him . . . Hey, Prokhor! Come over here a moment, will you? Take a look at this dog . . . One of yours, is it?'

'You must be joking! We've never had none like that!'

'Right, we can stop making enquiries,' says Moronoff. 'It's a stray! We can cut the chat . . . If everyone says it's a stray, it is a stray . . . So that's that, it must be put down.'

'No, it's not one of ours,' Prokhor continues. 'It belongs to the General's brother what come down the other day. Our General don't go much on borzois. His brother does, though –'

'You mean to say His Excellency's brother's arrived? Vladimir Ivanych?' asks Moronoff, his face breaking into an ecstatic smile. 'Well blow me down! And I didn't know! Come for a little stay, has he?'

'He's on a visit . . .'

'Well I never . . . So he felt like seeing his dear old brother again . . . And fancy me not knowing! So it's his little dog, is it? Jolly good . . . Take him away with you, then . . . He's a good little doggie . . . Pretty quick off the mark, too . . . Took a bite out of this

123

bloke's finger – ha, ha, ha! No need to shiver, little chap! "Grr-rrr"
... He's angry, the rascal ... the little scamp ...'

Prokhor calls the dog over and it follows him out of the wood-yard ... The crowd roars with laughter at Grunkin.

'I'll deal with you later!' Moronoff threatens him, and wrapping his greatcoat tightly round him, resumes his progress across the market square.

1884

Revenge

Mr Leo Turmanov, an ordinary fellow, with a tidy little sum in the bank, a young wife and a dignified bald patch, was playing vint at a friend's birthday party. After a particularly bad hand which made him break into a cold sweat, he suddenly remembered that it was high time he had some more vodka. He got up, tiptoed his way between the tables with a dignified, rolling gait, negotiated the drawing-room where the young people were dancing (here he smiled condescendingly at a weedy young chemist and gave him a fatherly pat on the shoulder), then nipped smartly through a small door into the pantry. Here on a small round table stood bottles and vodka decanters, while on a nearby plate, amid the other delicacies, a half-eaten herring peeped out from its green trimmings of chive and parsley ... After pouring himself some vodka and twiddling his fingers in the air as if about to make a speech, Leo knocked it back, pulled a frightful face, and had just stuck a fork into the herring when he heard voices on the other side of the wall ...

'Yes, by all means,' a woman's voice was saying pertly. 'Only when is it to be?'

'My wife,' thought Leo. 'But who's she with?'

'Whenever you like, dear,' replied a deep, fruity bass. 'Today's scarcely convenient, tomorrow I'm busy the whole blessed day ...'

'Why, that's Moorsky!' thought Turmanov, recognizing the bass voice as that of a friend of his. '*Et tu, Brute!* So she's got her

124

claws into you as well, has she? What a restless, insatiable creature! Can't let a day go by without some new affair!'

'Yes, I'm busy tomorrow,' the bass voice continued. 'But why not drop me a line instead? I'd look forward to that ... Only we must decide how we're going to communicate, think up a good dodge. The ordinary post is scarcely convenient. If I write to you, your old paunch of a husband may intercept the letter from the postman, and if you write to me, it'll arrive when I'm out and my better half is sure to open it.'

'What shall we do then?'

'We must think up a good dodge. It's no use relying on the servants, either, because Double-chins is bound to have your maid and footman under his thumb ... Where is he, by the way, playing cards?'

'Yes. Still keeps losing, the poor fool!'

'Unlucky at cards, lucky in love,' said Moorsky, laughing. 'Now here's what I suggest, my pet ... Tomorrow evening, when I leave the office, I shall walk through the park at exactly six o'clock on my way to see the keeper. What you must do, love, is put your note by six o'clock at the latest inside that marble urn – you know, the one to the left of the vine arbour ...'

'Yes, yes, I know the one ...'

'It'll be novel, poetic and mysterious ... Old Pot-belly won't find out, nor will my dearly beloved. All right?'

Leo downed another glass and made his way back to the card-table. His discovery had not shocked or surprised him or even upset him at all. The days when he became worked up, made a scene, used bad language and even fought duels, were long since past; he had given that up and now turned a blind eye to his wife's giddy affairs. But all the same he felt put out. Such phrases as 'Old Paunch', 'Double-chins' and 'Pot-belly' were a blow to his self-esteem.

'What a scoundrel that Moorsky is!' he thought, chalking up his losses. 'Meet him in the street and he's all smiles, taps you on the stomach, pretends he's your best friend – and now look at the names he comes out with! Calls me friend to my face, but behind my back I'm nothing but "Paunch" and "Pot-belly" ...'

As his ghastly losses kept mounting, so his feeling of injured pride grew ...

'Upstart,' he thought, angrily breaking the piece of chalk. 'Whipper-snapper ... If I didn't want to keep out of it, I'd give you Double-chins!'

Over supper he couldn't stand having to look at Moorsky's face, but the latter seemed to be going out of his way to pester him with questions: had he been winning? why was he so down in the mouth? etcetera. And he even had the nerve – speaking as an old friend, of course – to reproach Turmanov's wife in a loud voice for not looking after her husband's health properly. As for his wife, she just gave him her usual come-hither look, laughed cheerfully and chattered away innocently, so that the devil himself would never have suspected her of being unfaithful.

Returning home, Leo felt angry and dissatisfied, as if he'd eaten an old pair of galoshes instead of veal at supper. He might have managed to restrain himself and forget all about it, had not his wife's chatter and smiles constantly reminded him of 'Paunch', 'Fattie', 'Pot-belly' . . .

'I'd like to slap the blighter's cheeks,' he thought. 'Insult him in public.'

And he thought how pleasant it would be to give Moorsky a thrashing, to wing him in a duel like a sparrow . . . have him turfed out of his job, or put something foul and revolting in the marble urn – like a dead rat, for example . . . Or how about stealing his wife's letter from the urn in advance, and substituting for it some smutty poem signed 'Eliza', or something of that kind?

Turmanov paced up and down the bedroom for a long time, indulging in similar pleasing fancies. Suddenly he stopped and clapped his hand to his head.

'Got it, I've got it,' he exclaimed, and his whole face beamed with pleasure. 'That'll be perfect, ab-so-lutely perfect!'

When his wife had gone to sleep, he sat down at his desk and after much thought, disguising his handwriting and concocting various mistakes, wrote as follows:

'To the merchant Dulinov. Dear Sir! If before six this evening the twelfth of September you have not dipposited two hundrid roubles in the marbel vase what stands in the park to the left of the vine arber you will be killed and your abbingdashery shop blown up.'

On completing the letter, Leo jumped for joy.

'What a brainwave!' he muttered, rubbing his hands. 'Superb! Old Nick himself couldn't have thought up a better revenge. The old merchant boy's sure to take fright and run straight round to the police, and they'll be lying in wait at six in the bushes . . . then as soon as you go poking round for your letter, lad, they'll nab you! He'll get the shock of his life! And while they're sorting it all out, just think what the scoundrel will have to go through, sitting there in the cells . . . Oh, excellent!'

Leo stuck on the stamp and took the letter round to the post-box himself. He fell asleep with a most blissful smile on his lips and slept more sweetly than he had done for years. When he woke up next morning and remembered his plan, he purred merrily and even chucked his unfaithful wife under the chin.

On his way to work and then sitting at his office desk, he kept on smiling and picturing to himself Moorsky's horror when the trap was sprung . . .

After five he could bear it no longer and hurried off to the park to feast his eyes on the desperate plight of his enemy.

'A-hah . . .' he said to himself, as he passed a policeman.

On reaching the vine arbour, he hid behind a bush and gazing avidly at the urn, settled down to wait. His impatience knew no bounds.

Moorsky appeared on the stroke of six. The young man was obviously in a most excellent frame of mind. His top-hat was perched jauntily on the back of his head, and his coat was thrown wide open, so that not just his waistcoat but his very soul seemed to be displayed to the world. He was whistling and smoking a cigar . . .

'Now we'll see about Double-chins and Pot-belly!' thought Turmanov, with malicious glee. 'Just you wait!'

Moorsky went up to the urn and casually put his hand inside . . . Leo half rose, fastening his eyes on him . . . The young man pulled out of the urn a small packet, examined it this way and that, and shrugged his shoulders; then he unsealed it hesitantly, shrugging his shoulders yet again; and then the expression on his face changed to one of complete astonishment: the packet contained two multi-coloured hundred-rouble notes!

Moorsky studied these notes for a long time. Eventually, still shrugging his shoulders, he stuffed them into his pocket and said: '*Merci!*'

The unfortunate Leo heard that word. All the rest of the evening he spent standing opposite Dulinov's shop, shaking his fist at the sign and muttering indignantly:

'Coward! Money-grubber! Jumped-up little merchant! Chicken! Pot-bellied little coward! . . .'

1886

127

The Orator

One fine morning they buried Collegiate Assessor Kirill Ivanovich Babylonov. He died of two complaints so frequently encountered in our native land: a nagging wife and alcoholism. When the funeral procession moved off from the church on its way to the cemetery, one of the deceased's colleagues, a certain Poplavsky, hailed a cab and dashed round to his friend, Grigory Petrovich Vodkin. Vodkin is a young man, but has already made quite a name for himself. As many readers will know, he possesses a rare gift for making impromptu speeches at weddings, anniversaries and funerals. He can speak in any condition: half-asleep, on an empty stomach, drunk as a lord, or in a raging fever. Words flow as smoothly and evenly from his mouth as water from a drainpipe, and as copiously; black beetles in a tavern are not more numerous than the maudlin words in his vocabulary. He always speaks eloquently and at great length, so that sometimes, particularly at merchant weddings, the only way to stop him is to summon the police.

'I've come to ask you a favour, old man,' began Poplavsky, finding him at home. 'Put your coat on straight away and let's go. One of our lot has died, we're just seeing him off to the next world, and someone's got to whiffle a few words of farewell . . . We're banking on you, old man. We wouldn't have bothered you for one of the small fry, but this time it's our secretary – a pillar of the department, you might say. You can't bury a big shot like that without a speech.'

'Your secretary?' yawned Vodkin. 'The one who was always drunk?'

'Yes, him. There'll be pancakes and a good spread . . . cab fares on us. Come on, old son! Spin us some Ciceronian palaver by the grave, and we'll give you a right royal thank-you!'

Vodkin gladly agreed. He ruffled up his hair, put on a melancholy face and left with Poplavsky.

'I remember that secretary of yours,' he said, seating himself in

128

the cab. 'You'd have to go a long way to find a bigger cheat and swindler, God rest his soul.'

'Now then Grisha, one shouldn't speak ill of the dead.'

'Of course not – *aut mortuis nihil bene* – but the man's still a crook.'

The friends caught up with the funeral procession and joined it. The dead man was being borne along slowly, so that before reaching the cemetery they had time to nip into several pubs and knock back a quick one for the good of Babylonov's soul.

At the cemetery a short service of committal was held. Mother-in-law, wife and sister-in-law, following established custom, wept profusely. As the coffin was being lowered into the grave, the wife even shouted: 'Stand back – let me join him!' but did not, probably remembering the pension. Vodkin waited until everything had quietened down, then stepped forward, took in all his listeners at a glance, and began:

'Surely our eyes and ears deceive us? This grave, these tear-stained faces, this moaning and wailing: is it not all some terrible dream? Alas, it is no dream and our vision doth not deceive us! He whom we saw only the other day so cheerful, so youthfully fresh and pure, who only the other day, like the indefatigable bee, before our very eyes was bearing his honey to the hive of his country's common weal, he who – who – that man has now been reduced to dust, to an objective vacuum. Implacable Death placed its withering hand upon him at a time when, for all his ripeness of years, he was still at the height of his powers and full of the most radiant hopes. Oh, irreparable loss! Who can possibly replace him? We have no dearth of good civil servants, but there was only one Prokofy Osipych. He was devoted to his honourable duties heart and soul, never did he spare himself, many were the sleepless nights he spent, he was unselfish and incorruptible . . . How he despised those who tried to suborn him to the detriment of the common good, who sought with life's little comforts to lure him into betraying his duty! Why, with our very eyes we have seen Prokofy Osipych divide his meagre salary among his poorest colleagues, and you yourselves have just heard the wailing of the widows and orphans who depended upon his charity. Devoted as he was to the call of duty and to good works, he was a stranger to the joys of life and even turned his back on domestic felicity; as you know, he remained a bachelor to the end of his days! And who will replace him as a colleague? How clearly I can see before me now that tender, clean-shaven face, turned towards us with a kindly smile, how clearly I can hear the note of loving friendship in that gentle voice! May you rest in peace, Prokofy Osipych! Sleep well – thou true and faithful servant!'

As Vodkin proceeded, his listeners began to whisper among themselves. Everyone liked the speech, it even extracted a few tears, but there was a lot in it that seemed odd. First, no one could understand why the orator called the dead man Prokofy Osipovich, instead of Kirill Ivanovich. Secondly, everyone knew that the deceased had spent a lifetime warring with his lawful wedded wife and could not therefore be termed a bachelor; and thirdly, he had a bushy ginger beard and had never once used a razor, so that it was a mystery why the orator should describe him as clean-shaven. Perplexed, the listeners exchanged glances and shrugged.

'Prokofy Osipych!' continued the orator, staring raptly into the grave. 'Your face was plain – shall I say ugly? – you were stern and unbending, but we all knew that behind that outer shell there beat a heart of purest gold!'

Soon the audience began to notice something odd about the orator, too. His eyes were fixed on one point, he fidgeted restlessly and he himself began to shrug his shoulders. Suddenly he dried up, his mouth fell open in astonishment, and he turned round to Poplavsky.

'But he's alive!' he said, staring in horror.

'Who is?'

'Prokofy Osipych! He's standing over there by the headstone!'

'He's not the one who's dead, it's Kirill Ivanych!'

'But you said yourself your secretary had died!'

'Kirill Ivanych *was* our secretary – you've mixed them up, you clown! Prokofy Osipych was our secretary before, that's right, but he was transferred two years ago to the second section as head clerk.'

'Ah, God knows!'

'Why aren't you going on? This is getting embarrassing!'

Vodkin turned back to the grave and resumed with all his previous eloquence. Prokofy Osipych, an elderly civil servant with a clean-shaven countenance, was indeed standing by the headstone, looking at the orator and scowling.

'You put your foot in it there!' laughed the civil servants on their way back from the funeral with Vodkin. 'Fancy burying someone who's still alive.'

'A poor show, young fellow!' growled Prokofy Osipych. 'That

kind of speech may be all right when someone's dead, but when they're still alive – it's just poking fun, sir! How did you put it, for heaven's sake? Unselfish, incorruptible, doesn't take bribes! To say that of a living person you have to be joking, sir. And who asked you, young man, to sound off about my face? Plain and ugly it may be, but why draw the attention of all and sundry to it? No sir, I'm offended!'

1886

The Exclamation Mark
A Christmas Story

Yefim Fomich Perekladin, a collegiate secretary, went to bed on Christmas Eve feeling hurt and even insulted.

'Leave me alone, you witch!' he bellowed viciously at his wife when she asked him why he was so gloomy.

What had happened was that he had just come back from a party where a number of unpleasant and personally offensive things had been said. They had begun by talking in general terms about the usefulness of education, but then the conversation had shifted imperceptibly to the educational qualifications of the civil service fraternity, and many regrets, reproaches and even gibes had been directed at their low standards. At which point, as always happens when Russians are gathered together, they had moved on from the general to the personal.

'Now take you, for example, Yefim Fomich,' a young man said to Perekladin. 'You occupy a decent position, but what education did you have?'

'None whatsoever, I'm afraid. But education isn't necessary in our job,' Perekladin answered mildly. 'Write properly and that's all that matters . . .'

'Yes, but how did you learn to write properly?'

'By habit. After forty years in the service, you become a dab hand. Of course, it was hard going in the early days and I made mistakes, but then it became a habit and there was no problem.'

131

'And what about punctuation marks?'

'They're no problem either. I know when to use them.'

'I see,' said the young man, put out. 'But habit's not at all the same thing as education. Knowing when to use punctuation marks isn't enough – not by a long way! You must do it consciously. When you put in a comma, you must be consciously aware why you're doing it – that's the thing! This unconscious orthography of yours is a reflex, it's completely worthless. A mechanical activity and nothing more.'

Perekladin held his tongue and even smiled mildly (the young man was the son of a state counsellor and was himself entitled to a rank in grade 10 like Perekladin), but now, going to bed, he felt full of spite and indignation.

'Forty years I've been serving,' he thought, 'and no one's called me a fool before or come out with criticisms like that. "Unconscious! Preflex! Mechanical activity!" To hell with you! Why, I dare say I understand more than you, even if I haven't been to your universities!'

Having mentally vented all the swear-words in his vocabulary on his critic and warmed up under the blanket, Perekladin began to feel calmer.

'I do know . . . I do understand,' he thought, dropping off. 'I don't put in a colon where you need a comma, so that means I am aware, I understand. That's right . . . And as for you, young man, you need to grow up a bit and get some work in before you start judging us old ones . . .'

Through the crowd of darkly smiling clouds behind the drowsy Perekladin's closed eyes a fiery comma flashed past like a meteor. It was followed by a second and a third, and soon the whole limitless dark space unfolding in his imagination was covered by dense crowds of flying commas.

'Now take these commas,' thought Perekladin, feeling his limbs growing blissfully numb as sleep approached. 'I understand them perfectly, I can find a place for each one of them if you like . . . and consciously, not for no reason . . . Test me and you'll see . . . Commas are used in various positions, where they're necessary and where they're not. The more confused a document is, the more commas you need. You put them before "which" and "that". If a document lists a number of civil servants, each one of them must be separated off by a comma . . . I know!'

The golden commas spun round and disappeared. Some fiery full stops came flying in to take their place.

'A full stop is used at the end of a document. You also put one in when you need a good breathing space in which to glance up at your listener. After all long passages you need a full stop so that when a secretary's reading aloud, he doesn't run out of saliva. Full stops are not required anywhere else.'

The commas come flying in again: circling round, they mingle with the full stops, and Perekladin sees a whole throng of semi-colons and colons.

'I know them, too,' he thinks. 'If a comma's not enough and a full stop's too much, use a semi-colon. Before "but" and "consequently" I always put in a semi-colon. And what about a colon? A colon is placed after "it was resolved that", "it was decided that" . . .'

The semi-colons and colons faded out. Now it was the turn of the question marks. They jumped down from the clouds and began performing the can-can . . .

'Question marks, they're nothing! I could find room for a thousand of them. They're always put in when you're pursuing an inquiry or asking about some document . . . "Where has the balance for such-and-such a year been transferred to?" or "Would the Police Department not find it possible to apprehend the said Ivanova, and so on?" '

The question marks nodded their hooks approvingly, and as if on parade, straightened up instantly into exclamation marks.

'Hm . . . This punctuation mark is used frequently in letters. "My dear Sir!" or "Your Excellency, father and benefactor!" But what about documents?'

The exclamation marks straightened up still more and waited expectantly.

'In documents they're put in whenever you – when you want to . . . Hm . . . When *do* you use them in documents? Let me try and remember . . . Hm!'

Perekladin opened his eyes and turned over. But no sooner had he closed his eyes again than the exclamation marks reappeared on the dark background.

'To hell with them – when do you put them in?' he thought, trying to banish the unwanted visitors from his imagination. 'Don't say I've forgotten? Either I've forgotten or I've never put them in . . .'

Perekladin began recalling the contents of all the documents he'd written during his forty years' service, but however much he thought and furrowed his brow, he could not find in his past a single exclamation mark.

'What a rum business! I've been writing forty years and never once put in an exclamation mark ... So when do you use the tall blighter, eh?'

His youthful critic's ugly mug, laughing maliciously, showed up behind the row of fiery exclamation marks. The latter smiled in their turn and merged into one big exclamation mark.

Perekladin gave a shake of the head and opened his eyes.

'Damn it,' he thought, 'I must be up early for church and I can't get the wretch out of my mind ... When do you use the blasted thing? That's what habit does for you, becoming a dab hand! Would you believe it, forty years and not a single exclamation mark!'

Crossing himself, Perekladin closed his eyes, but reopened them immediately: the large exclamation mark was still standing there on the dark background.

'Hell, at this rate I shan't get any sleep at all. Martha dear,' he said, turning to his wife, who often boasted of her boarding-school education, 'you don't happen to know, do you, sweetheart, when an exclamation mark is used in documents?'

'Of course I do! I didn't spent seven years at boarding school for nothing. I remember all the grammar off by heart. This punctuation mark is used in forms of address, in exclamations and in expressions of delight, indignation, joy, rage and other feelings.'

'I see,' thought Perekladin. 'Delight, indignation, joy, rage and other feelings ...'

The collegiate secretary became thoughtful. He'd been writing documents for forty years, had written thousands of them, tens of thousands, yet he couldn't remember a single line expressing delight, indignation or anything of that kind.

'And other feelings,' he thought. 'But do you really need feelings in documents? Even an unfeeling person can write them.'

His youthful critic's ugly mug looked out again from behind the fiery exclamation mark, grinning maliciously. Perekladin sat up in bed. His head was aching, cold perspiration stood out on his brow. The icon-lamp in the corner of the room gleamed comfortingly, the furniture looked polished and festive, everything was pervaded by warmth and the presence of a female hand, but the poor pen-pusher felt cold and ill at ease, as if he had caught typhus. The exclamation mark was no longer standing behind his closed eyes but in front of him, in the room, by his wife's dressing-table, and it was winking at him mockingly ...

'Writing machine, you! Machine!' the apparition whispered, and the civil servant felt its cold dry breath. 'Unfeeling block of wood!'

The civil servant pulled the blanket over his head, but even underneath it he could still see the apparition; he pressed his face against his wife's shoulder, but it stuck up from behind there, too. Poor Perekladin was tormented all night, but even during the day the apparition would not leave him alone. He saw it everywhere: as he put on his boots, in the saucer he drank his tea from, in his St Stanislas medal.

'And other feelings,' he thought. 'It's true, there never were any feelings. Here I am about to go and sign the chief's visitors' book. Are feelings necessary for that? No, it's just done automatically . . . I'm a congratulating machine.'

When Perekladin went out and hailed a cab, it wasn't a cabby that he seemed to see driving up, but an exclamation mark. On reaching his chief's entrance hall, he saw the same mark instead of the doorkeeper. All this made him think of delight, indignation, rage . . . The penholder, too, looked like an exclamation mark. Perekladin picked it up, dipped the pen in the ink and signed himself:

'Collegiate Secretary Yefim Perekladin!!!'

And as he wrote those three marks, he felt delight and indignation, he was joyful and he seethed with rage.

'Take that, take that!' he muttered, pressing down hard on the pen.

The fiery mark was satisfied and disappeared.

1885

Notes from the Journal of a Quick-tempered Man

I am a serious person with a philosophical turn of mind. An accountant by profession, I am studying fiscal law and writing a thesis entitled: 'The Dog Tax: its Past and Future.' It's quite obvious I can have absolutely no interest in young ladies, love songs, the moon and suchlike nonsense.

At 10 a.m. my *maman* poured my coffee. I drank it and went out on to the balcony to get down to work on my thesis right away. I took a fresh sheet of paper, dipped my pen in the ink and put down the title: 'The Dog Tax: its Past and Future.' Then, after thinking for a while, I wrote: 'Historical Survey. Judging from certain passing references to be found in Herodotus and Xenophon the dog tax arose from –'

But at that point I heard footsteps of a highly suspicious nature. Looking down from the balcony I saw a young lady with an elongated face and elongated figure. I believe she is called Nadenka or Varenka (however, that is absolutely irrelevant). She was looking for something, pretending not to have noticed me, and singing: 'Dost thou recall that melody so full, so full of bliss . . .'

I re-read what I had written and was about to continue when the young lady suddenly pretended she had just noticed me, and said plaintively:

'Oh good morning, Nikolay Andreich! I'm awfully upset. I must have lost a bauble from my bracelet when I was out walking yesterday.'

I read the opening phrase of my thesis once again, touched up the crossbar on a 't' and was about to resume – but the young lady was not to be put off so easily.

'Nikolay Andreich,' she said, 'please come and see me back to the house. I'm so scared of passing that enormous dog of the Karelins I daren't go on my own.'

Well, there was no way out, so I replaced my pen and went down. Nadenka (or Varenka) took my arm and we set off towards her datcha.

Whenever it falls to my lot to have to walk arm-in-arm with a young girl or a lady, for some reason I always feel like a hook on which someone has hung a large fur coat. Nadenka (or Varenka) – who, between ourselves, has rather a passionate nature (her grandfather was Armenian) – is gifted with a way of leaning on your arm with the whole weight of her body and pressing herself to your side like a leech. So that was how we proceeded . . . As we walked past the Karelins' I saw their large dog. That reminded me of the dog tax and I sighed wistfully as I recalled my opening sentence.

'Why are you sighing?' asked Nadenka (or Varenka), and herself breathed a deep sigh.

A word of explanation here. Nadenka or Varenka (but now I seem to recall that her name is, in fact, Mashenka) for some reason has got it into her head that I am in love with her, and therefore considers it her duty, on humanitarian grounds, always to look at me with compassion in her eyes and to minister verbally to my wounded soul.

She stopped and said: 'Oh, I know why you are sighing. You love someone, that's what it is! But in the name of our friendship I beg you to believe that the girl whom you love holds you in great respect! She cannot answer your affection with like, but is the fault hers if her heart has long belonged to another?'

Mashenka's nose flushed and began to look puffy, and tears welled up in her eyes. She obviously expected me to reply, but fortunately just at that moment we arrived at her house . . . Mashenka's *maman* was sitting on the verandah. She is a kind woman, but with some funny ideas. Observing the signs of emotion in her daughter's face, she gave me a long hard look and sighed, as if to say: 'Ah, youth, youth! Too innocent even to conceal your feelings!' Apart from her there were several varie-gated young ladies sitting on the verandah, and in their midst the fellow who lives in the datcha next door to mine – an ex-army officer wounded during the last war in the left temple and right hip. Like me, this unfortunate had made up his mind to devote the summer to literary activity. He was writing the 'Memoirs of a Military Man'. Like me, he would set about his honourable task every morning and never get further than writing: 'I was born in . . .' when some Varenka or Mashenka would appear beneath his balcony and carry off the wounded warrior under escort.

The whole party sitting on the verandah were preparing some kind of ghastly berries for jam-making. I bowed with the intention of leaving them, but the variegated damsels seized my hat with a squeal and insisted I stay. So I sat down. I was given a plateful of berries and a hairpin. I started stoning the berries.

The variegated young ladies were discoursing on the subject of men: Mr A. was awfully sweet, Mr B. was good-looking but not very attractive, Mr C. wasn't good-looking but he was attractive, Mr D. wouldn't be bad if his nose wasn't so like a thimble, and so on.

'And you, *monsieur Nicolas*,' Varenka's *maman* said turning to me, 'aren't good-looking but you are attractive. You've an interesting face ... But of course,' she sighed, 'the most important thing in a man isn't his looks but his brain ...'

The young ladies all sighed and looked at the floor ... They too clearly agreed that the most important thing in a man wasn't his looks but his brain. At this point I took a sidelong glance at myself in the mirror to check how attractive I was. What I saw was a shaggy head of hair, a shaggy beard, moustache, eyebrows, hair on my cheeks, hairs under my eyes – a perfect thicket with a substantial nose sticking out of it like a forester's watch-tower. A fine-looking chap, I must say!

'But of course, *Nicolas*, it is your spiritual qualities that will win the day,' sighed Nadenka's *maman*, as if confirming some secret thought of her own.

Nadenka was sitting there suffering visibly on my behalf, but at the same time it clearly gave her the greatest satisfaction to know that opposite her was a man who was deeply in love with her. After they had finished with men, the young ladies got on to love. Then after a long conversation about love one of them stood up and left. The others immediately set about tearing her to pieces. They all agreed she was stupid, unbearable, a sight, and that one of her shoulder-blades stuck out.

Then at last, thank God, a maid appeared sent by my *maman* to call me for lunch. Now I could leave this objectionable company and go and get on with my thesis. So I stood up and bowed. But Varenka's *maman*, Varenka herself, and all the variegated young ladies surrounded me and declared I had no right at all to leave as I had firmly promised the previous day to have lunch and go out to the woods with them to pick mushrooms. So I bowed and sat down ... Hatred seethed within my breast – another minute of this and I felt I would not be answerable for myself, there would be an explosion. But a sense of delicacy and my fear of offending against social decorum always make me defer to the ladies. So I deferred.

We sat down for lunch. The ex-officer, whose jaws had seized up because of the wound in his head, ate as if he had a bit between his teeth. I rolled my bread into balls, thought about the dog tax, and knowing my tendency to be quick-tempered, tried not to say anything. Nadenka looked at me compassionately. There was cold soup, tongue with boiled peas, roast chicken and stewed fruit. I didn't feel like eating, but did so out of a sense of delicacy. After lunch, as I stood alone on the verandah smoking, Mashenka's *maman* came up to me, squeezed my hand and said in a breathless voice:

'Don't despair, *Nicolas*. . . Ah, what a loving nature she has, what a loving nature!'

So we went to the woods to pick mushrooms . . . Varenka hung on my arm and clung to my side. It was inexpressible torment, but I put up with it.

We entered the wood.

'Tell me, *monsieur Nicolas*,' sighed Nadenka, 'why is your face so sad? Why don't you speak?'

What an odd girl – what was there to speak to her about? What did we have in common?

'Please do say something,' she insisted.

I tried to think of some popular topic which she might be capable of understanding. So after much thought I said: 'The felling of forests is causing enormous havoc in Russia . . .'

'Oh, *Nicolas*,' Varenka sighed, and her nose began to flush. '*Nicolas*, I see you're avoiding a heart-to-heart conversation . . . It's as if you wanted to punish me with your silence. Your emotion is unrequited and you want to suffer in silence, alone . . . It's awful, *Nicolas*!' she exclaimed, suddenly grabbing me by the hand, and I could see her nose beginning to go puffy. 'But what would you say if the girl whom you love were to offer you Eternal Friendship?'

I mumbled something incoherent because I hadn't the faintest idea what to say to her . . . For goodness' sake – in the first place I wasn't in love with anyone, in the second place what on earth did I want with Eternal Friendship? And thirdly – I'm an extremely quick-tempered person. Mashenka (or Varenka) hid her face in her hands and said in an undertone, as if to herself:

'He does not answer . . . He obviously wants me to make a sacrifice. But how can I love him if I still love another! And yet . . . I'll think about it . . . Yes, I shall think about it . . . I shall summon up all the spiritual resources at my command and – perhaps, even at the cost of my own happiness, deliver this man from his suffering!'

It was all double Dutch to me. Some kind of mumbo-jumbo. We went on a bit further and started picking mushrooms. We said nothing. There were signs of inner conflict on Nadenka's face. I heard some dogs barking: that reminded me of my thesis and I sighed deeply. I saw the ex-officer between the tree-trunks. The poor fellow was limping painfully on both sides: he had his wounded hip on the right side and one of the variegated young ladies clinging to him on the left. His face expressed submission to Fate.

After the mushroom-picking we went back to the datcha for tea, then played croquet and listened to one of the variegated damsels singing a ballad: 'Sweet is my love, so sweet, so sweet!' Every time she sang 'sweet' her mouth curled right up to her ear.

'*Charmant!*' the other young ladies moaned in chorus. '*Charmant!*'

Darkness fell. The revolting moon was creeping up from behind the shrubbery. The air was still, with an unpleasant smell of fresh hay. I picked up my hat with the intention of going home.

'I have something to tell you,' Mashenka whispered to me significantly. 'Don't go.'

I had a nasty foreboding, but waited out of a sense of delicacy. Mashenka took my arm and led me off somewhere down an avenue of trees. Her whole being now expressed an inner conflict. She was pale, she breathed heavily and seemed intent on pulling my right arm off. What was the matter with the girl?

'I want to tell you,' she murmured. 'No, I can't . . . No, no.'

She wanted to say something, but kept hesitating. Then I saw from the expression on her face that she had made up her mind. With her eyes flashing and her nose all puffy she grabbed me by the hand and gasped: '*Nicolas,* I am yours! I cannot love you, but I promise to be faithful.'

She pressed herself up against my chest, then suddenly sprang back.

'Someone's coming,' she whispered. 'Farewell . . . I shall be in the summer-house tomorrow at eleven o'clock . . . Farewell – darling!'

And off she went. Completely at a loss, with my heart palpitating terribly, I made my way homeward. There 'The Past and Future of the Dog Tax' awaited me, but I couldn't do any work. I was furious. I would even go so far as to say I was fearsome in my wrath. Damn it, I will not permit people to treat me like a little boy! I'm quick-tempered, and woe betide anyone who plays games with me! When the maid came in to call me to supper I yelled at her: 'Get out!' Such quick-temperedness bodes ill.

Next morning we had typical summer holiday weather, i.e. temperature below freezing point, a cold, biting wind, rain, mud and the smell of mothballs caused by my *maman* dragging all her winter coats out of the chest. An absolutely foul morning. It was, to be precise, the 7th of August 1887, when there was to be an eclipse of the sun. I must point out that every one of us can do enormously important work during an eclipse even if we are not astronomers. For instance, each of us can: 1) measure the diameter of the sun and the moon, 2) sketch the sun's corona, 3) measure the temperature, 4) observe the behaviour of animals and plants at the moment of total eclipse, 5) note down his own personal impressions, etc. This was a matter of such importance that for the time being I decided to set aside 'The Past and Future of the Dog Tax' and observe the eclipse instead. We all got up very early. I had allocated the tasks to be performed as follows: I myself was to measure the diameter of the sun and moon, the wounded officer was to sketch the corona, and everything else was the responsibility of Mashenka and the variegated young ladies. So there we all were, waiting for it to begin.

'Why do eclipses happen?' Mashenka enquired.

I replied: 'An eclipse of the sun occurs when the moon, passing through the plane of the ecliptic, assumes a position upon the line joining the centres of the sun and the earth.'

'What does ecliptic mean?'

I explained. Mashenka listened attentively, then she asked: 'When you look through the smoked glass can you see the line joining the centres of the sun and the earth?'

I explained that this line is imaginary.

'But if it's imaginary,' said Varenka, completely bewildered, 'how can the moon assume a position on it?'

I did not answer. I could feel my spleen beginning to swell at the naïvety of such a question.

'All that's rubbish,' said Varenka's *maman*. 'No one can possibly foretell the future, and anyway you've never been in the sky, so how can you know what's going to happen to the moon and the sun? It's all make-believe.'

But soon a black spot began to move across the sun. The result was general consternation. Cows, sheep and horses bolted all over the fields with their tails in the air and bellowed in terror. Dogs howled. Bedbugs, thinking it was night again, crept out of their crannies and began biting anyone who was asleep. A local cleric, who was bringing home a load of cucumbers from his allotment, panicked, jumped off his cart and hid under a bridge, while his horse pulled the cart into someone else's yard where the cucumbers were devoured by pigs. An excise officer, who had been spending the night at a certain lady's datcha, ran out among the crowd in just his underwear, shouting wildly: 'Every man for himself!'

Many of the female occupants of the datchas, even some of the young and pretty ones, were woken by the noise and dashed out with no shoes on. And all sorts of other things occurred which I hesitate to recount.

'Ooh, I am scared!' squealed the variegated young ladies. 'Oh, isn't it awful!'

'*Mesdames*, please carry out your observations!' I shouted. 'Time is precious!'

I myself was making haste to measure the diameter . . . Remembering about the corona I looked for the ex-officer. He was standing doing nothing.

'What are you standing there for?' I shouted. 'What about the corona?'

He shrugged his shoulders and glanced down helplessly. Variegated damsels were clinging to both of the poor fellow's arms, pressing up against him in terror and preventing him from working. I took my pencil and noted the time precisely to the second: that was important. I noted down the geographical location of the observation point: that too was important. I was about to measure the diameter when Mashenka caught my arm and said: 'Don't forget: this morning at eleven!'

I freed my arm and knowing that every second counted, attempted to continue my observations, but Varenka seized my arm convulsively and pressed herself to my side. Everything – my pencil, my dark glasses and my drawings – fell on to the grass. For crying out loud! Whenever was this girl going to realize that I'm quick-tempered and once roused I go berserk and cannot answer for my actions?

I couldn't wait to continue – but the eclipse was already over!

'Look at me!' she whispered tenderly.

Oh, this was the absolute limit! It's perfectly obvious that anyone who tries a man's patience like that has got it coming to them. If I murder someone, don't blame me! Dammit, I will not allow myself to be made a fool of, and by God, when my hackles are up, I wouldn't advise anyone to come within a mile of me! I'm capable of anything!

One of the damsels, presumably seeing by my face that I was furious and obviously intending to mollify me, said: '*I* did as you told me, Nikolay Andreyevich. I observed the mammals. Just before the eclipse I saw a grey dog chasing a cat. Then it wagged its tail for a long time afterwards.'

So the eclipse came to nothing. I went home. But as it was raining I didn't go out on to the balcony to work. The wounded officer had risked coming out on to his and even got as far as writing 'I was born in . . .' when I saw one of the variegated damsels dragging him off to her datcha. I couldn't work because I was still livid and could feel my heart thumping. Nor did I go to the summer-house. Maybe that wasn't polite, but it's perfectly obvious I couldn't be expected to go in the rain, could I? At twelve o'clock I got a letter from Mashenka written as if we were the most intimate of friends, full of reproaches, and asking me to come to the summer-house . . . At one o'clock I received a second letter, at two yet another . . . I would have to go. But first I would have to consider what to say to her. I would act in an honourable manner. Firstly, I would tell her she was wrong in imagining that I loved her. Yet one cannot really say a thing like that to a woman. To say to a woman 'I do not love you' is as tactless as saying to a writer: 'You don't know how to write'. The best thing would be to explain to Varenka my views on marriage. So I put on my warm overcoat, took my umbrella and made my way to the summer-house. Knowing how quick-tempered I am, I was afraid of what I might come out with. I would try to restrain myself.

She was there in the summer-house waiting for me. Nadenka's face was pale and tear-stained. When she saw me she gave a shriek of joy and flung her arms round my neck, saying: 'Oh, at last! You're trying my patience so badly. I didn't sleep all night . . . I was thinking and thinking. And I feel if I got to know you better I would . . . would come to love you.'

I sat down and began to expound my views on marriage. To avoid going too deeply into the subject and in order to be as concise as possible, I put things briefly into their historical perspective. I spoke about marriage among the Hindus and Egyptians, then came on to more recent times with a few of Schopenhauer's ideas. Mashenka listened attentively, but suddenly she felt obliged to interrupt me with a curious *non sequitur*.

'*Nicolas*, give me a kiss!'

I was so embarrassed I didn't know what to say to her. She repeated her demand. So there was nothing else for it – I got up and put my lips to her elongated face, experiencing the same sensation I had as a child when I was made to kiss my dead grandmother's face at her funeral. Not satisfied with the kiss I had given her, Varenka leapt to her feet and impetuously flung her arms around me. At that moment Mashenka's *maman* appeared at the summer-house door ... She gave us a startled glance and saying to someone behind her: 'Shhhh!', vanished like Mephistopheles down a stage trapdoor.

I went back home feeling furious and embarrassed, only to find Varenka's *maman* there embracing my *maman* with tears in her eyes. My *maman* was saying tearfully: 'My dream has come true!'

And then – well, would you believe it? – Nadenka's *maman* came up to me, put her arms around me and said:

'May God bless you both! Take good care of her ... Never forget the sacrifice she is making ...'

So now I'm about to be married. As I write these lines the best man is looming over me telling me to hurry up. These people just don't know who they're dealing with! I am extremely quick-tempered and I can't answer for my actions! Dammit, you'd better watch out! Leading a quick-tempered, violent man to the altar – so far as I'm concerned it's as rash as sticking your hand into a frenzied tiger's cage. You'd better watch out, I tell you!

So here I am married. Everybody congratulates me and Varenka keeps pressing up to me and saying: 'Oh, to think that now you are mine, mine! Tell me you love me! Tell me, darling!'

And her nose goes all puffy.

I learned from the best man that the wounded officer had escaped Hymen's clutches by a cunning ruse. He produced for his variegated young lady a medical certificate to prove that as a result of the wound in his temple he was *non compos mentis* and therefore legally barred from getting married. Brilliant! I could have got a certificate too. One of my uncles drank like a fish, another was extremely absent-minded (he once put a lady's muff on his head instead of his fur hat) and my aunt was always playing the grand piano and sticking her tongue out at men in the street. Then there's my extreme quick-temperedness – that's another very dubious symptom. But why is it that good ideas always come too late? Why, why?

1887

A Man of Ideas

Midday. Not a sound, not a movement in the sultry air . . . The whole of nature resembles some huge estate, abandoned by God and men alike. Beneath the overhanging foliage of an old lime tree which stands near his quarters, prison superintendent Yashkin and his guest Pimfoff, the local headmaster, are sitting at a small three-legged table. They are both without jackets; their waistcoats are unbuttoned; their red, perspiring faces are immobile, rendered expressionless by the paralysing heat . . . Pimfoff's face has slumped into a state of complete apathy, his eyes are all bleary and his lower lip is hanging down loosely. Some signs of activity can still be detected, however, in Yashkin's eyes and forehead; he seems to be thinking about something . . . They gaze at each other in silence, expressing their torment by puffing and blowing and clapping in the air at flies. A carafe of vodka, some stringy boiled beef and an empty sardine tin encrusted with grey salt are standing on the table. Already they're on the fourth glass . . .

'Dammit,' Yashkin exclaims suddenly and so unexpectedly that a dog dozing by the table gives a start and runs off with its tail between its legs. 'Dammit! I don't care what you say, Filipp Maksimych, there are far too many punctuation marks in Russian!'

'How do you make that out, old man?' Pimfoff asks timidly, extracting the wing of a fly from his glass. 'There may be a large number, but each has its rightful place and purpose.'

'Oh, come off it now! Don't kid me your punctuation marks serve any purpose. It's just a lot of showing off . . . A chap puts a dozen commas in one line and thinks he's a genius. Take old Kastratoff, the deputy prosecutor – he puts a comma after every

145

word. What on earth for? Dear Sir, comma, while visiting the prison on such-and-such a date, comma, I observed, comma, that the prisoners, comma . . . ugh, it gives you spots before the eyes! And it's just the same in books . . . Colons, semi-colons, ordinary commas, inverted commas – it's enough to make you sick. And some smart alec isn't satisfied with one full stop, he has to go and stick in a whole row of them . . . Why, I ask you, why?'

'It's what the experts demand,' sighs Pimfoff.

'Experts? Charlatans, more likely. They only do it to show off, to pull the wool over people's eyes. Or take spelling, for example. If I spell "mediaeval" with "e" in the middle instead of "ae", does it really make a blind bit of difference?'

'Now you're going too far, Ilya Martynych,' says Pimfoff, offended. 'How can you possibly spell "mediaeval" with "e" in the middle? This is getting beyond a joke.'

Pimfoff drains his glass, blinks with a hurt expression and starts looking in the other direction.

'Yes, I've even been thrashed over that diphthong!' Yashkin continues. 'The teacher called me up to the blackboard one day and dictated: "Our beloved teacher is an outstanding paedagogue." I went and wrote "paedagogue" with just "e" at the beginning. Wrong, bend over! A week later he calls me out again and dictates: "Our beloved teacher is an outstanding paedagogue." This time I wrote "ae". Bend over again! "But sir," I said, "that's not fair. It was you told us 'ae' was correct!" "I was mistaken last week," he says, "yesterday I was reading an article by a member of the Academy which proves that 'paedagogue' is derived from the Greek *paidos* and should be spelt 'ai'. I am in agreement with the Academy of Sciences and it is therefore my bounden duty to give you a thrashing." Which he did. It's the same with my son Vasya. He's always coming home with a thick ear because of that diphthong. If I were Minister of Education, I'd soon stop you people having us on with your diphthongs.'

'I bid you good day,' sighs Pimfoff, blinking rapidly and putting on his jacket. 'When you start attacking education, that really is too much . . .'

'Oh, come, come, come . . . now you're offended,' says Yashkin, placing a restraining hand on Pimfoff's sleeve. 'You know I only say these things for something to talk about . . . Come on, sit down . . . Let's have another!'

The offended Pimfoff sits down, drains his glass and looks in the other direction. Silence descends. Martha, the cook, walks past the table carrying a bucketful of slops. A loud splash is heard, immediately followed by a dog's yelp. Pimfoff's lifeless face softens up even more; any moment now it will melt away completely in the heat and start running down his waistcoat. Furrows gather on Yashkin's brow. He gazes fixedly at the stringy beef and thinks . . . An old soldier comes up to the table, squints morosely at the carafe of vodka and seeing that it is empty, brings a fresh supply . . . They knock back another glass.

'Yes, dammit!' Yashkin says suddenly.

Pimfoff gives a start and looks up fearfully at Yashkin, anticipating new heresies.

'Yes, dammit!' Yashkin says again, gazing thoughtfully at the carafe. 'There are far too many sciences, that's what I reckon!'

'How do you make that out, old man?' Pimfoff asks quietly. 'Which sciences do you reckon are superfluous?'

'All of 'em . . . The more subjects a man knows, the more he starts thinking a lot of himself and becoming conceited . . . I'd scrap the whole lot of 'em, all the so-called learned sciences . . . Oh, come, come . . . now you're offended! You're so touchy, I daren't say a single word. Sit down, have another!'

Martha comes up to the table, and bustling about angrily with her plump elbows, places a pot of thick nettle soup in front of the two friends. Loud slurping and champing noises ensue. Three dogs and a cat appear from nowhere. They stand in front of the table and gaze imploringly at the chewing mouths. The soup is followed by a bowl of semolina pudding, which Martha bangs down on the table so viciously that all the spoons and crusts of bread jump off. Before turning to the pudding the friends knock back another glass in silence.

'Everything's superfluous in this world!' Yashkin remarks suddenly.

Pimfoff drops his spoon on to his lap, gazes fearfully at Yashkin and is about to protest, but his tongue has become weak from so much vodka and is all caught up in the semolina pudding . . . Instead of his usual 'How do you make that out, old man?', the only thing he can manage is a kind of bleat.

'Everything's superfluous,' Yashkin continues. 'The learned sciences, human beings . . . prisons, those flies . . . this pudding . . . And you're superfluous too . . . You may be a decent fellow and believe in God, but you're superfluous too . . .'

'Good day to you, old man!' Pimfoff mumbles, struggling to put on his jacket but completely failing to find the sleeves.

'Here we've been, stuffing and gorging ourselves, and what on earth for? No, it's all superfluous ... We eat and don't know ourselves why we're eating ... Oh, come, come ... now you're offended! You know I only say these things for something to talk about. And where can you go now? Come on, sit down and have a chat ... Let's have another!'

Silence descends, broken only occasionally by the clinking together of glasses and by drunken burps. The sun is already beginning to sink in the west and the shadow of the lime tree grows longer and longer. Martha comes out and spreads a rug by the table, snorting fiercely and jabbing her arms about. The friends knock back a final glass in silence, settle themselves on the rug and turning their backs to each other, begin to drop off ...

'Thank the Lord he didn't get round to the creation of the world or the hierarchy today,' thinks Pimfoff. 'That's enough to make anyone's hair stand on end ...'

1885

The Siren

After a session of the district court of N., the magistrates gathered in the conferring room to take off their uniforms and have a short rest before going home to dine. Their chairman, a very impressive man with bushy side-whiskers, who had failed to agree with his colleagues on one of the cases they had just been hearing, sat at a desk hastily writing down his dissenting opinion. One of the local magistrates, Mookin, a young man with a languid melancholy expression, reputed to be a philosopher at odds with circumstances and seeking the purpose of life, stood gazing mournfully out of a window. The other local magistrate and one of the honorary magistrates had already left. Sitting on a couch waiting for the chairman to finish before they all went off to dine together were the other honorary magistrate – a fat man of bloated appearance who had difficulty in breathing – and the deputy prosecutor, a young German with a catarrhal look. In front of them stood the court secretary, Zhilin, a little scrap of a fellow with short side-

148

burns and a sugary expression. He was looking at the fat man with a honeyed smile and saying in a low voice:

'We all feel hungry now, because we're tired and it's after three, but my dear Grigory Savvich, that's not real appetite. Real appetite, when you're so ravenous you could almost eat your own father, occurs only after physical exertion – after riding to hounds, for example, or bumping along in a peasant cart for a hundred versts without a breather. The imagination plays a big part, too, of course. If you're going home from the hunt, say, and want to have a good appetite, don't ever think about anything intellectual; anything learned or intellectual always spoils the appetite. You know yourself, where food's concerned, scholars and philosophers are the lowest of the low, and quite frankly, even the pigs eat better. On your way home try to think of your decanter and appetizer, nothing else. Once when I was travelling, I closed my eyes and imagined sucking-pig with horse-radish, and got such an appetite it made me quite hysterical. So, when you drive into your yard, there must be a good smell coming from the kitchen, you know, something like . . .'

'Roast goose takes a lot of beating,' said the honorary magistrate, breathing heavily.

'Goose, my dear Grigory Savvich? Dear me no, duck or snipe are streets ahead of goose. Goose has such a crude, unsubtle aroma. The most piquant of all is spring onion, just as it's beginning to turn brown and sizzle, you know, and the smell of the little rascal fills the whole house. So, when you step indoors, the table must already be set, and when you sit down, tuck your napkin into your collar straight away and reach slowly for the vodka decanter. Now don't pour the darling into an ordinary wine glass, but into a little silver beaker that's been in the family for generations, or one of those pot-bellied glasses with "Even The Monks Enjoy Their Tipple" inscribed on it, and don't down it immediately, but heave a contented sigh, rub your hands, glance casually at the ceiling, and only then, still taking your time, raise the vodka to your lips and at once you'll feel a fiery glow spread from your stomach right through your body . . .'

The secretary registered an expression of bliss on his sugary face.

'A fiery glow . . .' he repeated, half-closing his eyes. 'Then once you've had your drink, go straight on to the appetizers.'

'Can't you keep your voice down?' said the chairman, looking up at the secretary. 'You've made me spoil two sheets already.'

'I do apologize, Pyotr Nikolaich, I'll be very quiet,' said the secretary. 'So, my dear Grigory Savvich,' he went on in a half-whisper, 'you must choose your appetizers with real skill, too. I tell you the best appetizer of all and that's herring. Take a small piece with onion and mustard sauce, and while you've still got that glowing feeling in your stomach, help yourself straight away, my dear sir, to caviare, on its own or with lemon as you wish, then some plain radish with salt and then more herring. Even better, though, dear sir, are salted saffron milk-caps, chopped up as fine as caviare and served with onion and olive oil . . . delicious! As for liver of burbot – words fail me!'

'Mm-yes,' the honorary magistrate agreed, half-closing his eyes. 'And what about stewed white mushrooms . . . that's a good appetizer, too.'

'Yes, yes, yes, you're right, with onion and a bay leaf and all kinds of spices. When you lift off the lid and get that whiff of mushroom, it can even make you cry with pleasure sometimes. So, as soon as they've brought in the pie from the kitchen, don't waste a moment, drink a second glass.'

'Ivan Gurich!' moaned the chairman. 'You've made me spoil a third sheet!'

'The wretched man can only think of food!' grumbled Mookin the philosopher, scowling with contempt. 'Has life really nothing more to offer than pies and mushrooms?'

'So, before your pie have another drink,' the secretary continued in an undertone, so carried away that like a nightingale in full song he could hear nothing but his own voice. 'Your pie must be mouth-watering, it must tempt you by its sheer brazen nakedness. You wink at it, you cut off a huge slice about this size and you let your fingers play over it like this, because your heart's so full. You start eating and the butter oozes out like teardrops and the filling's rich and succulent, with eggs, giblets, onions . . .'

The secretary rolled his eyes heavenward and twisted his mouth right round to his ear. The honorary magistrate grunted and began twiddling his fingers, probably picturing the pie to himself.

'Intolerable,' grumbled Mookin, moving away to another window.

'You've eaten two slices and saved a third one for the shchi,' the secretary went on, fired with inspiration. 'Once you're through with the pie, don't let your appetite flag, but have the shchi brought in straight away and make sure it's piping hot. Even better, though, my dear sir, is borsch made of beetroot in the

Ukrainian style with ham and sausages in it. Serve it with sour cream and sprinkle fresh parsley and dill. Giblet soup with tender young kidneys is another excellent one, while the best broth is the one full of roots and vegetables like carrot, asparagus, cauliflower and all the rest of that jurisprudence.'

'Yes, that's excellent,' sighed the chairman, taking his eyes off his paper, but immediately recollected himself and groaned: 'For God's sake, have a care! At this rate I shall be here until evening writing this dissenting opinion. That's four sheets spoiled!'

'I do apologize, I shan't disturb you,' said the secretary and went on in a whisper. 'As soon as you've finished your borsch or your broth, have the fish course brought in straight away, my dear sir. The best of the dumb fishes is crucian fried in sour cream, but to get rid of that slimy smell and give it a delicate favour, you must keep it alive in milk for at least twenty-four hours.'

'And what about sterlet in a ring, that's good, too,' said the honorary magistrate, closing his eyes, but suddenly to everyone's astonishment he leapt to his feet, pulled a hideous face and roared at the chairman:

'Pyotr Nikolaich, how much longer are you going to be? I can't go on waiting, I can't!'

'Let me finish!'

'Oh to hell with you, I'm off!'

The fat man gave a dismissive wave, grabbed his hat and ran out of the room without saying goodbye. The secretary heaved a sigh, bent down to the deputy prosecutor's ear and went on in an undertone:

'Pike-perch is very good, too, or carp with tomato and mushroom sauce. But fish isn't going to satisfy your hunger, Stepan Frantsych, it's an insubstantial food, the main thing in a dinner isn't the fish or the sauces, it's the roast. What's your favourite bird?'

The deputy prosecutor pulled a sour face and said with a sigh:

'Unfortunately, I cannot enter into your feelings, I suffer from catarrh of the stomach.'

'Oh come now, sir! The doctors dreamed up that complaint. It comes mostly from too much pride and free-thinking. Ignore it. Suppose you're not hungry or you're feeling sick, just pay no attention, go ahead and eat. If you're offered a brace of snipe, with a partridge on top of that or a pair of plump little quails, you'll soon forget about catarrh of the stomach, I give you my word of honour. And how about roast turkey? One of those white, rich, succulent birds that remind you of a nymph . . .'

'Yes, that must be very good,' said the deputy prosecutor with a sad smile. 'Maybe I could manage some turkey.'

'And duck? Have you forgotten duck? Take a young bird that's just caught the ice during the first frosts, roast it in the griddle-pan with potatoes underneath, making sure your potatoes are chopped fine and brown nicely, then be sure to baste them with the duck fat, and then . . .'

Mookin the philosopher pulled a hideous face and was apparently about to say something, but suddenly he smacked his lips, probably picturing the roast duck to himself, and without saying a word, drawn by some unknown force, grabbed his hat and ran out.

'Yes, maybe I could manage some duck as well,' sighed the deputy prosecutor.

The chairman stood up, walked round the room and sat down again.

'After the roast a man is replete and falls into a state of sweet oblivion,' continued the secretary. 'He's physically satisfied and his soul feels transported. Now is the time to enjoy two or three glasses of fruit liqueur.'

The chairman grunted and put a line through his page.

'That's the sixth sheet,' he said angrily. 'This really is too bad!'

'You carry on, dear sir, you carry on,' whispered the secretary. 'I shan't disturb you, I'll be very quiet. I tell you in all honesty, Stepan Frantsych,' he continued in a barely audible whisper, 'home-made fruit liqueur is better than champagne. After the very first glass you're completely captivated by your sense of smell, by a kind of mirage, you forget you're at home in your armchair, and imagine you're sitting on a lovely soft ostrich somewhere in Australia . . .'

'Oh do let's be off, Pyotr Nikolaich!' said the prosecutor, jerking his leg impatiently.

'Yes, my friend,' the secretary continued, 'it's a good idea at the liqueur stage to light a cigar and blow rings, and then you'll have wonderful fantasies of being a generalissimo or married to the most beautiful woman in the world, and this beautiful creature spends her whole day floating beneath your windows in this amazing pool full of goldfish, and as she floats past, you call out: "Come and give me a kiss, darling!" '

'Pyotr Nikolaich!' groaned the deputy prosecutor.

'Yes, my friend,' the secretary continued, 'once you've had your smoke, gather up the skirts of your dressing-gown and it's off to bed with you! Lie there on your back, paunch upwards, and reach for a newspaper. When you're nodding off and feeling drowsy all over, you'll enjoy reading the political news – look, Austria's come a cropper, France is in someone's bad books, the Pope's stuck his neck out – it's really enjoyable.'

The chairman sprang to his feet, flung his pen aside and seized his hat with both hands. Forgetting about his catarrh and nearly fainting with impatience, the deputy prosecutor sprang to his feet, also.

'Let's go!' he shouted.

'But Pyotr Nikolaich, what about your dissenting opinion?' said the secretary in alarm. 'When are you going to finish it, dear sir? You know you've got to leave for town at six!'

The chairman gave a dismissive wave and made a dash for the door. The deputy prosecutor waved likewise, grabbed his brief-case, and vanished with the chairman. The secretary heaved a sigh, glanced reproachfully in their direction, and began tidying up the papers.

1887

The Burbot

A summer's morning. The only sounds in the still air are the chirping of a grasshopper on the river bank, and the timid purring somewhere of a turtle-dove. Feathery clouds hang motionless in the sky like scattered flakes of snow . . . Close to the bathing-hut that's being put up, Gerasim the carpenter, a tall scraggy peasant with a head of ginger curls and a face overgrown with hair, is wallowing about in the water under the green branches of some willows. Puffing and blowing, he is blinking furiously and trying to extract something from beneath the willow roots. His face is bathed in sweat. The carpenter Lyubim, a young hunchback peasant with a triangular face and narrow little oriental eyes, is standing two or three yards away, up to his neck in water. Both Gerasim and Lyubim are in shirts and trousers, and both are blue with cold. They have been in the water for over an hour . . .

'Why d'you keep poking about with your hand?' shouts Lyubim the hunchback, shaking like someone in a fever. 'Numskull! Get a grip on him, get a grip on him, or he'll escape, the blighter! You listening?'

'He won't escape. Where'd he go to? He's wedged hisself under the roots,' says Gerasim in a hoarse hollow bass that comes from the pit of his stomach, not his throat. 'He's a slippery devil, there's nothing to get hold of.'

'Grab him by the gulls, the gulls!'

'I can't see his gills . . . Hang on, I've got hold of something . . . It's his lip . . . Dammit, he's bitten me!'

'Don't pull him by the lip – you'll lose him! Grab him by the gulls, the gulls! Now you're poking your hand in again! Mother of God, what a daft peasant you are! Grab him!'

'Grab him,' Gerasim says mockingly. 'Look who's handing out the orders. Come and grab him yourself, you hunchback devil! What you waiting for?'

'Would if I could, but how'm I going to stand under the bank with my absence of stature? That's deep there!'

'Never mind that, you'll have to swim.'

The hunchback flaps his arms, swims up to Gerasim and grabs hold of some branches. At his first attempt to stand upright, his head disappears under the water and he emits a stream of bubbles.

'Told you that were deep,' he says, rolling the whites of his eyes angrily. 'Not going to sit on your shoulders, am I?'

'Try standing on a root under the water. There's lots of 'em, they're like stairs.'

The hunchback feels for a submerged root with his heel and by seizing hold firmly of several small branches at once, manages to stand on it. Balancing and steadying himself in his new position, he bends over and trying not to swallow any water, begins feeling round with his right hand among the roots. But his hand gets caught in the weed, slips on the moss-covered roots, and runs up against the jagged claws of a crayfish.

'We can do without *you*,' says Lyubim, hurling the crayfish on to the bank.

Eventually, his hand comes into contact with Gerasim's arm, moves down it, and reaches something cold and slippery.

'That's him!' Lyubim says, smiling. 'What a beaut . . . Open your fingers out, lemme get hold of his gulls . . . Can't you stop elbowing me? Now lemme just . . . just get a grip . . . he's gone further under the root, blast him, there's nothing to get hold of. His head's out of reach, all you can feel is his belly ... Kill that mosquito, it's biting my neck! If I can just get my hands under his gulls ... Give him a shove from the side, worry him with your finger!'

Puffing out his cheeks, holding his breath and opening his eyes wide, the hunchback seems on the point of getting his fingers 'under his gulls' when the twigs he's gripping with his left hand break off, he loses his balance and goes plop into the water. Startled ripples run away from the river bank and bubbles appear at the place where he fell in. The hunchback comes snorting to the surface and grabs some more branches.

'If you drown, you devil, they'll blame me!' Gerasim wheezes. 'Climb out, blast you! Let me get him!'

They start swearing at each other. Meanwhile the sun burns ever more fiercely. The shadows grow shorter and withdraw into themselves like the horns of a snail. Warmed by the sun, the tall grass begins to give off a thick cloying smell of honey. Soon it will be midday, and Gerasim and Lyubim are still wallowing about beneath the willow. The hoarse bass and the shrill frozen tenor go on rending the silence of the summer day.

'Drag him by the gulls, drag him! Hold on, I'll give him a nudge. Don't shove your great fist in, use your finger – pigface! Get at him from the side! No, from the left, the left, there's a pothole on the right. You'll make a meal for the sprites that way. Pull him by the lip.'

Someone can be heard cracking a stock-whip. Wandering lazily down the slope to their watering place come the animals, driven by Yefim the herdsman. A decrepit old man with one eye and a lopsided mouth, Yefim is walking along with head bowed, gazing in front of him. First to go down to the water are the sheep, then the horses and finally the cows.

'Give him a shove from underneath!' he hears Lyubim's voice. 'Push your finger through! What's the matter, damn you, you deaf? Useless!'

'Hey, what are you after, lads?' shouts Yefim.

'A burbot! We just can't drag him out! Wedged hisself under a root, he has! Go in from the side! The side, the side!'

Yefim focuses his eye for a minute on the fishermen, then removes his bast shoes, takes his knapsack off his shoulders and removes his shirt. Too impatient to take off his trousers, he crosses himself and goes straight into the water, using his thin swarthy arms to maintain balance. For about fifty paces he walks along the silty bottom and then he starts swimming.

'Hold on, boys!' he shouts. 'Hold on! Don't drag him out any old how, you'll lose him. You must do it the right way!'

Yefim joins the carpenters and all three jostle about on one spot, digging their knees and elbows into each other, panting and swearing. Lyubim the hunchback swallows some water the wrong way, and the air resounds with his sharp convulsive coughing.

'Where's the herdsman?' comes a shout from the river bank. 'Yefi-im! Where are you, herdsman? The animals are in the garden! Get them out of there, get them out! Where on earth is he, the old rascal?'

Men's voices are heard, then a woman's. The master, Andrey Andreich, comes out through the garden gate, wearing a dressing-gown cut from a Persian shawl and holding a newspaper. He looks enquiringly in the direction the shouts are coming from and hurries off with short quick steps towards the bathing-hut.

'What's going on here? Who's that yelling?' he asks sternly, catching sight of the fishermen's three wet heads through the branches of the willow. 'What are you playing at down there?'

'Ca-catching a fish,' Yefim says in a lisping voice, without looking up.

'I'll give you catching a fish! The animals have strayed into the garden and he's catching a fish! And when's the bathing-hut going to be ready, you devils? Two days you've been working and what have you to show?'

'It'll be re-ready,' wheezes Gerasim. 'Summer's long, yeronner, you'll still have time for your wash ... Brrrr ... It's this burbot, we can't get to grips with him. He's taken cover under this root like it was a burrow, we can't move him this way nor that ...'

'A burbot?' asks the master, his eyes lighting up. 'What are you waiting for? Pull him out!'

'If you could give us half a rouble ... we'd oblige ... Strong as a merchant's wife he is ... Our labour's worth half a rouble, yeronner ... Don't squeeze him, Lyubim, don't squeeze him or you'll wear him out! Support him from below! You, old fellow – what's your name? – pull the root up. Up, blast you, not down! Stop wobbling your legs!'

Five minutes pass, then ten. The master can't stand it any longer.

'Vasily!' he shouts, turning towards the house. 'Vaska! Send Vasily to me!'

Vasily the coachman comes running up. He's chewing something and breathing heavily.

'Get into the water,' the master orders, 'and help them with this burbot. They can't even pull out a burbot.'

Vasily quickly takes off his clothes and gets into the water.

'Leave it to me,' he mumbles. 'Where's the burbot? Leave it to me. Won't be a tick. You clear off, Yefim, there's no point an old boy like you barging in. Where's this burbot then? Leave him to me. There he is! You let go now!'

'What do you mean, let go? We don't need telling that. You try pulling him out!'

'You're going about it the wrong way. You must grab his head.'

'But can't you see, his head's under the root, you idiot!'

'Watch your tongue or you'll get more than you bargained for. Swine!'

'Fancy using words like that in the master's presence,' lisps Yefim. 'You'll not get him out, lads, he's got himself into a really clever corner there.'

'Just one moment,' says the master and starts hastily taking off his clothes. 'There are four of you fools and you can't pull out a burbot.'

After undressing, Andrey Andreich gives himself time to cool down and then climbs into the water. But his intervention has no effect, either.

'We must cut through the root a bit!' Lyubim finally decides. 'Gerasim, fetch the axe! Give it here!'

'Mind you don't chop your fingers off!' says the master, as the axe is heard striking the root under the water. 'Yefim, clear off! Hold on, let me pull out the burbot. I'll do it better . . .'

Once the root has been notched, they break it back slightly, and to his enormous pleasure Andrey Andreyich feels his fingers close round the burbot's gills.

'He's coming, lads! Don't crowd me . . . keep still . . . he's coming!'

On the surface a large burbot head appears, followed by a black body thirty inches long. The burbot is writhing its heavy tail and trying to escape.

'He's playing up . . . You're wasting your time, my friend. Don't you know you're caught? Oh yes you are!'

A honeyed smile spreads across the faces of all present. A minute passes in silent observation.

'That's some burbot!' lisps Yefim, scratching his chest. 'Reckon he must be about ten pounds.'

'Mm-yes,' agrees the master. 'Look at that swollen liver, it's fit to burst. A-ah-akh!'

All of a sudden the burbot gives an exceptionally sharp twist of its tail and the fishermen hear a loud splash. They all throw their arms forward, but too late: the burbot's got clean away.

1885

The Civil Service Exam

'That geography teacher Dawkin's really got it in for me. I know his questions are going to trip me up.'

Mr Yefim Fendrikov, counter-clerk at the post office in the town of X., a grey-haired, bearded man with a very worthy bald patch and a comfortable paunch, was sweating and rubbing his hands nervously.

'I'm going to fail this exam, so help me I am. And why's he got this grudge against me? All because of a silly little trifle. He comes in one day with this registered letter and shoves his way past everyone so's I'll deal with him first. Now that's just not good enough ... He may be one of the educated class but he's got to abide by the rules and take his turn like the rest of them. So I tells him off quite politely. "Wait your turn, sir," I says, "if you don't mind." Then he flared up and his wrath's been kindled against me like Saul ever since. He gives my kid Yegor bad marks for geography and spreads all kinds of names for me round the town. Do you know, I was walking past Kukhtin's tavern one day when he sticks his head out of the window with a billiard cue in his hand, and bawls across the square in a voice full of liquor: "Take a good look, everyone! Here comes the used postage stamp!" '

Boozin, the Russian language teacher, who was standing in the entrance hall of X. district school next to Fendrikov and had graciously accepted the latter's cigarette, shrugged his shoulders and said reassuringly:

'No need to worry. We've never had one of you chaps fail an

exam yet. It's a pure formality.'

This made Fendrikov feel easier, but not for long. Dawkin, the geography teacher, came into the entrance hall. A young man with a thin little beard that looked as if it had been plucked, he was wearing linen trousers and a new dark blue tail-coat. He glanced sternly at Fendrikov and walked on.

Then word went round that the Inspector was arriving. Fendrikov felt cold all over and began waiting with that sense of dread so familiar to the prisoner in the dock or the candidate taking his first examination. Dimvitsky, the superintendent, dashed through the entrance hall on his way to meet the Inspector. He was hastily followed by the scripture teacher, Venomovsky, wearing his priest's skull-cap and a pectoral cross, with the various other teachers in close pursuit. The loud voice of Agagin, the Inspector of State Schools, could be heard exchanging greetings with everyone and complaining bitterly about the dusty state of the roads. Then he went into the school. Five minutes later the exams began.

The first two candidates were priests' sons hoping to become village teachers. One of them passed but the other failed. The unsuccessful candidate took out a red handkerchief, blew his nose, stood there for a while lost in thought and went away. Next, two short-service army volunteers were examined. Then it was Fendrikov's turn . . .

'Where are you employed?' asked the Inspector.

'I'm counter-clerk at the local post office, your excellency,' he replied, standing very upright and trying to conceal the trembling in his hands. 'I've served for twenty-one years, your excellency, and now credentials are required for promotion to the clerical grade of the civil service, 14th class, for which purpose I venture to present myself to be examined for the rank of collegiate registrar.'

'I see . . . The dictation, please.'

Boozin stood up, cleared his throat and began reading the dictation passage in a deep penetrating bass, trying to catch the candidate out on words where the spelling did not correspond to the sound: 'They ceased to believe . . . that the thief . . . had been seized', etc. But in spite of all Boozin's most cunning efforts, the dictation went well. Even if he did concentrate more on forming the letters beautifully than on grammar, the aspiring collegiate registrar made few mistakes. He had written 'extremely' with double 'e' in the middle, 'worst' came out as 'worsed', and the

Inspector could not help smiling when he saw that for 'recent investigations' Fendrikov had written 'recent infestigations', but none of these were gross errors.

'The dictation is satisfactory,' announced the Inspector.

'May I venture to bring to the attention of your excellency,' Fendrikov said more confidently, casting sidelong glances at his enemy Dawkin, 'the fact that I learned geometry from Davydov's textbook, with additional instruction from my nephew Varsonofy when he came back on holiday from the Trinity-Sergius or Bethanian Seminary. I learned both plane and solid geometry . . . everything as required . . .'

'I'm afraid solid geometry isn't in the syllabus.'

'Not in the syllabus? And I spent a whole month on it . . . What a shame!' sighed Fendrikov.

'But let us leave geometry for the moment and turn instead to that science which you, as a Post Office employee, must no doubt love – geography, the postman's science.'

All the teachers simpered respectfully. Fendrikov did not agree that geography was the postman's science (it didn't say anything about that in the Post Office Guide or in regional regulations), but out of respect he said 'Yessir', and clearing his throat nervously, awaited the questions in terror. His enemy Dawkin leaned back in his chair and without looking at him, drawled:

'Ah . . . tell me now, what kind of government do they have in Turkey?'

'Well, er . . . surely they've got a Turkish government . . .'

'Hm, yes . . . ah, Turkish . . . a somewhat elastic term. In Turkey they have a *constitutional* government. Which tributaries of the Ganges can you name?'

'I learned geography from Smirnov's book but begging your pardon, with insufficient clarity . . . The Ganges, that's the river in India . . . the one what flows into the ocean.'

'I didn't ask you that. I asked you the names of its tributaries. You don't know? Well, what about the Aras, where does *it* flow? You don't know that, either? Very strange . . . In which province is the town of Zhitomir?'

'Route 18, area 121.'

Fendrikov broke into a cold sweat. His eyes blinked and he gulped so hard it looked as if he'd swallowed his tongue.

'Almighty God be my witness, your excellency,' he began mumbling. 'Even his reverence the archpriest will bear me out . . . I've served for twenty-one years and now there's this . . . which

... I shall pray for your excellency till my dying day ...'

'Very well then, let us leave geography. What have you prepared in arithmetic?'

'I did arithmetic with insufficient clarity, too ... Even his reverence the archpriest will bear me out ... I shall pray for your excellency till my dying day ... Been at it ever since Feast of the Intercession I have, and it's no good ... I'm too old for learned stuff ... Be gracious, your excellency, cause me to remember you in my prayers for ever.'

Tears hung on Fendrikov's eyelashes.

'I've served honest and above reproach ... Every year I observe all the fasts ... Even his reverence the archpriest will bear me out ... Be lenient, your excellency.'

'So you haven't prepared anything?'

'Oh yes sir, I've prepared everything, but I can't remember nothing, sir ... I'm nearly sixty, your excellency, how can I be expected to go in for learning? Please be generous.'

'He's even ordered a new cap with his badge of rank,' said Archpriest Venomovsky with a laugh.

'Very well then, you may go,' said the Inspector.

Half an hour later Fendrikov was walking along with the teachers to Kukhtin's tavern to drink tea and feeling on top of the world. His face was bright, his eyes shone with happiness, but it was clear from the way he kept scratching the back of his head that some thought was troubling him.

'What a waste!' he muttered. 'I ask you, though, wasn't that a damned silly thing to do?'

'Now what are you on about?' asked Boozin.

'Why ever did I go and learn solid geometry if it's not in the syllabus? I spent a whole month on blooming solid geometry. What a waste!'

1884

Boys

'Volodya's here!' someone outside shouted.

'Master Volodya's here!' shrieked Natalya, running into the dining-room. 'Oh my goodness!'

All the members of the Korolyov family, who had been expecting their Volodya to arrive at any moment, rushed to the windows. A wide peasant sledge was standing by the entrance, and steam was rising in a dense cloud from the troika of white horses. The sledge was empty, because Volodya was already standing in the porch untying his hood, his fingers red and numb with cold. His school greatcoat and peaked cap, his overshoes and the hair on his temples, were covered in rime, and the whole of him from head to foot was giving off such a delicious frosty smell that looking at him, you felt you wanted to hug yourself with cold and go 'brrr!' His mother and aunt rushed to embrace and kiss him, Natalya flung herself down at his feet and began pulling off his felt boots, his sisters started squealing, doors creaked and slammed, and Volodya's father ran into the entrance hall in his shirtsleeves, a pair of scissors in his hands, and shouted anxiously:

'We were expecting you yesterday! You got here all right? Safe journey? Oh come on, let him say hello to his father! I am his father, for heaven's sake!'

'Garf! Garf!' bayed the huge black dog Milord, thumping his tail against the walls and furniture.

Everything merged into one continuous joyful sound, which lasted a couple of minutes. When the first rush of joy was over, the Korolyovs noticed that in addition to Volodya the entrance hall contained another young person, muffled up in scarves, shawls and hoods, and covered in rime. He was standing motionless in the corner, in the shadow cast by a large fox-fur coat.

'Volodya dear,' Mother whispered, 'who's your companion?'

'Oh sorry!' Volodya recollected himself. 'Allow me to introduce my friend Lentilov from second year. I've brought him to stay with us.'

'Delighted, you're most welcome!' Father said joyfully. 'I'm sorry I'm not properly dressed. Come on in! Natalya, help Mr Dentilov with his outdoor clothes! For heaven's sake, can't anyone get rid of that damned dog?'

Not long afterwards, Volodya and his friend Lentilov, reeling from their noisy reception and still pink with cold, were sitting at the table drinking tea. A wintry sun penetrated the snow and tracery on the window-panes, played over the samovar and bathed its pure rays in the rinsing bowl. The room was warm, and the boys felt a tickling sensation in their numbed bodies as the warmth and chill competed for supremacy.

'So, Christmas is almost upon us!' Father was intoning, rolling a cigarette from some dark reddish-brown tobacco. 'It seems no time since last summer, when your mother was in tears seeing you off, and lo and behold, you're back again. How time does fly! Before you can say knife, old age is upon you. Mr Reptilov, do help yourself to anything you want. We don't stand on ceremony.'

Volodya's three sisters, Katya, Sonya and Masha – Katya, the eldest, was eleven – sat at the table with their eyes fixed on the new acquaintance. Lentilov was the same age and height as Volodya, but where Volodya was plump and fair-skinned, he was thin, swarthy and covered in freckles. He had bristly hair, narrow eyes and thick lips, he was really very ugly, and but for his school jacket, you might have taken him from outward appearances for a cook's son. He was sullen, said nothing and did not once smile. Looking at him, the girls reckoned straight away that he must be very clever and learned. He was so preoccupied with his own thoughts that whenever he was asked something, he started, shook his head and asked for the question to be repeated.

The girls noticed that Volodya, who was always jolly and talkative, on this occasion likewise said little, never smiled and did not even seem pleased to be home. While they were having tea, he addressed his sisters only once, and even then his words were strange. Pointing at the samovar, he said:

'In California they don't drink tea, they drink gin.'

He too was preoccupied, and judging by the glances that he exchanged from time to time with his friend Lentilov, they shared the same thoughts.

After tea everyone went into the nursery. Father and the girls sat down at the table and took up the work that had been interrupted by the boys' arrival. They were making flowers and a fringe for the Christmas tree out of coloured paper. It was noisy, exciting work. The girls greeted each newly completed flower with cries of delight, even of horror, as if the flower had fallen from the sky. Papa was also in raptures and every so often would throw the scissors down on the floor, complaining angrily that they were not sharp enough. Mamma would run into the nursery looking very worried and ask:

'Who's pinched my scissors? Ivan Nikolaich, have you pinched my scissors again?'

'For heaven's sake, am I to be deprived of scissors?' Ivan Nikolaich replied in a tearful voice, leaning back on his chair and striking an offended pose, but a minute later he was in raptures again.

On previous arrivals Volodya had also helped to dress the Christmas tree or had run outside to see how the coachman and shepherd were getting on with the snow hill, but now he and Lentilov completely ignored the coloured paper and did not visit the stables even once; instead, they sat by the window and began whispering, then they opened up an atlas together and began studying a map.

'First get to Perm,' Lentilov said quietly. 'Next Tiumen ... Tomsk ... then on to ... Kamchatka. From there the Samoyeds take you by boat across the Bering Straits, and that's it, you're in America. There are lots of fur-bearing animals in that area.'

'What about California?' Volodya asked.

'California's lower down. Once you're in America, California's no distance. Then we can earn a living by hunting and robbing.'

All day long Lentilov avoided the girls and glared at them, but after evening tea he happened to be left alone in their company for five minutes. He coughed sternly, rubbed his left hand with his right palm, looked gloomily at Katya and asked:

'Have you read Mayne Reid?'

'No, I haven't ... Tell me, can you skate?'

Absorbed in his own thoughts, Lentilov did not answer this question, but merely puffed out his cheeks and sighed as if he felt very hot. Looking up again at Katya, he said:

'When a herd of bison runs across the pampas, the whole earth shakes and the mustangs take fright and buck and neigh.'

Lentilov gave a sad smile and added:

'Then there are the Red Indians, they attack trains. But worst of all are the mosquitoes and termites.'

'Termites? What are they?'

'They're like little ants, only with wings. They've got a vicious bite. Do you know who I am?'

'You're Mr Lentilov.'

'No, I'm not, I'm Montihomo Hawk's Claw, Leader of the Unconquerables.'

Masha, the youngest girl, glanced at him, then at the window, where evening was already drawing in, and said dreamily:

'We had lentils for lunch yesterday.'

Lentilov's incomprehensible words, his constant whispering with Volodya, and Volodya being too preoccupied to play with them – all this was strange and mysterious, and the two older girls, Katya and Sonya, began to keep a close watch on the boys. That evening, when the boys went to bed, the girls crept up to their door and overheard their conversation. And what secrets they found out! The boys were planning to run away to somewhere in America to look for gold, and had already prepared everything for their journey: a pistol, two knives, some rusks, a magnifying glass to make fire with, a compass and four roubles in cash. They found out how the boys would have to cover several thousand versts on foot, fighting against tigers and savages along the way, then look for gold and ivory, kill their enemies, join some pirates, drink gin and finally marry beauties and cultivate plantations. Volodya and Lentilov were so carried away that they kept interrupting each other. Lentilov referred to himself as 'Montihomo Hawk's Claw' and to Volodya as 'my palefaced brother'.

'Whatever you do, don't tell Mamma,' Katya said to Sonya as they went back to bed. 'Volodya will bring us gold and ivory from America, but if you tell Mamma, they won't let him go.'

On the day before Christmas Eve Lentilov spent the whole time studying the map of Asia and making notes, while Volodya, looking languid and puffy, like someone stung by a bee, walked moodily about the house and ate nothing. Once he even stopped in front of the icon in the nursery, crossed himself and said:

'Oh Lord, forgive me my sins! Oh Lord, look after my poor unhappy Mamma!'

Towards evening he burst into tears. Before going to bed, he spent a long time embracing his father, mother and sisters. Katya and Sonya knew what it was all about, but Masha, the youngest, who hadn't the faintest idea what was going on, simply looked thoughtfully at Lentilov and said with a sigh:

'Nanny says, in Lent we should eat peas and lentils.'

Early on the morning of Christmas Eve Katya and Sonya climbed quietly out of bed and went to spy on the boys as they ran away to America. They crept up to the door.

'So you're not going?' Lentilov was asking angrily. 'Say it: you're not going?'

'Oh Lord!' Volodya was crying quietly. 'How can I go? I feel so sorry for Mamma.'

'My palefaced brother, please let's go! It was you said you were going and talked me into it, and now the time's come, you're in a funk.'

'I'm not in a funk, it's just . . . I'm sorry for Mamma.'

'Are you going or aren't you?'

'I am going, only . . . only not just now. I want to spend some time at home first.'

'In that case I'll go by myself!' Lentilov decided. 'I'll manage without you. And it was you said you wanted to hunt tigers and fight! In that case, give me back my pistol caps.'

Volodya began crying so bitterly that the sisters couldn't help crying quietly themselves. There was a silence.

'So you're not going?' Lentilov asked again.

'Oh . . . all right.'

'Get dressed then!'

To win Volodya over, Lentilov began praising America, roared like a tiger, described a steamboat, began swearing, and promised to let Volodya have all the ivory, and all the lion and tiger skins.

In the girls' eyes this thin little boy with the swarthy face, bristly hair and freckles was someone unusual, remarkable. He was a hero, a decisive, fearless individual, and he roared so convincingly that from outside the door it really did seem that there was a tiger or lion inside.

When the girls returned to their room and got dressed, Katya's eyes filled with tears and she said:

'Ooh, I do feel scared!'

Everything was quiet until two o'clock when they sat down to eat, but then it suddenly became clear that the boys were missing. They were sought in the servants' quarters, the stable and the steward's fliegel: they were not there. They were sought in the village: not there, either. Tea was drunk without them, and by the time supper was served, Mamma was extremely worried and even crying. That night they searched again in the village, and a party went to the river with lanterns. Heavens, what a hullabaloo!

Next morning the village constable arrived, and some document was being drawn up in the dining-room. Mamma was crying.

But now a wide peasant sleigh stops in front of the porch, and there's steam pouring off the troika of white horses.

'Volodya's here!' someone outside shouts.

'Master Volodya's here!' shrieks Natalya, running into the dining-room.

'Garf! Garf!' bays Milord.

It turned out that the boys had been detained in town in the shopping Arcade (they'd been walking up and down asking everyone where they could buy gunpowder). As soon as he entered the hall, Volodya burst out sobbing and threw himself round his mother's neck. Trembling with horror at the thought of what was about to happen, the girls heard Papa take Volodya and Lentilov into his study and talk to them for a long time; Mamma was there, too, talking and crying.

'How *could* you do such a thing?' Papa was saying. 'Let's hope to goodness the school doesn't hear about it or you'll be expelled. Mr Lentilov, you should be ashamed of yourself! It was too bad, sir! You were the ringleader and I hope you'll be punished by your parents. How could you do such a thing? Where did you spend the night?'

'At the station!' Lentilov replied proudly.

Afterwards Volodya went to lie down with a towel soaked in vinegar pressed to his head. A telegram was sent off somewhere, and next day a lady arrived, Lentilov's mother, and took her son away.

On leaving, Lentilov's expression was stern and haughty, and when he was saying goodbye to the girls, he did not utter a single word, but took Katya's exercise book and wrote in it as a memento:

'Montihomo Hawk's Claw.'

1887

A Drama

'If you please, sir, there's this lady wants to speak to you,' announced Luka. 'She's been waiting a good hour . . .'

Pavel Vasilyevich had just finished lunch. Hearing of the lady, he frowned and said:

'To hell with her! Say I'm busy.'

'But she's been here four times already, sir. Says she simply must speak to you . . . Almost in tears, she is.'

'Hm . . . Oh well, all right, ask her into the study.'

Taking his time, Pavel Vasilyevich put on his frock-coat, picked up a pen in one hand and a book in the other, and giving the appearance of being extremely busy, walked into the study. His visitor had already been shown in: a large stout lady with fleshy red cheeks and wearing glasses, clearly a person of extreme respectability and more than respectably dressed (she was wearing a four-flounced bustle and a tall hat surmounted by a ginger bird). On seeing the master of the house, she rolled her eyes heavenward and clasped her hands together as if in prayer.

'You won't remember me, of course,' she began in a kind of mannish falsetto, visibly agitated. 'I-I had the pleasure of making your acquaintance at the Khrutskys . . . My name is Medusina . . .'

'Ah . . . aha . . . mm . . . Do take a seat! And how can I be of service to you?'

'Well, you see, I . . . I . . .' the lady continued, sitting down and becoming even more agitated. 'You won't remember me . . . My name is Medusina . . . You see, I'm a great admirer of your talent and always read your articles with such enjoyment . . . Please don't think I say that to flatter – Heaven forbid – I'm only giving credit where credit's due . . . I read every *word* of yours. I am not a complete stranger to authorship myself . . . That's to say, I naturally wouldn't dare call myself a writer . . . but nevertheless I have added my own drop of honey to the comb. I've had three children's stories published at various times – you won't have read them, of course . . . and a number of translations . . . and my late brother worked on *The Cause.*'

'Aha . . . mm . . . And how can I be of service to you?'

'Well, you see,' (Medusina looked down bashfully and blushed) 'knowing your talent . . . and your views, Pavel Vasilyevich, I should like to find out your opinion, or should I say, seek your advice. I must tell you that I have recently – *pardon pour l'expression* – conceived and brought forth a drama, and before sending it to the censor, I should like to have your opinion.'

Fluttering about like a trapped bird, Medusina began rummaging nervously in her skirts and pulled out a huge fat exercise book.

Pavel Vasilyevich liked only his own articles, and whenever he had to read or listen to other people's, he always felt as if the mouth of a cannon were being aimed straight at his head. Scared by the sight of the exercise book, he said quickly:

'Very well, leave it with me . . .I'll read it.'

'Pavel Vasilyevich!' moaned Medusina, rising to her feet and clasping her hands together as if in prayer. 'I know how busy you are, how every minute is precious to you . . . and I know that in your heart of hearts you must be cursing me at this moment, but please let me read my drama to you now . . . Please!'

'I'd be delighted,' stammered Pavel Vasilyevich, 'but my dear lady, I'm . . . I'm busy . . . I'm about to – about to leave town.'

'Pavel Vasilyevich,' the good lady groaned, and her eyes filled with tears. 'I'm asking for a sacrifice. Call me brazen and importunate, but be magnanimous! I'm leaving for Kazan tomorrow and that's why I'd like to hear your opinion today. Spare me your attention for half an hour – just half an hour! I implore you!'

Pavel Vasilyevich was a spineless fellow and did not know how to refuse; so when the lady seemed on the point of bursting into tears and falling on her knees, he lost his nerve and mumbled helplessly:

'Very well then, please do . . . I'm listening . . . I can spare half an hour.'

With a squeal of delight, Medusina took off her hat, settled herself more comfortably and began to read. First she read how a maid and a footman, as they were tidying up a magnificent drawing-room, had a long conversation about their young mistress, Anna Sergeyevna, who had just built a school and a hospital for the village peasants. When the footman had gone off, the maid delivered a monologue on the theme that 'knowledge is

light and ignorance darkness'; then Medusina brought the footman back into the drawing-room and made him recite a long
monologue on their master, the General, who could not abide his
daughter's convictions, intended to marry her to a rich Groom of
the Chamber, and believed that the salvation of the peasantry lay
in total ignorance. After the servants had made their exit, the
young lady herself entered and informed the audience that she
had lain awake all night thinking of Valentine Ivanovich, the son
of the impecunious schoolmaster, who assisted his sick father
with no thought of reward. Valentine had studied all the sciences,
but believed neither in love nor friendship, had no aim in life and
longed for death, and therefore she, the young lady, had to save
him.

Pavel Vasilyevich listened and thought back fondly to his sofa.
He glared at Medusina, felt his eardrums being battered by her
strident voice, took in nothing and thought to himself:

'Why pick on me? ... Why should I have to listen to your
drivel? Is it my fault you've written this "drama"? Heavens, look
how fat that exercise book is! This is torture!'

Pavel Vasilyevich glanced at his wife's portrait which hung
between the windows, and remembered that she had instructed
him to buy four yards of braid, a pound of cheese and some tooth-
paste, and bring them back with him to their datcha.

'Hope to goodness I haven't lost the sample for the braid,' he
thought. 'Where did I put it? In my blue jacket, I think ... Those
wretched flies have sprinkled full stops all over her portrait again.
I must tell Olga to wipe the glass ... She's on to Scene Twelve, so
it'll soon be the end of Act One. How could anyone be inspired in
this heat, let alone a mountain of flesh like her? Instead of writing
dramas, she'd be better off drinking iced soup and having a nap
in the cellar ...'

'You don't find this monologue a trifle long?' Medusina asked
suddenly, looking up.

Pavel Vasilyevich had not heard the monologue. Caught off his
guard, he answered so apologetically that one might have
thought the monologue had been written by him, not the lady.

'No, indeed, not in the least ... It's most charming.'

Medusina beamed with happiness and continued reading:

'*Anna.* Analysis has eaten into your soul. You ceased too soon
living by the heart and put all your faith in the intellect. *Valentine.*
What do you mean by the heart? It's a concept in anatomy. As a
conventional term to describe what are referred to as the feelings,

I refuse to acknowledge it. *Anna (in confusion).* And love? Is that too only a product of the association of ideas? Tell me frankly: have you ever loved? *Valentine (bitterly).* Let us not open up old wounds, wounds yet barely healed. (*Pause.*) What are you thinking about? *Anna.* It seems to me that you are unhappy.'

During the course of Scene Sixteen Pavel Vasilyevich yawned, and his teeth inadvertently produced the kind of noise that dogs make when they are snapping at flies. Scared by the impropriety of this noise, he tried to cover it up by assuming an expression of rapt attention.

'Scene Seventeen. When on earth's it going to finish?' he thought. 'Good God, if this torment goes on another ten minutes, I'll have to shout for help. This is too much!'

But now at last the good lady began reading faster and more loudly, raised her pitch and announced: 'Curtain.'

Pavel Vasilyevich breathed a sigh of relief and was about to get up, but straight away Medusina turned over the page and carried on reading:

'Act Two. The stage represents the village street. Right a school, left a hospital. On the steps of the hospital sit the village lads and lasses.'

'Pardon me for interrupting,' said Pavel Vasilyevich, 'but how many acts are there altogether?'

'Five,' answered Medusina, and straight away, as if fearing her listener might leave the room, hurried on: 'Valentine is looking out of a window in the school. Upstage villagers can be seen taking their goods and chattels into the village tavern.'

Like a condemned man who knows he cannot be reprieved, Pavel Vasilyevich abandoned all hope, gave up wondering when the play would end, and was concerned only to keep his eyes from sticking together and to preserve the expression of interest on his face. The future, when this lady would finish reading and depart, seemed so remote that he could not even contemplate it.

'A-blah-bla-bla-bla...' Medusina's voice reverberated in his ears. 'Blah-bla-bla...Zzzzz...'

'I forgot to take my soda,' he thought. '...Er, what was that? Oh yes, my soda...I've probably got a stomach ulcer...It's an extraordinary thing, Smirnovsky guzzles vodka all day long, and his stomach's still all right...Some little bird's settled on the window-sill...A sparrow...'

Pavel Vasilyevich forced himself to keep his aching, drooping eyelids apart, yawned without opening his mouth and looked at

Medusina. She was becoming blurred, started wobbling, grew three heads, towered up and touched the ceiling . . .

'*Valentine.* No, you must allow me to go away . . . *Anna (alarmed).* But why? *Valentine (aside).* She blanched! *(To Anna.)* Do not force me to explain my reasons. I would rather die than let you know those reasons. *Anna (after a pause).* You cannot leave now . . .'

Medusina began to swell again, expanded to gigantic proportions and merged with the grey atmosphere of the study; all he saw now was her mouth opening and closing; then suddenly she became very small, like a bottle, started to wobble and together with the desk receded to the far end of the room . . .

'*Valentine (holding Anna in his arms).* You have resurrected me, you have shown me life's purpose! You have revived me as the spring rain revives the awakening earth! But it is too late – ah, too late! An incurable malady gnaws at my breast . . .'

Pavel Vasilyevich gave a start and stared at Medusina with dull, bleary eyes; for a whole minute he gazed at her fixedly, as if in a complete stupor . . .

'Scene Eleven. Enter the Baron and a police officer with witnesses. *Valentine.* Take me away! *Anna.* I am his! Take me too! Yes, take me too! I love him, love him more than my own life. *The Baron.* Anna Sergeyevna, does your father's suffering mean nothing to you –'

Medusina began to swell again . . . Gazing round wildly, Pavel Vasilyevich half rose, gave a deep-chested, unnatural yell, seized a heavy paperweight from the table and completely beside himself, swung it round with all his strength at Medusina's head . . .

'Tie me up, I've killed her!' he said when the servants ran in a minute later.

He was acquitted.

1887

The Malefactor

Before the examining magistrate stands a short, extremely skinny little peasant wearing a shirt made of ticking and baggy trousers covered in patches. His face, which is overgrown with hair and pitted with pockmarks, and his eyes, which are barely visible beneath their heavy, beetling brows, wear a grim, sullen expression. He has a whole shock of tangled hair that has not seen a comb for ages, and this lends him an even greater, spider-like grimness. He is barefoot.

'Denis Grigoryev!' the magistrate begins. 'Stand closer and answer my questions. On July 7th of this year Ivan Semyonov Akinfov, the railway watchman, was making his morning inspection of the track, when he came across you at verst 141 unscrewing one of the nuts with which the rails are secured to the sleepers. This nut, to be precise! . . . And he detained you with the said nut in your possession. Is that correct?'

'Wossat?'

'Did all this happen as Akinfov has stated?'

'Course it did.'

'Right. So why were you unscrewing the nut?'

'Wossat?'

'Stop saying "Wossat?" to everything, and answer my question: why were you unscrewing this nut?'

'Wouldn't have been unscrewing it if I hadn't needed it, would I?' croaks Denis, squinting at the ceiling.

'And why did you need it?'

'What, that nut? We make sinkers out of them nuts . . .'

'Who do you mean – "we"?'

'Us folks . . . Us Klimovo peasants, I mean.'

'Listen here, my friend, stop pretending you're an idiot and talk some sense. I don't want any lies about sinkers, do you hear?'

'Lies? I never told a lie in my life . . .' mutters Denis, blinking. 'We got to have sinkers, haven't we, your honour? If you put a live-bait or a worm on, he won't sink without a weight, will he?

173

Hah, "lies" ...' Denis sniggers. 'Ain't no use in a live-bait that floats on the top! Your perch, your pike and your burbot always go for a bait on the bottom. Only a spockerel takes one that's floating on top, and not always then ... There aren't no spockerel in our rivers ... He likes the open more, does that one.'

'Why are you telling me about spockerels?'

'Wossat? You asked me, that's why! The gents round here fish that way, too. Even a little nipper wouldn't try catching fish without a sinker. 'Course, those as don't understand anything about it, they might. Fools are a law unto 'mselves ...'

'So you are saying you unscrewed this nut in order to make a sinker out of it?'

'What else for? Not for playing fivestones with!'

'But you could have used some lead for a sinker, a piece of shot ... or a nail ...'

'You don't find lead on the railway, you got to buy it, and a nail's no good. You won't find anything better than a nut ... It's heavy, and it's got a hole through it.'

'Stop pretending you're daft, as though you were born yesterday or fell off the moon! Don't you understand, you blockhead, what unscrewing these nuts leads to? If the watchman hadn't been keeping a look-out, a train could have been derailed, people could have been killed! You would have killed people!'

'Lord forbid, your honour! What would I want to kill people for? Do you take us for heathens or some kind of robbers? Glory be, sir, in all our born days we've never so much as thought of doing such things, let alone killed anyone ... Holy Mother of Heaven save us, have mercy on us ... What a thing to say!'

'Why do you think train crashes happen, then? Unscrew two or three of these nuts, and you've got a crash!'

Denis sniggers, and peers at the magistrate sceptically.

'Hah! All these years our village's been unscrewing these nuts and the Lord's preserved us, and here you go talking about crashes – me killing people ... Now if I'd taken a rail out, say, or put a log across that there track, then I grant you that'd brought the train off, but a little nut? Hah!'

'But don't you understand, it's the nuts and bolts that hold the rails to the sleepers!'

'We do understand ... We don't screw them all off ... we leave some ... We're not stupid – we know what we're doing ...'

Denis yawns and makes the sign of the cross over his mouth.

'A train came off the rails here last year,' says the magistrate.

'Now we know why ...'

'Beg pardon?'

'I said, now we know why the train came off the rails last year ... I understand now!'

'That's what you're educated for, to understand, to be our protectors ... The Lord knew what he was doing, when he gave you understanding ... You've worked out for us the whys and wherefores, but that watchman, he's just another peasant, he has no understanding, he just grabs you by the collar and hauls you off ... First work things out, then you can haul us off! It's as they say, if a man's a peasant, he thinks like a peasant ... You can put down as well, your honour, that he hit me twice on the jaw and in the chest.'

'When your hut was searched, they found a second nut ... Where did you unscrew that one, and when?'

'You mean the nut that was lying under the little red chest?'

'I don't know where it was lying, but they found it in your hut. When did you unscrew that one?'

'I didn't; Ignashka, One-Eye Semyon's son, gave it me. The one under the little red chest, that is. The one in the sledge out in the yard me and Mitrofan unscrewed.'

'Which Mitrofan is that?'

'Mitrofan Petrov ... Ain't you heard of him? He makes fishing nets round here and sells them to the gents. He needs a lot of these here nuts. Reckon there must be ten to every net ...'

'Now listen ... Article 1081 of the Penal Code says that any damage wilfully caused to the railway, when such damage might endanger the traffic proceeding on it and the accused knew that such damage would bring about an accident – do you understand, *knew*, and you couldn't help but know what unscrewing these nuts would lead to – then the sentence is exile with hard labour.'

'Well, you know best, of course ... We're benighted folks ... you don't expect us to understand, do you?'

'You understand perfectly! You're lying, you're putting all this on!'

'Why should I lie? You can ask in the village, if you don't believe me ... Without a sinker you'll only catch bleak, and they're worse'n gudgeon – you'll not catch gudgeon without a sinker, either.'

'Now you're going to tell me about those spockerels again!' smiles the magistrate.

'Spockerel don't live in our parts . . . If you float your line on the water with a butterfly on it, you might catch a chub, but seldom even then.'

'All right, now be quiet . . .'

There is silence. Denis shifts from foot to foot, stares at the green baize table-top, and blinks strenuously, as if he's looking into the sun rather than at a piece of cloth. The magistrate is writing quickly.

'Can I go?' asks Denis after a while.

'No. I have to take you into custody and commit you to gaol.'

Denis stops blinking and, raising his thick brows, looks at the official in disbelief.

'How do you mean, gaol? I ain't got time, your honour, I've got to go to the fair, I've got to pick up three roubles off Yegor for some lard –'

'Quiet, you're disturbing me.'

'Gaol . . . If there was due cause I'd go, but . . . I ain't done nothing! What do I have to go for, eh? I haven't stole anything, I haven't been fighting . . . And if it's the arrears you're worried about, your honour, then don't you believe that elder of ours . . . You ask the zemstvo gentleman what deals with us . . . He's no Christian, that elder of ours –'

'Be quiet!'

'I am being quiet . . .' mutters Denis. 'And I'll swear on oath that elder fiddled our assessment . . . There are three of us brothers: Kuzma Grigoryev, Yegor Grigoryev, and me, Denis Grigoryev . . .'

'You're distracting me . . . Hey, Semyon!' shouts the magistrate. 'Take him away!'

'There are three of us brothers,' Denis mutters, as two brawny soldiers grab hold of him and lead him from the courtroom. 'One brother doesn't have to answer for another . . . Kuzma won't pay, so you, Denis, have to answer for him . . . Call that justice! The general our old master's dead, God rest his soul, or he'd show you, you "judges" . . . A judge must know what he's doing, not hand it out any old how . . . He can hand out a flogging if he knows he's got to, if a man's really done wrong . . .'

1885

No Comment

In the fifth century, just as now, every morning the sun rose, and every evening it retired to rest. In the morning, as the first rays kissed the dew, the earth would come to life and the air be filled with sounds of joy, hope and delight, while in the evening the same earth would grow quiet again and be swallowed up in grim darkness. Each day, each night, was like the one before. Occasionally a dark cloud loomed up and thunder growled angrily from it, or a star would doze off and fall from the firmament, or a monk would run by, pale-faced, to tell the brethren that not far from the monastery he had seen a tiger – and that would be all, then once again each day, each night, would be just like the one before.

The monks toiled and prayed, while their Abbot played the organ, composed music and wrote verses in Latin. This wonderful old man had an extraordinary gift. Whenever he played the organ, he did so with such art that even the oldest monks, whose hearing had grown dull as they neared the end of their lives, could not restrain their tears when the sounds of the organ reached them from his cell. Whenever he spoke about something, even the most commonplace things, such as trees, the wild beasts, or the sea, it was impossible to listen to him without a smile or a tear; it seemed that the same chords were sounding in his soul as in the organ. Whereas if he was moved by anger, or by great joy, or if he was talking about something terrible or sublime, a passionate inspiration would take hold of him, his eyes would flash and fill with tears, his face flush and his voice rumble like thunder, and as they listened to him the monks could feel this inspiration taking over their souls; in those magnificent, wonderful moments his power was limitless, and if he had ordered the fathers to throw themselves into the sea, then, to a man, they would all have rushed rapturously to carry out his will.

His music, his voice, and the verses in which he praised God, the heavens and the earth, were for the monks a source of constant joy. As life was so unvaried, there were times when spring and autumn, the flowers and the trees, began to pall on them, their ears tired of the sound of the sea, and the song of the birds became irksome; but the talents of the old Abbot were as vital to them as their daily bread.

Many years passed, and still each day, each night, was just like the one before. Apart from the wild birds and beasts, not a single living soul showed itself near the monastery. The nearest human habitation was far away, and to get to it from the monastery or vice versa, meant crossing a hundred versts or so of wilderness on foot. The only people who ventured to cross the wilderness were those who spurned life, had renounced it, and were going to the monastery as though to the grave.

Imagine the monks' astonishment, therefore, when one night a man knocked at their gates who, it transpired, came from the town and was the most ordinary of sinful mortals who love life. Before asking the Abbot's blessing and offering up a prayer, this man called for food and wine. When he was asked how he, a townsman, came to be in the wilderness, he answered with a long sportsman's yarn about how he had gone out hunting, had too much to drink, and lost his way. To the suggestion that he take the monastic vow and save his soul, he replied with a smile and the words: 'I'm no mate of yours.'

After he had eaten and drunk his fill, he looked around at the monks who had been waiting on him, and shaking his head reproachfully, he said:

'What a way to carry on! All you monks bother about is eating and drinking. Is that the way to save your souls? Just think, whilst you're sitting here in peace and quiet, eating, drinking, and dreaming of heavenly bliss, your fellow humans are perishing and going down to hell. Why don't you look at what's going on in the town! Some are dying of hunger there, others have more gold than they know what to do with, and wallow in debauchery till they die like flies stuck to honey. People have no faith or principles! Whose job is it to save them? To preach to them? Surely not mine, when I'm drunk from morning till night? Did God give you faith, a humble spirit and a loving heart just to sit around here within four walls twiddling your thumbs?'

Although the townsman's drunken words were insolent and profane, they had a strange effect upon the Abbot. The old man glanced round at his monks, paled, and said:

'Brothers, what he says is right! Through their folly and their frailty, those poor people are indeed perishing in sin and unbelief, whilst we sit back, as though it had nothing to do with us. Should I not be the one to go and recall them to Christ whom they have forgotten?'

The townsman's words had carried the old man away, and the very next morning he took his staff in his hand, bade the brethren farewell, and set off for the town. And the monks were left without his music, his verses, and his fine speeches.

A month of boredom went by, then another, and still the old man did not return. At last, after the third month, they heard the familiar tapping of his staff. The monks rushed to meet him and showered him with questions, but he, instead of being glad to see them again, broke into bitter tears and would not say a single word. The monks saw he had aged greatly and grown much thinner; his face was strained and full of a deep sorrow, and when he broke into tears he looked like a man who had been mortally offended.

The monks too burst into tears and began begging him to tell them why he was weeping, why he looked so downcast, but he would not say a word and locked himself away in his cell. Seven days he stayed there, would not eat or drink or play the organ, and just wept. When the monks knocked at his door and implored him to come out and share his grief with them, they were met with a profound silence.

At last he came out. Gathering all the monks about him, he began with a tear-stained face and an expression of sorrow and indignation to tell them what had happened to him in the past three months. His voice was calm and his eyes smiled while he described his journey from the monastery to the town. As he went along, he said, the birds had sung to him and the brooks babbled, and tender young hopes had stirred in his soul; as he walked, he felt like a soldier going into battle, confident of victory; and in his reverie he walked along composing hymns and verses and did not notice when his journey was over.

But his voice trembled, his eyes flashed, and his whole being burned with wrath when he started talking of the town and its people. Never in his life had he seen, never durst imagine, what confronted him when he entered the town. Only now, in his old age, had he seen and understood for the first time how mighty was the devil, how beautiful wickedness, and how feeble, cowardly and faint-hearted were human beings. As luck would have it, the first dwelling that he went into was a house of ill fame.

Some fifty people with lots of money were eating and drinking immoderate quantities of wine. Intoxicated by the wine, they sang songs and bandied about terrible, disgusting words that no God-fearing person could ever bring himself to utter; completely uninhibited, boisterous and happy, they did not fear God, the devil or death, but said and did exactly as they wished, and went wherever their lusts impelled them. And the wine, as clear as amber and fizzing with gold, must have been unbearably sweet and fragrant, because everyone drinking it smiled blissfully and wanted to drink more. In response to men's smiles it smiled back, and sparkled joyfully when it was drunk, as if it knew what devilish charm lurked in its sweetness.

More and more worked up and weeping with rage, the old man continued to describe what he had seen. On a table among the revellers, he said, stood a half-naked harlot. It would be difficult to imagine or to find in nature anything more lovely and captivating. This foul creature, young, with long hair, dusky skin, dark eyes and full lips, shameless and brazen, flashed her snow-white teeth and smiled as if to say: 'Look at me, how brazen I am and beautiful!' Silk and brocade hung down in graceful folds from her shoulders, but her beauty would not be hid, and like young shoots in the spring earth, eagerly thrust through the folds of her garments. The brazen woman drank wine, sang songs, and gave herself to anyone who wished.

Then the old man, waving his arms in anger, went on to describe the horse races and bull fights, the theatres, and the artists' workshops where they made paintings and sculptures in clay of naked women. His speech was inspired, beautiful and melodious, as if he were playing on invisible chords, and the monks, rooted to the spot, devoured his every word and could scarcely breathe for excitement . . . When he had finished describing all the devil's charms, the beauty of wickedness and the captivating graces of the vile female body, the old man denounced the devil, turned back to his cell and closed the door behind him . . .

When he came out of his cell next morning, there was not a single monk left in the monastery. They had all run away to the town.

1888

180

Sergeant Prishibeyev

'Staff-Sergeant Prishibeyev! You are accused of using insulting language and behaviour on the 3rd of September of this year towards Police Officer Zappsky, District Elder Berkin, Police Constable Yefimov, Official Witnesses Ivanov and Gavrilov, and six other peasants; whereof the first three aforenamed were insulted by you in the performance of their duties. Do you plead guilty?'

Prishibeyev, a shrivelled little sergeant with a crabbed face, squares his shoulders and answers in a stifled, croaky voice, clipping his words as though on the parade ground:

'Your Honour Mr Justice of the Peace – sir! What it says in the law is: every statement can be mutually contested. I'm not guilty – it's them lot. This all came about because of a dead corpse, God rest his soul. I was walking along on the 3rd – quiet and respectable like – with my wife Anfisa, when suddenly I spy this mob of varied persons standing on the river bank. "What perfect right has that mob got to be assembled there?" I ask myself. "What do they think they're up to? Where's it written down that common folk can go around in droves?" So I shout, "Hey, you lot – disperse!" I started shoving them, to get them to go indoors, I ordered the constable to lay into them, and –'

'Just one moment. You're not a police officer or elder: is it your business to be breaking up crowds?'

'No, it ain't! It ain't!' voices cry from different corners of the courtroom. 'He's the bane of our lives, yeronner! Fifteen years we've put up with him! Ever since he gave up work and came back here the village ain't been worth living in. He's driving us mad!'

'It's quite true, yeronner,' says the elder who is one of the witnesses. 'The whole village complains of him. He's impossible to live with. Whether we're taking the icons round the village, or there's a wedding, or some do on, say, he's out there shouting at us, kicking up a row and calling for order. He goes about pulling the kids' ears, he spies on our womenfolk to see they're not up to something, like he was their own father-in-law ... The other day he went round the huts ordering everyone to stop singing and put all their lights out. "There's no law permitting you to sing songs," he says.'

'All right, you'll have time to give evidence later,' says the magistrate. 'At the moment let's hear what else Prishibeyev has to say. Go on, Prishibeyev.'

'Yessir!' croaks the sergeant. 'You were pleased to observe, your honour, that it's not my business to be breaking up crowds ... Very good, sir ... But what if there's a disturbance? We can't allow them to run riot, can we? Where's it written down that the lower orders can do what they like? I can't let them get away with that, sir. And if I don't tell them to break up, and give them what for, who will? No one round here knows what proper discipline is, you might say I'm the only one, your honour, as knows how to deal with the lower orders, and, your honour, I know what I'm talking about. I'm not a peasant, I'm a non-commissioned officer, a Q.M.S. retired, I served in Warsaw as a staff-sergeant, sir, after I got an honourable discharge I worked in the fire brigade, sir, then I had to give up the fire brigade by virtue of health and worked for the next two years as janitor in an independent classical school for young gentlemen ... So I know all about discipline, sir. But a peasant's just a simple fellow, he doesn't know any better, so he must do what I tell him – 'cause it's for his own good. Take this business, for example. I break up the crowd and there lying in the sand on the river bank is the drownded corpse of a dead man. On what possible grounds can he be lying there, I ask myself. Do you call that law and order? Why's the officer just standing there? "Hey, officer," I say, "why aren't you informing your superiors? Maybe this drownded corpse drowned himself, or maybe it smacks of Siberia – maybe it's a case of criminal homicide ..." But officer Zappsky doesn't give a damn, he just goes on smoking his cigarette. "Who's this bloke giving orders?" he says. "Is he one of yours? Where'd he spring from? Does he think we don't know what to do without his advice?" he says. "Well you can't do, can you, dimwit," says I, "if you're just standing there and don't give a damn." "I informed the inspector yesterday," he says. "Why the inspector?" I ask him. "According to which article of the code? In cases like this, of people being drowned or strangulated and such-like and so forth, what can the inspector do? It's a capital offence," I says, "a case for the courts ... You'd better send a dispatch to his honour the examining magistrate and the justices straightaway," I says. "And first of all," I says, "you must draw up a document and send it to his honour the Justice of the Peace." But the officer, he just listens to me and laughs. And the peasants the same. They were all laughing, your honour. I'll testify to that on oath. That one there laughed – and this one – and Zappsky, he laughed too. "What are you all grinning at?" I says. Then the officer says: "Such matters," he says, "are nothing to do with the J.P." Well, the blood rushed to my head when I heard him say that. That is what you said, isn't it, officer?' the sergeant asks, turning to Zappsky.

'That's what I said.'

'Everyone heard you say them words, for all the common people to hear. "Such matters are nothing to do with the J.P." – everyone heard you say them words . . . Well, the blood rushed to my head, your honour, I went quite weak at the knees. "Repeat to me," says I, "repeat, you . . . so-and-so, what you just said!" He comes out with them same words again . . . I goes up to him. "How dare you say such things," says I, "about his honour the Justice of the Peace? A police officer and you're against authority – eh? Do you know," I says, "that if he likes, his honour the Justice of the Peace can have you sent to the provincial gendarmerie for saying them words and proving unreliable? Do you realize," says I, "where his honour the Justice of the Peace can pack you off to for political words like that?" Then the elder butts in: "The J.P.," he says, "can't deal with anything outside his powers. He only handles minor cases." That's what he said, everyone heard him . . . "How dare you," says I, "belittle authority? Don't you come that game with me, son," I says, "or you'll find yourself in hot water." When I was in Warsaw, or when I was janitor at the independent classical school for young gentlemen, soon as I heard any words as shouldn't be said I'd look out on the street for a gendarme and shout, "Step in here a minute, will you, soldier?" — and report it all to him. But who can you tell things to out here in the country? . . . It made me wild. It really got me, to think of the common people of today indulging in licence and insubordination like that, so I let fly and – not hard of course, just lightly like, just proper, so's he wouldn't dare say such things about your honour again . . .The officer sided with the elder. So I gave the officer one, too . . . And that's how it started . . . I got worked up, your honour. But you can't get anywhere without a few clouts, can you? If you don't clout a stupid man, it's a sin on your own head. Especially if there's good reason for it – if he's been causing a disturbance . . .'

'But there are other people appointed to keep public order! That's what the officer, the elder and the constable are there for –'

'Ah, but the officer can't keep an eye on everybody, and he don't understand what I do . . .'

'Well understand now that it's none of your business!'

'Not my business, sir? How do you make that out? That's queer . . . People behave improperly and it's none of my business? What am I supposed to do – cheer them on? They've just been complaining to you that I won't let them sing songs . . . And what good is there in songs, I'd like to know? Instead of getting on with something useful, they sing songs . . . Then they've got a new craze for sitting up late with a light burning. They ought to be in bed asleep, but all you hear is laughing and talking. I've got it all written down!'

'You've got what written down?'

'Who sits up burning a light.'

Prishibeyev takes a greasy slip of paper from his pocket, puts his spectacles on, and reads:

'Peasants what sit up burning a light: Ivan Prokhorov, Savva Mikiforov, Pyotr Petrov. The soldier's widow Shustrova is living in illicit union with Semyon Kislov. Ignat Sverchok dabbles in black magic, and his wife Mavra is a witch, she goes around at night milking other people's cows.'

'That's enough!' says the magistrate and turns to examining the witnesses.

Sergeant Prishibeyev pushes his glasses on to his forehead and stares in amazement at the J.P. – who is evidently not on his side. His eyes gleam and start out of his head, and his nose turns bright red. He looks from the J.P. to the witnesses and simply cannot understand why the magistrate should be so het up and why from every corner of the courtroom comes a mixture of angry murmurs and suppressed laughter. The sentence is equally incomprehensible to him: one month in custody!

'For what?!' he asks, throwing up his arms in disbelief. 'By what law?'

And he realizes that the world is a changed place, a place impossible to live in. Dark, gloomy thoughts possess him. But when he comes out of the courtroom he sees some peasants huddled together talking about something and by force of a habit which he can no longer control, he squares his shoulders and bawls in a hoarse, irate voice:

'You lot – break it up! Move along! Diss-perse!'

1885

Encased

After returning late, the hunters had decided to bed down for the night in a barn belonging to village elder Prokofy on the very edge of Mironositskoye village. There were only two of them: Ivan Ivanych, a veterinary surgeon, and Burkin, a schoolmaster. Ivan Ivanych had a rather strange, double-barrelled surname, Chimsha-Himalaisky, which did not suit him at all, and everyone in the province knew him simply as Ivan Ivanych. He lived on a stud-farm close to the town and had come on this expedition to enjoy some fresh air, whereas Burkin, the schoolmaster, spent every summer as a guest of Count P.'s family and was very much at home in these parts.

They were not asleep. Ivan Ivanych, a tall thin old man with a big moustache, was sitting outside the barn smoking a pipe in the moonlight, while Burkin lay inside on the hay, invisible in the darkness.

They were telling various stories. The conversation turned to Mavra the village elder's wife, a healthy woman of normal intelligence, who had never once been outside her own village, had never seen a town or railway, and for the past ten years had sat behind her stove and only ever gone out at night.

'Nothing so remarkable in that,' Burkin said. 'There are plenty of people in the world who are solitary by nature and try to retire into their shells, like hermit-crabs or snails. Maybe it's some kind of atavistic throwback to the time when our ancestors were not social animals but lived in their own solitary lairs, or maybe it's just one of the variants of human nature – who knows? I'm not a natural scientist and such questions aren't in my line. All I'm saying is that people like Mavra aren't uncommon. I can think of one straight away. Name of Belikov. He was the Greek master at our school and died in the town two months ago. You'll have heard of him, no doubt. The remarkable th:ng about him was that even in the hottest weather he would go out in galoshes and with an umbrella and always wearing a warm padded coat. He had a cover for his umbrella, a grey shammy-leather case for his pocket-watch, and when he took out his penknife to sharpen a pencil, even that had a little case of its own. His face, too, seemed encased, as he always hid it in his upturned collar. He wore dark glasses and a pullover, stuffed his ears with cotton-wool, and whenever he took a cab, gave orders for the hood to be raised. In brief, the man displayed a persistent, insuperable urge to surround himself with a membrane, to make a kind of casing that would isolate and protect him from external influences. Reality irritated and scared him, kept him in a state of permanent anxiety, and perhaps it was to justify his timidity and revulsion from the present that he always praised the past and a world that had never existed. The ancient languages, which he taught, were essentially just like the galoshes and umbrella in which he took refuge from the real world.

"Oh, how sonorous and beautiful the Greek language is!" he would say with a sugary expression; and as if to prove his point, he would half-close his eyes, raise his finger and say the word *anthropos*.

His thoughts, too, Belikov endeavoured to encase. The only things clear to him were official regulations and newspaper articles in which something was forbidden. If there was an official regulation banning pupils from being out after nine at night, or some article appeared banning sexual intercourse, that was clear and definite: it's banned, the matter's settled. But in anything that was authorized or permitted he always detected a dubious element, something not fully spelled out and unclear. Whenever an amateur dramatic society or a reading-room or a tea-shop was authorized in the town, he would shake his head and say quietly:

"Well, yes, it's a good idea, of course – but what if it leads to something?"

Any infringement of the rules, any deviation or departure from them, would make him despondent, however little it might have to do with him. If a colleague was late for church service, or the boys were rumoured to have been up to some prank, or a member of staff from the girls' school was seen out late with an officer, he became very worried and kept saying that it might lead to something. At staff meetings he simply wore us down with his cautious, suspicious attitude, with those encased ideas of his about bad behaviour in the boys' and girls' schools, and the awful din in the classrooms – oh dear, suppose the authorities hear about this, suppose it leads to something – and wouldn't it be a good idea to expel Petrov from the second year and Yegorov from the fourth? And what happened? With his sighs and his whining, his dark glasses on that pale little face – it was a small kind of face like a ferret's – he put such pressure on us that we caved in, gave Petrov and Yegorov bad marks for conduct, put them in detention and eventually expelled them both. He had a strange habit of going round our lodgings. He'd call on a teacher, sit down and say nothing, and appear to be making an inspection. He'd sit like that in silence for an hour or two and go away. He called this "maintaining good relations with his colleagues", but it was obvious he found it a strain visiting us and sitting like that, and did so only because he considered it his duty as a colleague. We teachers were scared of him. Even the headmaster was scared of him. Just imagine, our teachers are thoroughly decent, thinking people, brought up on Turgenev and Shchedrin, and yet this little man with his galoshes and umbrella held the whole school under his thumb for all of fifteen years! And not only the school, the whole town! Our ladies never arranged any home theatricals on a Saturday in case he found out, and the clergy took care not to eat meat on fast days or play cards when he was around. Because of Belikov and his like, during the past ten or fifteen years people in our town have become scared of everything. Scared of talking in a loud voice, of sending letters, making new acquaintances, reading books, afraid of helping the poor, of teaching people to read and write . . .'

Ivan Ivanych wanted to say something and cleared his throat, but first lit his pipe, glanced at the moon and only then said in measured tones:

'Yes. Decent, thinking people, they read their Shchedrin and Turgenev, their Henry Buckle and the rest of them, and yet they submitted, they put up with it . . . Yes, that's the way things are.'

'Belikov and I lived in the same house,' Burkin continued, 'on the same floor. Our doors were facing, so we often met, and I knew his domestic life. It was the same story there: dressing-gown and nightcap, shutters and bolts, a whole series of bans and restrictions of every kind, and worrying about what things might lead to. Fasting is bad for you, but you mustn't eat meat on fast days or people will say Belikov doesn't observe the fasts, so he ate perch fried in butter, which wasn't Lenten food, but wasn't exactly prohibited either. For fear of gossip he did not keep any female servants, only a cook, Afanasy, a drunken old half-wit of about sixty, who had once served as a batman and could knock up a meal of sorts. This Afanasy usually stood outside the door with his arms folded, forever mumbling the same words and sighing deeply:

"Far too many of *them* around these days!"

Belikov's bedroom was small and box-like, and his bed was a four-poster. When he lay down, he pulled the bedding over his head. It was hot and stuffy, the wind was knocking on the closed doors and droning in the stove. Sighs came from the kitchen, ominous sighs ... He felt scared beneath his blanket. He was afraid something might happen, that Afanasy might cut his throat or thieves break in, and all night long he had nightmares, so that in the morning, when we walked to school together, he was pale and lifeless, he was obviously terrified of the school he was going to with its masses of people, all this was deeply repellent to him, and even having to walk alongside me was a strain for a solitary nature like his.

"What an awful din from the classrooms," he would say, as if trying to find an explanation for his depressed mood. "Indescribable."

And believe it or not, this teacher of Greek, this man in a case, nearly got married.'

Ivan Ivanych glanced quickly into the barn and said:

'You're joking!'

'No, he nearly got married, strange as it may seem. A new master was appointed to teach history and geography, name of Kovalenko, Mikhail Savvich, a Ukrainian. When he arrived, he had his sister Varenka with him. He was a tall, swarthy young man with huge hands, his face alone told you he had a bass voice and so he had, boom-boom-boom, like something from a barrel ... She wasn't young, about thirty, but tall and well built like him, with dark eyebrows and red cheeks. In brief, not a maiden but a ripe peach, full of noise and energy, singing Ukrainian songs all the time and laughing ... The least thing and she'd go off into peals of loud laughter: ha-ha-ha! The first time, I remember, that we really got to know the Kovalenkos was at the head's name-day party. Amid those grim, bottled-up old teachers, for whom parties were more like an official duty, suddenly we see a new Aphrodite rising from the foam: arms on hips, laughing, singing and dancing ... She gave a heartfelt rendering of "Winds A-blowing", then another song, and a third, and bowled us all over, Belikov included. He sat down next to her and said with a sugary smile:

"The delicacy and pleasing sonority of Ukrainian remind me of ancient Greek."

She was flattered, and began telling him with great intensity of feeling about the farm she owned in the Gadyach district, it was where her dear mother lived, and you should just see the pears they have down there, and the melons, and the pumpkins! And did he know the Ukrainians have a word for "pumpkin" which is the same as the Russian word for "pub", and the borsch they make using tomatoes and egg-plants is "so tasty, so tasty, it's simply terrific!"

We listened and listened and suddenly we all had the same thought.

"Why don't we get them married?" the head's wife said to me quietly.

For some reason we all called to mind that our Belikov was a bachelor and were puzzled we'd never noticed this before, had somehow quite overlooked this important detail in his life. What was his attitude to women, how did he resolve this vital question? Previously it hadn't been of the slightest interest to us; maybe we couldn't even conceive that a man who wore galoshes in all weathers and slept in a four-poster could love anyone.

"He's well over forty, she's thirty," the head's wife elaborated. "I think she'd have him."

What a lot of stupid, unnecessary things we get up to in the provinces out of sheer boredom! And all because we fail to do what *is* necessary. Why this sudden need to marry off Belikov when you couldn't even imagine him as a married man? The head's wife, the inspector's wife and all the school ladies perked up and even looked prettier, as if they'd discovered a purpose in life. The head's wife takes a box at the theatre, and whom do we see sitting there but Varenka, holding this fan if you please, beaming and happy, with the small, hunched-up Belikov beside her, looking as if he'd been prised from home with a pair of pincers. I throw a party and the ladies insist that I invite Belikov and Varenka. In brief, the wheels began to turn. Varenka, it emerged, was quite keen to get married. Living with her brother was no great fun, they did nothing but argue and swear at each other for days on end. Here's a typical scene. Kovalenko's walking down the street, healthy, tall and gangling, wearing an embroidered shirt, with a quiff of hair pushing out from under his cap. He's carrying a parcel of books in one hand and a thick knobbly stick in the other. His sister is walking behind him, also carrying books.

"But you haven't read it, Mikhailik!" she's arguing loudly. "I tell you, I swear to you, you simply haven't read it!"

"And I say I have!" Kovalenko shouts, banging his stick on the pavement.

"Oh, for heaven's sake, Minchik! Why get so worked up when we're talking about a matter of principle?"

"And I tell you I have read it!" Kovalenko shouts even louder.

At home, as soon as anyone turned up, they immediately began squabbling. She was probably tired of living like that and wanted a place of her own, and there was also her age to consider: she was in no position to pick and choose, but must take anyone going, even a teacher of Greek. For most of our young ladies getting married, after all, is what matters, and never mind to whom. Be that as it may, Varenka began to show our Belikov a marked partiality.

And Belikov? He used to call on Kovalenko, as he did the rest of us. He'd arrive, sit down and say nothing. And while he sat there in silence, Varenka would sing him "Winds A-blowing", or gaze at him thoughtfully with her dark eyes, or suddenly burst out laughing:

"Ha-ha-ha!"

Where love is concerned and especially marriage, people are easily influenced. All his colleagues and all the ladies began to assure Belikov that he ought to marry, that he had no other alternative in life; we all congratulated him, and uttered various po-faced banalities about marriage being a serious step and so on; and Varenka *was* quite good-looking, an interesting person, the daughter of a state counsellor with her own farm, and most important of all, she was the first woman who had shown him genuine affection – his head was turned and he decided he really must marry.'

'That was the time to get his galoshes and umbrella off him,' said Ivan Ivanych.

'Couldn't be done, would you believe it? He put a portrait of Varenka on his desk, kept coming in to talk to me about Varenka and family life and marriage being a serious step, visited the Kovalenkos frequently, but didn't change his way of life in the slightest. On the contrary, his decision to marry seemed to affect his health, he became thin and pale and appeared to retreat even further into his shell.

"I like Varvara Savvishna," he said to me, twisting his face into a weak little smile, "and I know everyone must marry, but . . . but all this, you know, has been rather sudden . . . I must think it over."

"What's there to think over?" I reply. "Just get married."

"No, marriage is a serious step, one must first weigh up one's future duties and responsibilities . . . in case it should lead to anything later. I'm so worried, I can't sleep at all now. To be honest, I'm apprehensive. She and her brother have such strange views, they look at things in such a strange kind of way somehow, they've got lively characters. Get married, and before you know what's happening, you'll be caught up in some incident."

And he didn't propose but kept delaying, much to the annoyance of the head's wife and all our ladies; kept weighing up his future duties and responsibilities, while at the same time he went out with Varenka almost every day, perhaps because he felt he had to in his position, and came in to talk to me about family life. In all probability he would eventually have proposed, and one of those stupid, unnecessary marriages would have taken place that occur by the thousand because we're bored and have nothing better to do, had not the most *kolossalische Skandal* suddenly erupted. I should mention that Varenka's brother, Kovalenko, had hated Belikov from the first day of their acquaintance and couldn't stand him.

"I don't know how you put up with that loathsome little sneak," he would say to us, shrugging his shoulders. "Gentlemen, gentlemen, how can you go on living in such a foul, stifling atmosphere? You're not educators or teachers, you're time-servers. This isn't a temple of learning, it's a police station, it smells as sour as a sentry-box. No, my friends, I'll spend a while longer with you, then I'm off to the farm to catch crayfish and teach the local boys. And you can stay on here with that Judas of yours, blast him."

Or else he'd laugh, laugh until he cried, first in a deep bass, then in a squeaky little treble.

"Why does he just sit there?" he would ask me, reverting to his native Ukrainian accent and gesturing helplessly. "What does he want? He just sits and stares."

He even nicknamed Belikov "The Bloodsucker". Needless to say, we refrained from mentioning that his sister Varenka was intending to marry this same "Bloodsucker". And when the head's wife said to him once what a good idea it would be to fix up his sister with such a reliable, universally respected man as Belikov, he scowled and muttered:

"No concern of mine. Let her marry a viper if she wants to. I don't stick my nose into other people's business."

Now on with the story. Some joker drew a caricature. It showed Belikov in galoshes with his trousers rolled up, carrying his umbrella and walking arm in arm with Varenka. Underneath was the caption "The Lovesick Anthropos". It had caught his expression to a T. The artist must have been hard at it for several nights, because we all received a copy – all the teachers at the boys' and girls' schools and the theological college, plus the town officials. Belikov received one, too. The caricature had a profoundly depressing effect on him.

So, it's May 1st, a Sunday, and he and I are leaving the house together. Masters and boys have arranged to meet at the school and then all go walking to a small wood beyond the town. Belikov's face is green and gloomier than a thunder-cloud.

"What bad, wicked people there are in the world!" he said, and his lips trembled.

I even felt sorry for him. Then as we were walking along, who should suddenly appear but Kovalenko, riding a bicycle, and behind him, also on a bicycle, Varenka, red in the face and exhausted, but cheerful and happy.

"We're going on ahead!" she shouts. "Isn't it a *wonderful* day? Simply terrific!"

And they disappeared from view. My Belikov's face turns from green to white. He stops dead in his tracks, looks at me and asks:

"What *is* going on? Or do my eyes deceive me? Can bicycling be regarded as a proper activity for schoolmasters and for women?"

"What's improper about it?" I said. "Let them ride as much as they like."

"But how can you say that?" he shouted, astonished by my calmness. "What on earth do you mean?"

And he was so overcome that he refused to go on and returned home.

Next day he was rubbing his hands nervously all the time and shaking, and looked obviously unwell. For the first time in his life he cancelled his classes and went home. He did not have a meal, but towards evening wrapped himself up well, even though it was a perfect summer's day, and took himself off to the Kovalenkos. He found only the brother at home, Varenka was out.

"Please take a seat," Kovalenko said coldly and frowned. He looked half-asleep, having only just finished resting after his meal, and was in a very bad temper.

Belikov sat there in silence for about ten minutes and then began:

"I have come here to relieve my mind of a very, very heavy burden. Some lampoonist has made a comic representation of myself and another individual, who is close to both of us. It is my duty to assure you that I am in no way to blame. I never gave the least grounds for such ridicule. On the contrary, I behaved throughout with perfect propriety."

Kovalenko sat there fuming and said nothing. Belikov waited a while, then went on quietly in a sorrowful voice:

"There is something else I have to say to you. I have been teaching a long time, whereas you are only just starting in the profession, and it is my duty as a senior colleague to give you a warning. You go bicycling, and such an amusement is most improper in one who bears responsibility for educating the young."

"Why so?" Kovalenko said in a deep voice.

"Do I really need to go into explanations, Mikhail Savvich, isn't it obvious? If a teacher goes bicycling, then what can be expected from the pupils? Next thing we know, they'll be walking on their heads! And if it's not been officially sanctioned, it's not allowed. I was appalled yesterday! When I caught sight of your sister, I nearly fainted. A woman or a girl on a bicycle is quite shocking."

"What exactly is it you want?"

"One thing only, Mikhail Savvich, to warn you. You are a young man with your future ahead of you, you must behave with very, very great caution, but you – you don't bother, oh dear me no, you don't bother at all! You wear an embroidered shirt, you're always carrying books around in the street, and now on top of everything there's this bicycle. The headmaster will find out that you and your sister ride bicycles, then it'll reach the school governor . . . That won't be so pleasant."

"The fact that my sister and I ride bicycles is no one's concern but ours!" Kovalenko said, turning crimson. "If anyone starts interfering in my domestic and family life, I'll see him in hell."

Belikov turned pale and stood up.

"If you adopt that tone with me, I cannot continue," he said. "I must ask you never to express yourself like that in my presence about our superiors. You must show proper respect for the authorities."

"When did I say anything critical of the authorities?" Kovalenko asked, glaring at him. "Please leave me in peace. I'm an honest man and have no wish to talk to a gentleman of your sort. I don't like informers."

Belikov fussed about nervously and began hastily putting on his coat, an expression of horror on his face. No one had ever used such strong language to him before.

"You may say what you wish, but I must warn you of one thing," he said, going out on to the landing from the hall. "Someone may have been listening to us, and in case they misinterpret our conversation and it might lead to something, I shall have to report its substance to the headmaster ... in general terms. It is my bounden duty."

"Go on then, report away!"

Seizing him from behind by the collar, Kovalenko gave him a push and Belikov tumbled downstairs, his galoshes thumping. It was a long steep staircase, but he reached the bottom safely, stood up and felt his nose to see if his glasses were broken. But at the very moment when he was tumbling down, Varenka came in with two ladies. They were standing at the bottom watching. For Belikov this was the worst thing that could have happened. Better to break his neck or both legs than become a laughing-stock: now the whole town's going to find out, it'll reach the headmaster and the governor – oh dear, what will that lead to – they'll draw a new caricature, and it'll end up with him being forced to resign ...

When he had got to his feet, Varenka saw who it was and looking at his comic face, his rumpled coat and his galoshes, and not realizing what had happened but assuming he had fallen downstairs by accident, she could not contain herself. Her laughter echoed all over the house:

"Ha-ha-ha!"

And that peal of loud laughter brought everything to an end: the courtship and Belikov's earthly existence. He did not hear what Varenka was saying to him, he did not see anything. Returning home, he first removed her portrait from the desk, then lay down and was never to rise again.

Three days later Afanasy came in to ask me if he should send for the doctor, as something was wrong with the master. I went in to Belikov. He was lying in the four-poster, covered with a blanket, and not speaking; in answer to my questions he said yes or no – and nothing more. Meanwhile Afanasy was prowling round, gloomy, scowling, sighing deeply and stinking to high heaven of vodka.

A month later Belikov died. We all attended his funeral: both schools, that is, and the theological college. Now that he was lying in his coffin, his expression was mild, pleasant, and even cheerful, as if he were glad to have been put at last in a case from which he would never emerge. Yes, he had attained his ideal! As if in his honour, the weather during the funeral was dull and rainy, and we were all wearing galoshes and carrying umbrellas. Varenka was at the funeral, too, and when the coffin was lowered into the grave, she burst into tears. I've noticed that Ukrainian women either laugh or cry, they don't have a mood in between.

Burying people like Belikov is a great pleasure, I have to admit. On the way back from the cemetery, our faces wore expressions of modest sobriety; no one wanted to reveal this feeling of pleasure, the kind of pleasure we had experienced long long ago as children, when the grown-ups went out and we ran round the garden for an hour or two enjoying absolute freedom. Freedom, freedom! Even a hint, even a faint hope of its possibility, makes the spirit soar, doesn't it?

We got back from the cemetery in an excellent mood. But not a week had gone by before life was as grim, tiring and fatuous as ever, a life that was not banned officially, but was not fully authorized either; there was no improvement. We might have buried one Belikov, but how many other encased men had been left behind, and how many more are still to come!'

'Yes, that's the way things are,' said Ivan Ivanych and lit his pipe.

'How many more are still to come!' Burkin repeated.

The schoolmaster came out of the barn. He was a short fat man, completely bald, with a black beard almost down to his waist. Two dogs came out with him.

'That's quite a moon!' he said, looking upwards.

It was already midnight. To the right the whole village was visible, the long road stretching five versts into the distance. A deep quiet sleep pervaded everything; there was no sound or movement; how could everything in nature be so quiet? The sight of a wide village road in the moonlight with its huts, its hayricks and its sleeping willows has a quieting effect on the soul; that sense of repose, of being sheltered by the darkness of night from toil, worry and grief, give it a sad gentle beauty, the stars seem to look down on it with tender kindness, evil is no more and all's well in the world. Beyond the edge of the village to the left, open fields began, stretching far away to the horizon, and there, too, no sound or movement came from the whole of that wide moonlit expanse.

'Yes, that's the way things are,' Ivan Ivanych repeated. 'And what of our own lives, crowded together in towns without fresh air, compiling useless reports and playing cards – isn't that a kind of case? Spending all our time among idlers and pettifoggers, and stupid empty-headed women, talking and hearing all kinds of rubbish – isn't that a kind of case? If you like, I'll tell you a very instructive story.'

'No, it's time to go to sleep,' Burkin said. 'Tell me tomorrow.'

They both went into the barn and lay down on the hay. Both had covered themselves and dozed off when suddenly they caught the tip-tap of light footsteps ... Someone was walking near the barn, taking a few steps, stopping, then a minute later, tip-tap ... The dogs began growling.

'That's Mavra,' Burkin said.

The footsteps died away.

'To see and hear people lying,' Ivan Ivanych said, turning over, 'and to be called a fool because you put up with such lies; to bear insults and humiliations, not to dare to proclaim that you are on the side of free, honest people, but to lie and smile yourself, and all for the sake of a crust of bread, a roof over your head, some worthless rank – no, it's impossible to go on living like that!'

'Now you're on to a different theme, Ivan Ivanych,' the school-master said. 'Let's get some sleep.'

Ten minutes later Burkin was already sleeping. But Ivan Ivanych kept turning over and sighing, then he got up, went outside again and sat down in the doorway to light his pipe.

1898

The Darling

Olenka, the daughter of retired collegiate assessor Plemyannikov, sat on the porch in her yard, lost in thought. It was hot, the flies wouldn't leave her alone, and it was bliss to think it would soon be evening. Dark rain-clouds were moving up from the east, preceded by occasional wafts of humid air.

In the middle of the yard Snookin, manager-proprietor of the Tivoli Pleasure Gardens, who lodged across the yard in Olenka's fliegel, stood gazing at the sky.

'Not again!' he was saying in despair. 'Not rain again! Day after day, day after day, rain, rain, rain! Just my luck! What I have to put up with! I'm ruined! I'm losing huge sums every day!'

Throwing up his hands, he turned to Olenka and said:

'You see what our life's like, Olga Semyonovna. Enough to make you weep! You work hard and do your best, you worry and have sleepless nights, you're always thinking of improvements – and what's the result? Take audiences for a start. They're nothing but ignorant savages. I give them the best operetta and pantomime, top-quality burlesque, but is that what they want? Do they appreciate it? No, they want some vulgar little peepshow. Then take the weather. Rain almost every evening. May 10th it started, and it's been at it right through May and June. Appalling! The public stays away, but who has to pay the rent, I ask you? Who has to pay the performers?'

Clouds began gathering at the same time next day.

'Oh yes, let it all come!' Snookin said, laughing hysterically. 'Let it flood the whole Gardens and take me with it! I don't deserve any happiness in this world or the next! Let the performers take me to court! Why stop at that? Make it penal servitude in Siberia! The scaffold! Ha-ha-ha!'

It was the same next day . . .

Olenka said nothing but listened to Snookin gravely, and sometimes tears came to her eyes. In the end his misfortunes moved her and she fell in love with him. He was short and skinny, with a sallow complexion and hair combed back off the temples, he spoke in a high-pitched tenor, twisting his mouth as he did so, and his face wore an expression of permanent despair – yet he aroused in her deep and genuine emotion. She was constantly in love with someone and could not live otherwise. Previously she had loved her Papa, now an invalid sitting in his armchair in a darkened room and breathing with difficulty; then she had loved her aunt, who came to visit them every other year from Bryansk; and earlier still she had loved the French master at her school. She was a quiet, good-natured, tender-hearted girl, with soft gentle eyes, and in the best of health. Looking at her plump rosy cheeks and soft white neck with its dark birthmark, at the innocent, kindly smile on her face whenever she was listening to something pleasant, men said to themselves, 'yes, not a bad one, that,' and smiled, too, while her female visitors could not refrain from seizing her by the hand in the middle of a conversation and exclaiming with delight:

'You're such a darling!' .

The house she had lived in all her life and was due to inherit stood on the edge of town in Gypsy Lane, not far from the Tivoli, so that in the evenings and at night, hearing the band playing and the rockets going off with a bang, she imagined this was Snookin challenging his fate and taking his chief enemy, the indifferent public, by storm; her heart would melt, she didn't feel a bit sleepy, and when he returned home in the early hours, she would knock softly on her bedroom window and letting him see through the curtains only her face and one shoulder, smile affectionately . . .

He proposed and they were married. Now that he could see her neck and both her plump healthy shoulders properly, he threw up his hands and said:

'You darling, you!'

He was happy, but since it rained on the wedding day *and* on the wedding night, the look of despair never left his face.

Life went well after the marriage. She sat in his box office, supervised the Gardens, wrote down expenses and paid out salaries, and you'd catch a glimpse of her rosy cheeks and sweetly innocent, radiant smile at the box office window one moment, behind stage the next, and now in the refreshment bar. Already she was telling her friends that nothing in the world was so remarkable, so important and necessary as the theatre, and only in the theatre could you experience real enjoyment and become an educated, civilized human being.

'But does the public appreciate that?' she would say. 'What they want is a peepshow. Yesterday we did *Faust Inside Out* and almost all the boxes were empty, but if we'd put on something vulgar, me and Vanya, we'd have been packed out, I can tell you. Tomorrow we're doing *Orpheus in the Underworld*, me and Vanya, why don't you come?'

Whatever Snookin said about the theatre and the actors, she repeated. Like him, she despised the public for its indifference to art and its ignorance, interfered in rehearsals, corrected the actors and made sure the musicians behaved, and whenever there was a bad notice in the local press, she would cry and then go round to the editorial office to have it out with them.

The actors were fond of her and called her 'Me and Vanya' and 'The Darling'. She felt sorry for them and gave them small loans, and if they let her down, she just had a quiet cry and said nothing to her husband.

Life went well that winter, too. They hired the town theatre for the whole season and rented it out for short periods to a Ukrainian troupe, a conjuror, and the local amateur dramatic company. Olenka put on weight and positively radiated well-being, but Snookin looked thin and sallow, and complained of huge losses, even though business was quite good all winter. At night he coughed and she gave him raspberry or lime-blossom tea to drink, rubbed him with eau-de-Cologne and wrapped him in her soft shawls.

'My wonderful little man!' she would say with complete sincerity, as she stroked his hair. 'My handsome little man!'

During Lent he went off to Moscow to engage a new company, and in his absence she couldn't sleep, but sat by the window look-ing at the stars. She was like the hens, she thought, which stay awake all night and are restive when the cock isn't in the hen-house. Snookin was delayed in Moscow but said he'd be back by Easter, and his letters were already giving her instructions about the Tivoli. But on the Sunday before Easter, late at night, there was a sudden ominous knocking outside. Someone was banging on the gate until it started booming like a barrel. The sleepy cook ran to answer, her bare feet splashing in the puddles.

'Open up, please!' someone outside was saying in a deep bass. 'Telegram for you!'

Olenka had received telegrams from her husband before, but now for some reason she felt petrified. She opened it with trem-bling hands and read as follows:

'Ivan Petrovich died suddenly today suchly await instructions funreal Tuesday.'

That was what the telegram said, 'funreal' and the other meaningless word 'suchly'; it was signed by the producer of the operetta company.

'My darling!' Olenka sobbed. 'My sweet darling little Vanya! Why did I ever meet you? Why did I come to know you and love you? Who's going to look after your poor wretched Olenka now you've abandoned her?'

Snookin was buried on the Tuesday at the Vagankovo Cemetery in Moscow. Olenka returned home on Wednesday and as soon as she entered her room, flung herself down on the bed and sobbed so loudly she could be heard in the street and the neighbouring yards.

'Poor darling!' the women neighbours said, crossing themselves. 'She *is* taking it badly, poor darling Olga Semyonovna!'

Three months later Olenka, in full mourning, was returning home sadly one day from church. It so happened that a neighbour of hers, Vasily Andreich Pustovalov, manager of the merchant Babakayev's timber-yard, was also returning from church and walking alongside her. He was wearing a straw hat and a white waistcoat with a gold watch-chain, and looked more like a landowner than a tradesman.

'Everything has to take its proper course, Olga Semyonovna,' he was saying soberly, with a sympathetic note in his voice, 'and if someone dear to us dies, that means it is God's wish, so we must contain ourselves and bear it with resignation.'

After seeing Olenka to her gate, he said goodbye and walked on. For the rest of the day she kept hearing that sober voice, and she had only to close her eyes to picture his dark beard to herself. She liked him very much. Evidently she had made an impression on him, too, for not long afterwards an elderly lady, whom she scarcely knew, came to drink coffee with her, and had no sooner sat down at the table than she started talking about Pustovalov, what a good, reliable man he was and how any young lady would be delighted to have him for a husband. Three days later Pustovalov himself paid her a visit, stayed no more than about ten minutes and said little, but Olenka fell for him so completely that she lay awake all night feeling hot and feverish, and next morning sent for the elderly lady. The match was quickly arranged, then came the wedding.

Life went well for Pustovalov and Olenka after their marriage.

He would usually stay at the timber-yard until lunch and then go out on business, whereupon Olenka would take his place and stay in the office until evening, doing the accounts and dispatching orders.

'Timber's going up by twenty per cent a year now,' she would tell customers and friends. 'In the past we used to get our timber locally, but now, imagine, my Vasya has to fetch it every year from Mogilyov Province. And the freight charges!' she would say, covering both cheeks with her hands in horror. 'The freight charges!'

She felt that she had been dealing in timber for ages and ages, and it was the most vitally important thing in life, and the words joist, batten, offcut, purlin, round beam, short beam, frame and slab, were like dear old friends to her. At night she dreamed of whole mountains of boards and battens, of never-ending convoys of carts carrying timber somewhere far beyond the town; she dreamed of a whole regiment of beams, thirty feet by nine inches, marching upright into battle against the timber-yard, and how beams, joists and slabs banged together with the resounding thud of dry wood, falling over and then righting themselves, piling up on top of each other. Olenka would cry out in her sleep and Pustovalov would say to her tenderly:

'What's the matter, Olenka dear? Better cross yourself!'

Whatever thoughts her husband had, she had also. If he thought the room was too hot or business had become quiet, she thought the same. Her husband did not like any entertainments and on holidays stayed at home; so did she.

'You're always at home or in the office,' friends said to her. 'You should go to the theatre, darling, or the circus.'

'Me and Vasya have no time for theatres,' she replied soberly. 'We're working folk, we can't be bothered with trifles. What do people see in those theatres, anyway?'

On Saturdays she and Pustovalov attended the all-night vigil, and on feast days early-morning service. Afterwards, walking home side by side, they both looked deeply moved, they smelt fragrant, and her silk dress rustled agreeably. At home they drank tea, with rich white bread and various jams, then they had pie. Every day at noon the yard and the street outside the gates were filled with the appetizing smell of borsch and roast lamb or duck, or fish on fast days, and no one could walk past without beginning to feel hungry. In the office the samovar was always on the boil, and customers were treated to tea and buns. Once a week the couple went to the baths and walked home side by side, both red in the face.

'We're not complaining,' Olenka told her friends. 'Life's going well, praise be to God. May God grant everyone as good a life as me and Vasya.'

When Pustovalov went off to Mogilyov Province for timber, she missed him terribly and could not sleep at night for crying. Sometimes she had an evening visit from the young man renting her fliegel, a regimental vet called Smirnin. He would tell her about something or they'd play cards, and this cheered her up. She was particularly interested to hear about his own family life: he was married with a son, but had separated from his wife because she'd been unfaithful, and now he hated her and sent her forty roubles a month for the boy's maintenance. As she listened, Olenka sighed and shook her head, and felt sorry for him.

'The Lord be with you,' she would say, bidding him good night and lighting him to the top of the stairs with a candle. 'It was kind of you to while away your time with me, may God and the Holy Mother watch over you . . .'

She always expressed herself in the same sober, judicious tones, imitating her husband. The vet was already disappearing behind the downstairs door when she would call him back and say:

'Vladimir Platonych, don't you think you should make it up with your wife? Forgive her, if only for your son's sake! That little chap knows just what's going on, be sure of that.'

When Pustovalov returned, she would tell him in a hushed voice about the vet and his unhappy family situation, and both would sigh, shake their heads and talk of how the boy must be missing his father; then, by some strange association of ideas they would both kneel before the icons, prostrate themselves and pray that God might send them children.

Thus did the Pustovalovs live for six years, quietly and peacefully, in love and complete harmony. But one winter's day at the yard Vasily Andreich went out bare-headed to dispatch some timber after drinking hot tea, caught cold and fell ill. He was treated by the best doctors, but the illness took its course and he died four months later.

Olenka had become a widow again.

'Who will look after me now, my darling?' she sobbed, after burying her husband. 'How can I possibly live without you? I'm so wretched and unhappy! Pity me, good people, I'm all alone now ...'

She wore a black dress with weepers, having vowed never to wear a hat or gloves again, went out seldom and then only to church or to her husband's grave, and lived at home like a nun. Six months passed before she discarded the weepers and began opening her shutters. Some mornings she was to be seen shopping for food in the market with her cook, but people could only surmise how she was living now and what her domestic arrangements were. They surmised when they saw her, for example, sitting in her little garden drinking tea with the vet while he read the newspaper out to her, and also when she bumped into a female friend at the post office and was heard to say:

'Our town has no proper veterinary inspection and that gives rise to many illnesses. You're always hearing of people being infected by milk or catching diseases from horses and cows. We really ought to treat the health of domestic animals as seriously as we do that of human beings.'

She repeated the vet's thoughts and now shared his opinions on everything. It was clear that she could not survive even for a year without an attachment and had found her new happiness in the fliegel next door. Anyone else would have been condemned for this, but no one could think ill of Olenka, her whole life was so transparent. She and the vet did not tell anyone about the change that had taken place in their relationship and tried to conceal it, but without success, because Olenka could not keep a secret. When regimental colleagues came to visit him and she was pouring out their tea or serving supper, she would start talking about cattle plague, pearl disease, and the municipal slaughterhouses. This made him terribly embarrassed, and as they were leaving, he would seize her by the arm and hiss angrily:

'Haven't I told you before not to talk about things you don't understand? When we vets are talking shop, please don't butt in. It's extremely tedious.'

She would look at him in alarm and astonishment, and say:

'But Volodya dear, what *am* I to talk about?!'

With tears in her eyes she embraced him and begged him not to be angry, and they were both happy.

But this happiness did not last long. The vet departed with his regiment, and since they had been transferred somewhere very distant, practically to Siberia, his departure was permanent.

Olenka was left on her own.

This time she was completely on her own. Her father had long since died, and his armchair, with one leg missing, was gathering dust in the attic. She became plain and thin, and people meeting her in the street no longer looked at her and smiled as they used to; her best years were evidently gone for good, now a new, unknown life was beginning that did not bear thinking about. In the evenings Olenka sat on her porch and could hear the band playing and the rockets going off at the Tivoli, but this no longer made her think of anything. She gazed apathetically at her empty yard, had no thoughts or desires, and when night fell, went to bed and dreamed of her empty yard. She seemed reluctant even to eat or drink.

But the worst thing of all was no longer having any opinions. She saw objects round her and understood everything that was going on, but she could not form opinions about anything and did not know what to talk about. How awful it is not to have an opinion! You see a bottle, for example, standing there, or the rain falling, or a peasant going along in his cart, but what the bottle or rain or peasant are for, what sense they make, you can't say and couldn't say, even if they offered you a thousand roubles. In Snookin's and Pustovalov's time, and then with the vet, Olenka could explain everything and give her opinion on any subject you liked, whereas now her mind and heart were as empty as the yard outside. It was a horrible, bitter sensation, like a mouthful of wormwood.

The town has gradually expanded in all directions. Gypsy Lane is now called a street, and where the Tivoli and the timber-yards once stood, houses have sprung up and there are a number of side streets. How time flies! Olenka's house looks dingy, the roof has rusted, the shed is leaning to one side, and the yard is completely overgrown with weeds and stinging nettles. Olenka herself has grown older and plainer. In summer she sits on her porch, with the same feeling of emptiness, boredom and bitterness in her soul as before, in winter she sits by her window gazing at the snow. If she feels the breath of spring, or hears the sound of cathedral bells carried on the wind, memories suddenly flood in, tugging at her heart-strings, and copious tears stream down her face; but this lasts only a minute, then the same emptiness and sense of futility returns. Her black cat Bryska snuggles up to her, purring softly, but Olenka is unmoved by these feline caresses. Is that what she needs? No, she needs the kind of love that will possess her completely, mind and soul, that will provide her with thoughts and a direction in life, and warm her ageing blood. She bundles black Bryska off her lap and says irritably:

'Go away . . . I don't want you here!'

It's the same day after day, year after year – she doesn't have a single joy in life or a single opinion. Whatever Mavra the cook says is good enough.

One hot July day, towards evening, when the town cattle were being driven past and clouds of dust had filled the yard, all of a sudden someone knocked at the gate. Olenka went to open it herself, took one look and was completely dumbfounded: Smirnin the vet was standing there, grey-haired and in civilian clothes. Suddenly everything came back to her, she broke down and burst into tears, laid her head on his chest without saying a word, and was so overcome that afterwards she had no recollection of how they went into the house together and sat down to drink tea.

'Vladimir Platonych,' she murmured, trembling with joy, 'dearest! Whatever brings you here?'

'I'd like to settle down here permanently,' he told her. 'I've resigned my commission and come to try my luck as a civilian, leading a settled life. Then there's my son, he's growing up and it's time he went to grammar school. I've made it up with my wife, you know.'

'And where is she now?' Olenka asked.

'At the hotel with the boy while I go round looking for lodgings.'

'But good heavens, have *my* house, dear! Far better than lodgings. Oh heavens above, I don't want any rent,' Olenka went on, becoming agitated and bursting into tears again. 'You live here and the fliegel will do for me. Wonderful!'

Next day they were already painting the roof and whitewashing the walls, and Olenka was walking about the yard, arms on hips, giving orders. Her face shone with its old smile, and everything about her was fresh and lively, as if she had just woken from a long sleep. The vet's wife arrived, a thin, unattractive woman with short hair and a peevish expression. With her came the boy, Sasha, who was small for his age (he was over nine) and chubby, with bright blue eyes and dimpled cheeks. He had no sooner set foot in the yard than he began chasing the cat, and his merry, joyful laughter rang out.

'Is that your cat, Auntie?' he asked Olenka. 'When it has babies, will you give us one, please? Mamma's scared stiff of mice.'

Olenka chatted to him and gave him tea, and suddenly felt a warm glow and pleasurable tightening in her heart, as if this boy were her own son. And when he was sitting in the dining-room repeating his lessons in the evenings, she would look at him with tenderness and pity, and whisper:

'My darling, my pretty little child . . . You're so clever and your skin is so fair.'

'An island,' he read out, 'is an area of dry land surrounded on all sides by water.'

'An island is an area of dry land . . .' she repeated, and this was the first opinion she had expressed with confidence after all those years of silence and emptiness of mind.

Now she had her own opinions and talked to Sasha's parents over supper about how hard children had to work at grammar school these days, but all the same a classical education was better than a modern one, because every career was open to you afterwards – doctor, engineer, whatever you wished.

Sasha had begun attending the grammar school. His mother went away to her sister's in Kharkov and did not come back, his father went off somewhere every day to inspect herds and might be away for three days at a time, and Olenka felt that Sasha was being completely neglected, his parents didn't want him and he must be starving to death; so she transferred him to her fliegel and fixed him up in a little room there.

Six months have now passed since Sasha began living in her fliegel. Every morning Olenka goes into his room: he is fast asleep with his hand under his cheek, breathing imperceptibly. She is sorry to have to wake him.

'Sashenka,' she says sadly, 'get up, dear! Time for school.'

He gets up, dresses, says his prayers, and then sits down to drink tea; he drinks three glasses and consumes two large rolls and half a French loaf with butter. Still not fully awake, he is in a bad mood.

'You didn't learn your fable properly, you know, Sashenka,' Olenka says, looking at him as if about to see him off on a long journey. 'What a worry you are to me. You *must* make an effort to learn, dear, and do as the teachers say.'

'Oh, stop nagging!' says Sasha.

Then he walks along the street to school, a small boy in a big cap, with a satchel on his back. Olenka follows silently behind.

'Sashenka-a!' she calls.

He looks round, and she pops a date or a caramel into his

hand. When they turn into the school street, he feels ashamed at being followed by this tall, stout woman, looks round and says:

'You go home now, Auntie, I'll do the last bit on my own.'

She stops and keeps her eyes fixed on him until he disappears through the school entrance. Oh, how she loves him! Not one of her previous attachments has been so deep, never before has she surrendered herself so wholeheartedly, unselfishly and joyfully as now, when her maternal feelings are being kindled more and more. For this boy, who is not hers, for his cap and his dimpled cheeks, she would give away her whole life, and do so with gladness and tears of emotion. Why? Who can possibly say why?

After seeing Sasha off, she returns home quietly, feeling so calm and contented, and overflowing with love. In these last six months her face has become younger, she is smiling and radiant, and people meeting her in the street feel pleasure as they look at her, and say:

'Olga Semyonovna darling, good morning! How are you, darling?'

'They have to work so hard at grammar school these days,' she tells them in the market. 'It's no laughing matter. Yesterday the first year had a fable to learn by heart *and* a Latin translation *and* a maths problem . . . How can a small boy cope?'

She goes on to talk about teachers and lessons and textbooks – repeating exactly what Sasha tells her.

Between two and three they have their meal together, and in the evening they do Sasha's homework together and cry. Putting him to bed, she spends a long time making the sign of the cross over him and whispering a prayer, then, on going to bed herself, she pictures that distant hazy future when Sasha has finished his degree and become a doctor or an engineer, has his own large house with horses and a carriage, marries and has children . . . She falls asleep still thinking about it all, and tears run down her cheeks from her closed eyes. The black cat lies purring by her side: mrr, mrr, mrr . . .

Suddenly there's a loud knock at the gate. Olenka wakes up, too terrified to breathe. Her heart is thumping. Half a minute passes, then there's another knock.

'It's a telegram from Kharkov,' she thinks, beginning to tremble all over. 'Sasha's mother wants him to live with her in Kharkov . . . Oh heavens!'

She is in despair. Her head, arms and legs turn cold, she feels the unhappiest person in the world. But another minute passes and she hears voices. It's the vet, he's come back from his club.

'Oh, thank God,' she thinks.

Gradually the pressure on her heart eases and she feels relaxed again. She lies down and thinks of Sasha, who is sleeping soundly in the room next door. From time to time he starts talking in his sleep:

'I'll show you! Get out! Stop fighting!'

1899

Notes

An asterisk before a title indicates that the version first appeared in *Chekhov: The Early Stories 1883–88*, translated by Patrick Miles and Harvey Pitcher (John Murray, 1982, reprinted by Sphere Books under the Abacus imprint, 1984, and by Oxford University Press in their World's Classics series, 1994), and is reproduced here by kind permission of Patrick Miles and Oxford University Press.

All the translations are based on *A.P.Chekhov: Complete Collection of the Works and Letters in Thirty Volumes* (Moscow, 1974–82). Chekhov himself selected and revised the stories for his *Collected Works* of 1899–1902. Except as indicated below, the texts used here are the revised versions as published in *Collected Works*.

The system of transliteration is that of *The Oxford Chekhov*, but the following words of Russian origin have been treated as English by adoption and spelt accordingly: borsch (beetroot soup), datcha (summer residence), droshky (light carriage), feldsher (semi-qualified doctor's assistant), kopeck (hundredth part of a rouble), shchi (cabbage soup), troika (team of three horses abreast; vehicle drawn by three horses), verst (two-thirds of a mile) and zemstvo (organ of rural self-government). To these has been added a word that has yet to appear in English dictionaries: fliegel. Derived from the German *Flügel*, it can mean the wing of a house, but is used by Chekhov to denote a small house in the grounds of a larger one. It may be in the town or the country; hence the difficulty of finding a suitable equivalent in English. The fliegel might be lived in by part of the family or by employees, it might be reserved for visitors, or rented out, as in 'The Darling'.

Apart from verst, other units of measurement have been converted into British equivalents. The civil service ranks, ranging from 1 to 14, that figure so prominently in the comic stories, are sometimes translated in full and sometimes simplified to 'a Number 3' etc., depending on context.

Chekhov delighted in unusual names, of places as well as

people, and always chose them with great care. The characters' names in his comic stories are outlandish but never quite impossible. Sometimes they simply sound odd/comic, provoking the reaction: what extraordinary names you come across, what strange words they must come from! But they may also allude to some foible or weakness in a person's character, or contain some other, often quite subtle, meaning. These names are a nightmare for the translator. Transliterating them misses the point; translating them into English looks and sounds absurd. The only answer is to go for the Anglo-Russian hybrid, in which the English element is used to suggest the comic allusion or meaning, while the Russian element – one of the unfortunately small number of surname endings – makes the name look and sound more or less Russian.

The liberal use of exclamation marks and question marks, and of the pregnant three dots, was one of those hackneyed conventions that Chekhov followed as a young writer. Later he had second thoughts. When he revised 'A Dreadful Night', he replaced three dots by a full stop on no fewer than 55 occasions, but this still left 34 instances; in the English version they have been reduced to 30. There is a place for 'expressive' punctuation in the comic stories, even in English, but as the sniffy young man says in 'The Exclamation Mark': 'Knowing when to use punctuation marks isn't enough – not by a long way! You must do it consciously.'

In compiling these Notes good use has been made of the extensive notes and commentaries in the 30-volume *Works*, and of two other helpful publications: Lehrman, Edgar H., *A Handbook to Eighty-Six of Chekhov's Stories in Russian* (Columbus, Ohio, 1985), and Birkett, G.A. and Struve, Gleb (eds.), *Anton Chekhov: Selected Stories* (Oxford, 1951).

Introduction

Some parts of this Introduction were adapted from my article, 'Chekhov's Humour', in *A Chekhov Companion*, ed. Clyman (Westport, Connecticut, 1985), pp.88–103.

p. 2 In claiming that he never wrote a novel, Chekhov ignored his remarkable whodunnit, *Drama na okhote* (1884–85): translated into English as *The Shooting Party* by A.E. Chamot (1926), reissued in a revised translation and with an introduction by Julian Symons (André Deutsch, 1986).

p. 6 The quotation from V. B. Kataev is in the section *O*

prirode komicheskogo u Chekhova ('On the Nature of the Comic in Chekhov') in his book, *Proza Chekhova: problemy interpretatsii*, 'Chekhov's Prose: Problems of Interpretation' (Moscow, 1979), p.55.

'He Quarrelled with his Wife' *S zhenoy possorilsya* (1884)
Not included in *Collected Works*; first known translation into English.

'Notes from the Memoirs of a Man of Ideals' *Iz vospominany idealista* (1885)
Revised in 1899 for *Collected Works*, but eventually excluded; first known translation into English.

* 'A Dreadful Night' *Strashnaya noch* (1884)
Horror stories, spiritualism and the paranormal were much in vogue in the Moscow of the 1880s. The words 'The end of your life is at hand' (p. 16) were addressed to Chekhov himself at a seance by the spirit of Turgenev. This was one of the first of Chekhov's comic stories to be translated into English ('Fugitive coffins: a weird Russian tale' by Anton Petrovitch (*sic*) Tschechoff. Translated from the Russian by Grace Eldredge. *Short Stories: a magazine of select stories*, New York, 1902, July, pp.50–53).

'From the Diary of an Assistant Book-keeper' *Iz dnevnika pomoshchnika bukhgaltera* (1883)
p. 23 'Grabsky . . . has his St Stanislas': the order of St Stanislas was a standard award for government service (cf. 'Fat and Thin', 'The Exclamation Mark').
    The prescription for catarrh of the stomach was based on the mixture sold by Chekhov's father in his Taganrog shop. A *zolotnik* and a *shtof* were old units of measurement. 'Seven brothers blood' was a name for insoluble coral.

* 'An Incident at Law' *Sluchay iz sudebnoy praktiki* (1883)
The text is the revised version prepared by Chekhov in 1886 for his *Pyostrye rasskazy* ('Motley Tales'); the story was not included in *Collected Works*.

* 'The Daughter of Albion' *Doch Albiona* (1883)
p. 28 'Wilka Charlesovna Tvice': partial repatriation of the

strictly transliterated Uilka Charlzovna Tfays. 'Uilka' is perhaps Gryabov's version of Willa, 'Charlzovna' is the patronymic meaning 'daughter of Charles', and 'Tfays' perhaps Gryabov's attempt at pronouncing Twiss or Thwaites; although the general opinion is that Chekhov coined the surname from 'twice'.

p. 30 'Bit different from England, eh?!' Now a set expression, applied scathingly to things Russian.

'Foiled!' *Neudacha* (1886)
p. 30 N. A . Nekrasov (1821–77): well-known poet and radical.
p. 31 I. I. Lazhechnikov (1792–1869): historical novelist, one of the Russian followers of Sir Walter Scott.

'A Woman Without Prejudices' *Zhenshchina bez predrassudkov* (1883)
Not included in *Collected Works*.

* 'The Complaints Book' *Zhalobnaya kniga* (1884)

'The Swedish Match' *Shvedskaya spichka* (1883)
Also known in English as 'The Phosphorus Match' and 'The Safety Match'. The proper names, many of them comic-sounding, have been strictly transliterated, except that the unwieldy Klyauzov has been simplified to Klauzov.

p. 38 'witnesses' (*ponyatye*): members of the public who have to be present when a police search is taking place.

p. 43 'used to call her Nana': the prostitute heroine of Zola's novel, *Nana*, published in 1880 and in Russian translation in the same year.

p. 47 'not to mention Leskov and Pechersky': N.S. Leskov (1831–95) was well known as the author of novels and stories concerned with the church and clergy, and with popular beliefs and superstitions; Pechersky was the pseudonym of P. I. Melnikov (1819–83), whose works describe the life of the Old Believers.

p. 51 'the novels of Gaboriau': Emile Gaboriau (1832–73), first practitioner in France of the *roman policier* and widely translated into Russian.

* 'Rapture' *Radost* (1883)

'Vint' *Vint* (1884)
When a public reading of this story was proposed in 1890, the

theatre censor, dismayed by its lack of respect for the civil service, found it 'completely unsuitable for public performance'.

Vint: a popular card game resembling auction bridge.

'On the Telephone' *U telefona* (1886)
Not included in *Collected Works*; first known translation into English. The first (manually operated) telephone exchanges appeared in Russia in 1882–3. The 'Slavic Bazaar' was one of Moscow's best-known hotel-restaurants, the 'Hermitage' a famous restaurant.

* 'Romance with Double-Bass' *Roman s kontrabasom* (1886)

* 'The Death of a Civil Servant' *Smert chinovnika* (1883)
p. 71 *'The Chimes of Normandy'*: English title of *Les Cloches de Corneville* (1877), operetta by Planquette.

'Overdoing It' *Peresolil* (1885)
This appears to be the first of Chekhov's comic stories to have been translated into English: 'Two tales from the Russian of Anton Tschechow. The biter bit. Sorrow.' *Temple Bar; a London magazine*, 1897, vol.III, pp.104–13. (No translator given.)

'Surgery' *Khirurgiya* (1884)
Candidates for the priesthood often had their surnames changed to more impressive religious-sounding ones. The sexton's name, Vonmiglasov, consists of the Church Slavonic *vonmi* ('hear') and *glas* ('voice'); it has been Latinized in translation. Chekhov and his elder brother Alexander are said to have enacted this story as a party piece.

'In the Dark' *V potyomkakh* (1886)

'Kashtanka' *Kashtanka* (1887)
First published 25 December 1887 in Suvorin's newspaper *New Times* under the title *V uchonom obshchestve* ('In Learned Society'); published as a separate illustrated edition for children by Suvorin in 1892 (reprinted six times 1893–9) and in 1903 by Marx, publisher of the *Collected Works*. In 1892 Chekhov changed the title to *Kashtanka*, dividing the story into 7 chapters (instead of 4), of which No. 6, 'A Troubled Night' – very

reminiscent of Chapter 5 in *Skuchnaya istoriya* ('A Boring Story', 1889) – was newly written.

Rival prototypes have been proposed for Kashtanka, but no such controversy surrounds Fyodor Timofeich. This was the Chekhov family cat, of which Chekhov wrote on 13 September 1887: 'He occasionally comes home to eat, but spends the rest of his time wandering over the roofs, gazing dreamily at the sky. Evidently he has become aware of the emptiness of life.'

The name Kashtanka derives from *kashtan* ('chestnut'), but is here transliterated, since the story is well known in English by this name.

p. 87 'In her sins . . .': garbled version of Psalm 50, verse 7 in the Russian Bible (English Psalm 51, verse 5). The joiner confuses *giyena* (hyena) with *geyenna* (Gehenna).

p. 93 'Now imagine you're a jeweller . . .': this was changed for the children's edition from 'Now imagine you come home from the club and discover your dearly beloved wife with the family friend.'

p. 103 'the Kamarinskaya': a Russian folk dance.

* 'Grisha' *Grisha* (1886)

* 'Fat and Thin' *Tolsty i tonky* (1883)
p. 108 'Herostratos': Ephesian who set fire to the temple of Diana.
'Ephialtes': Greek traitor at Thermopylae, 480 BC.

* 'The Objet d'Art' *Proizvedeniye iskusstva* (1886)
p. 110 'No. 223 of the *Stock Exchange Gazette*': this No. contained an instalment of Zola's novel *L'Oeuvre*, which concerns a painter who transfers his affections from his wife to his paintings of the female nude.

'A Horsy Name' *Loshadinaya familiya* (1885)
For Russians this is one of Chekhov's best-known comic stories, but how can one translate 42 horsy names into English? Even if it were possible, concocting that number of Anglo-Russian hybrids would be a clumsy solution, whereas the use of English surnames may at least capture something of the flavour of Chekhov's original. Amazingly, the last name of all translates straight into English.

'At the Bath-house' *V bane* (1885)

For the *Collected Works* Chekhov combined this story with *Otnositelno zhenikhov* ('With Regard to Suitors', 1883), which is told in a bath-house, but *V bane* works much better on its own.

p. 119 Saint Dimitry of Rostov: Dmitry Savvich Tuptalo (1651–1709), Metropolitan of Rostov (1702) and Russian Orthodox saint (1757), the compiler of lives of the saints.

Innocent of Kherson: Ivan Alekseyevich Borisov (1800–57), Archbishop of Kherson and Tauris (1848), famous preacher who published many books on religious themes.

Filaret of Moscow: Vasily Mikhaylovich Drozdov (1783–1867), Metropolitan of Moscow (1821), who published religious works and in February 1861 wrote final draft of the edict for the emancipation of the serfs.

* 'The Chameleon' *Khameleon* (1884)

* 'Revenge' *Mest* (1886)

* 'The Orator' *Orator* (1886)

p. 129 '*aut mortuis nihil bene*'. Nonsense version of *De mortuis aut nihil aut bene* ('Of the dead speak well or not at all').

'The Exclamation Mark' *Vosklitsatelny znak* (1885)

First known published translation into English.

* 'Notes from the Journal of a Quick-tempered Man' *Iz zapisok vspylchivogo cheloveka* (1887)

* 'A Man of Ideas' *Myslitel* (1885)

p. 146 'Or take spelling, for example.' What Yashkin objects to in Russian spelling concerns the redundant letter *yat*, which was abolished in the spelling reform of 1918. It is translated here into a roughly comparable feature of English spelling.

'The Siren' *Sirena* (1887)

p. 152 'Take a young bird that's just caught the ice during the first frosts . . .': in other words, one that has been shot at the point of maximum fatness before migrating to warmer climes for the winter.

'The Burbot' *Nalim* (1885)

'The Civil Service Exam' *Ekzamen na chin* (1884)

'Boys' *Malchiki* (1887)
Chekhov changed the ending on revision: previously, the girls gave the game away before the boys could leave. A *gimnazist* (grammar-school boy) in his second year would be aged about ten.

p. 163 'the rinsing bowl': a metal or china bowl in which glasses were rinsed and then carefully dried by the hostess/tea-pourer as part of the tea ritual.

'a cook's son': this expression had a special significance. In June 1887 the reactionary Minister of Education Delyanov issued a circular making access to secondary education more difficult for children of plebeian origins; it became known as the 'cooks' children' circular.

p. 164 'the snow hill': artificially built snow hill used for toboganning.

'Have you read Mayne Reid?' Thomas Mayne Reid (1818–83), of Anglo-Irish descent, emigrated to the United States and after a dozen years of adventure, including active service, settled in England in 1850 and wrote enormously popular adventure stories for boys; a 20-volume edition of his works was published in St Petersburg (1864–76).

* 'A Drama' *Drama* (1887)
p. 169 *'The Cause'*: radical literary periodical published in St Petersburg from 1866 to 1888. Medusina's play is a parody of the 'ideologically committed' drama of Chekhov's day.

* 'The Malefactor' *Zloumyshlennik* (1885)
p. 174 'a spockerel': the Russian fish known to science as the 'asp' (*Aspius aspius*).

* 'No Comment' *Bez zaglaviya* (1888)

* 'Sergeant Prishibeyev' *Unter Prishibeyev* (1885)
This meaningful name has not been rendered, partly because it appears to be impossible (it manages to convey bruising, intim-idating, depressing and actually killing all in one word), and

partly because the story is already well known in English by this title.

'Encased' *Chelovek v futlyare* (1898)

The first of three linked stories published in 1898 and now known as 'The Little Trilogy', the others being *Kryzhovnik* ('Gooseberries') and *O lyubvi* ('About Love').

Chekhov's title became part of the Russian language, but is difficult to translate. It covers both the particular 'man in a case', Belikov, and the social or psychological type that he represents. 'Encased' is intended to bring out the more abstract second meaning. It also has the advantage of brevity: Chekhov always preferred laconic titles.

p. 187 'Our ladies never arranged any home theatricals on a Saturday . . .': the Russian Orthodox Sabbath begins at dusk on Saturday.

'They read their Shchedrin and Turgenev, their Henry Buckle'. The novelist I.S. Turgenev (1818–83) and the satirist M. Ye. Saltykov-Shchedrin (1826–89) were literary heroes of Russia's liberal intelligentsia. So was the British free-thinker, Henry Thomas Buckle (1821–62), author of *History of Civilization in England* (1857–61). Much admired by Darwin, Buckle was especially popular in Russia. In Act II of *The Cherry Orchard* (1904) the lovesick Yepikhodov asks the maid Dunyasha if she has read Buckle, but gets no reply.

'The Darling' *Dushechka* (1899)

p. 199 *Faust Inside Out*: title of Russian translation of Herve's *Le Petit Faust* (1869), a take-off of Gounod's *Faust* (1859).

Orpheus in the Underworld: Offenbach's operetta of 1858.